CONTENT WARNING

This book contains spice and suspense and also include scenes that may be triggering to some people including;

- Drug Use
- Blackmail
- Assault/Violence

1

VALERIE VAN CLEEF

The room falls quiet as I squint at my father over our meal, wondering if I heard him right.

"You heard me. You're getting married," my father says, as my small, forced smile disappears.

"Excuse me?" I ask, taken aback. *What did he just say?* Mouth agape, I look at my stepmother, who is finishing off her glass of wine and already asking Dennis, our butler, for another.

"I have found you a husband." He stabs his carrots with the crystal-encrusted fork from the formal cutlery set Abigail brought home from Italy last month. Not to be confused with the special Sunday cutlery set they already had, which is gold-plated and from Paris.

"Oh," I sigh, with a small smile coming to my lips as my racing heart slows. "I thought you were serious for a moment there." I shake my head at how silly I was for believing him. It isn't like my father to joke. Actually, it isn't like him to talk to me much at all. I can't remember the last time we had a nice conversation. Dinners like tonight are few and far between.

A small growl emits from my feet, and I look down to see my little guard dog sitting up with his ears high. Bordeaux is a purebred Pomeranian, a ball of fluff, and my best friend. Good to know even he didn't like my father's odd sense of humor.

"Valerie. I am serious. You will be wedded in a few months," he deadpans, and I sit up straight, looking at him, wide-eyed. *He's serious?* My fork drops from my grip and clatters on the plate of perfectly seared sea bass untouched in front of me.

"What?" I can barely get the word out as my breaths suddenly feel sparse.

"Valerie. You will do this. It is what I expect of you." He stabs his fish to punctuate his stern order, his dining manners now out the window. He is quick to anger these days. The father I grew up loving is no longer the man who sits at the dining table.

"But I don't want to get married. Not to a stranger!" Heart pounding, my stomach churns with my argument. I'm too young. I'm only twenty-five. I haven't found the love of my life yet. I want to fall in love, travel, and see the world together. This can't be happening.

"It isn't really about what you want, dear. It is about what is good for the business," Abigail pipes up, and my eyes snap to her. Sure, she has never been a feminist, but I expected *some* support. She has filled the role of a mother for over a decade now since my own mother died. She hasn't been overly loving, but she hasn't been a total ogre either.

"But I want to choose my own husband. I want to fall in love." Sitting forward, my flight-or-fight kicks in as my sweaty hands grip on to the edge of the table. This is my worst nightmare. I'm not stupid; I know arranged marriages still happen. But my father has never made mention of it before, so I just didn't think it was in the cards for me. I should have known better.

My father huffs. "Of course, you don't get a choice. We need to align ourselves with other families of similar caliber. The Rothschilds are growing, and we need to assure our business interests too. Van Cleef Corp must flourish and thrive well into the future." He's dismissing me, like my own wants are of no concern. Probably because, in his mind, they aren't.

"But why do I need to marry for that? I can run the business. I don't need to marry someone to do that..." This isn't making any sense. I have a law degree. I have worked in the business for years. I worked every summer, every school break. I went into the legal department straight out of college, and I have been there, working full-time, ever since. My goal was always to take over for him. I want to be CEO.

"You can't run the business." My father blows out a breath, shaking his head, almost in a mock laugh. I feel every muscle in my body lock tight.

"What?" I ask, my brow pinching. "I am your only child. The business has been passed down from female to female for generations. I have experience, I have the desire, I have the skills." My body is growing hot and my hands are starting to shake. Everything I imagined about my future is unraveling right before my eyes.

"Once you are married, you won't work. You will need to produce heirs yourself." Placing his cutlery on his plate, he wipes his lips with the French linen napkin.

"I don't understand?" I look between him and Abigail, utterly confused. My mind is spinning. I don't know what in the world is going on. He paid for me to go to college. He supported me and encouraged me... Was my law degree simply for appearances?

"Oh, dear. Women of our stature don't work," my stepmother says a little more firmly, and things start to click into place.

"The Rothschild women do," I state just as firmly. *My mother did,* I think to myself, but don't dare say her name at the dinner table.

"Tsk. They married money, they *aren't* money." She takes another big gulp of wine as I fist my hands in my dress under the table. *She* married money. My mother's family money. So did my father, for that matter. Van Cleef Corp was built by the strong women in my maternal family line. Not by the two people sitting at this table. My father took over when my mom died, holding the role until I was older. I am ready now.

"But I want to work. I am good at what I do. I love Van Cleef Corp," I plead with them, feeling my independence slip through my fingers with every passing second.

I love the business. We are predominantly in mergers and acquisitions, but also own interests in a wide variety of other sectors, including hospitality, manufacturing, and, of course, a lot of charity work. I love working. I love contributing. Until five seconds ago, I thought my life was near perfect. Great friends, great career, great opportunities, and soon to step up into my rightful position as CEO. Sure, I was yet to meet Mr. Right, but I was positive that he was coming for me, too.

"Nonsense. You will have babies and run the charity luncheons with Abigail," my father says in a way that signals this is the end of the conversation. I look at Abigail, her pursed lips turned up in a smile, and I suppress a groan. I enjoy helping charities and I go to every event I can. But I don't want to be just a Stepford wife like her. I want to work. I want to run Van Cleef Corp.

"I don't understand. Van Cleef Corp is *my* family business. I am meant to be there. I am meant to be the CEO!" I push, my voice rising with my frustration. My father sighs like I am being disobedient and looks at me with cold eyes. I gulp a little because his eyes tell me everything I need to know. He never had any intention of letting me run the business, regardless of if it is my birth right.

"You will marry the man I selected for you. You will be a wife and a mother, and you'll do what he says when he says it. You will not involve yourself with business affairs; you will not step out of line. You will remain well kept in appearance. You *will* do this for me." I swallow roughly at the threat in his tone. *Well kept in appearance? What's wrong with my appearance?* I look down at myself in my day dress. My hair is blow waved, my nails manicured. My weight has been the same for years, a perfect size four, as he always required. The familiar feeling of not being good enough crawls up my throat. Never good enough for my father. It is an unachievable target and one that I will never meet, no matter how hard I try.

"And if I don't?" I ask, trying to act confident. I am a lawyer. I have my own money. My own apartment. As the only child of the Van Cleef family, the family business *should* be mine. But I have never gone against my father's wishes. *Ever.* I have always done what he has asked. Now I understand that it didn't benefit me whatsoever, and our relationship is just as broken as it has always been.

"There is no choice here, Valerie. I want to grow our empire. This is how I am going to do it." And with that, he stands from the table. I am such an idiot. He has had this planned for years, no doubt. He just never told me about it.

"By marrying me off to some rich businessman who doesn't care about me at all?" I ask, standing with him, throwing my napkin on my plate.

"Oh, Valerie. Stop being so childish. It is unbecoming," Abigail scolds me, and I bite my tongue so hard I taste blood.

"Yes, Valerie. That is exactly how I am doing it. Abigail has already added you to the charity committee and scheduled your time accordingly. May I suggest you lose a few pounds. I want you to be perfect for your wedding. Lord knows, you have let yourself go these past few months." My father scoffs, looking me up and down, his lips curling slightly in disgust. I try to blink through the hurt as my eyesight becomes blurry, not wanting him to see any tears fall. It is like I mean nothing to him anymore. I'm nothing but a pawn in his business strategy, it seems.

I remember a time when he used to look at me adoringly. Bounce me on his knee, take me for ice cream on Sundays. It all changed once I was shipped off to boarding school when my mother died. I came home the next summer and Abigail was here. Nothing has been the same since.

"I don't want to..."

"Dammit, Valerie!" he shouts, slamming his fist on the table so hard the dishes clash together, and out the corner of my eye, I see Abigail grab her wineglass. Heaven forbid she spills a drop.

My body jolts at the violent outburst, and Bordeaux growls again at my feet, ready to bite his ankles if I need protection. I have heard him yell at others, people in the office or on the phone, but he's never directed that anger toward me. He usually ignores me, or speaks sharply, but never raises his voice like this.

"Just do as you're damn well told!" Without another word or look my way, he stalks out of his formal dining room and down the hall to his office. I watch the back of him and don't breathe again until I hear his office door slam.

"Well, Dennis, this glass isn't going to fill itself." Abigail motions for Dennis, and he fills her glass for a third time in half an hour. I look over at them and meet Dennis' gaze. He has been here since I was a kid. My mom hired him. And the look in his eyes is murderous. So I give him a small smile. I don't want him to worry.

Sitting back down slowly, I take a deep breath as despair crawls up my throat.

"The sea bass was lovely tonight, Dennis," Abigail

says as she places her napkin on the table and stands up. "Good to see you, Valerie. Talk soon." She smiles like my world didn't just crumble, and she walks out the door with her glass of wine, leaving me sitting alone at the large timber table.

The familiar feeling is nothing new. The large room is ostentatious, renovated by Abigail. There isn't anything left of my mother here. Actually, there is nothing left in this house that reminds me of my mother at all.

"Are you alright, Miss Valerie?" Dennis asks quietly as he starts to clear the dishes.

"I'm sure everything will be fine," I say shakily, looking at him. His face is set, deep concern etched into his brow.

"Your mother wouldn't have wanted this," he says as his eyes search mine. I don't see Dennis much these days because I am very rarely in this house anymore. But I grew up with him, and we both miss my mother.

"I need to figure a way out of this. This can't be happening..." I'm still reeling in disbelief. My heart still races. I need to think, to strategize. I can't marry a man I don't love. And I need to be CEO. Dennis is right, my mother would not have wanted this, and neither do I.

"I know you never defy your father, but maybe on this, you need to. Perhaps George can help?" Giving me a look of support, he picks up the dishes and retreats out of the room. I think about his suggestion. George is the VP of Operations at Van Cleef Corp and the only person still in the company that knew my mother just as well as my father did. He has always been a support to me, and

Dennis is right. George can help me figure a way out of this mess.

"How about we go home Bordeaux?" I whisper to my little companion at my feet. Bile rises up my throat as the panic inside me continues to swirl, so I grab my bag, deciding to get out of here.

He said I have a few months. I still have time to turn this around.

2

AJ STEELE

As my fists hit the bag, it's like music to my ears. My rhythm is good, my mind focused.

"That's it, my boy!" Marcus, my fight promoter, says as he stalks into the gym. I stop punching and look up, watching his shit-eating grin as he walks toward me.

"What are you doing here?" I grit out. Marcus is not good news. Sure, he has connections, puts together fights, but he pits everyone against each other. His mantra in life: *As long as my pocket is lined with cash, I have no allegiance.*

"I came to see how you're training. You're the favorite. I'm putting my money on you. So I want the inside knowledge," he says, not even trying to hide how underhanded he is.

"We were fucking fine before you walked in the door," my best friend, Brady, calls out as he comes to my side. The two of us have been friends since we could talk and always have each other's backs.

"Well, I didn't ask you, Brady, did I? I asked *AJ*." Marcus' condescending manner has Brady lifting his shoulders back, and I slap his chest to stop him throwing a punch to Marcus' face.

"Just book the fights, Marcus, and leave my fitness up to me." I roll my own shoulders to relieve the tension building. I am too old for this shit. I started boxing when I was thirteen, and now almost two decades later, my body is sore, and I am sick of dealing with piece-of-shit promoters like Marcus.

"Ahhh, you will beat Rago easily. He was half limping when I saw him this morning. You are the most powerful boxer we have in the mix. It will be easy money." I have no idea if anything he says is the truth. Maybe my opponent, Rago, is sporting an injury, maybe he isn't. It doesn't matter. I learned a long time ago not to focus on anyone else. That just leads to problems. Now I just focus on me.

Brady smirks. "Rago is fucking dead and buried before he even enters the fucking ring. He should just give up now."

"But what fun would that be?" Marcus says with a sly glint in his eyes. "I don't know how you do it." He looks me up and down. My top half is naked, my skin glistening with sweat running down my abs, and my eyes thin in his direction.

"Do what?" I spit out, wishing he would leave already.

"Go without sex for so long." I breathe out slowly as I flex my fist.

"Because he is committed and a fucking fitness freak and a goddamn professional," Brady speaks up for me. I spot Cody out of the corner of my eye, watching closely. He's ready to step in if needed.

Boxing is about fitness, but also mental toughness. "I box better with blue balls," I tell him, a smirk coming to my lips. It has been about two months since I touched a woman, and I am on the edge. But that's what I need, an edge. No other boxer I know takes fights as seriously as I do, and I one hundred percent know that staying celibate during my training gets me the advantage in all my fights. That is why I am undefeated. That is why I am the underground champion.

"A hell of a lot more mental strength than me. I like pussy too much. Way too fucking much," Marcus says with a chuckle.

"About time you fucked off now." Cody, my other best friend, enters the conversation, and the three of us stand side by side. Our arms crossed in front of our chests, we look like the security team we are.

"Ahh, if it isn't the Big, Bad Baltimore Boys all trying to be intimidating," Marcus teases as he throws a cigarette into his mouth. I step forward then, right into his space, and push my shoulders back, arms lowered to my sides. I have had enough. He needs to leave.

"Fine. Just take Rago down in round three when you meet in a few weeks, and I will leave you the fuck alone." Marcus has rigged the fights since I started. I nod to him in understanding, because if he wins, then I win. He lines my pockets well, and I desperately need the money. Besides, I know that I can make this fight last as long as I need to. I watch him retreat, his ill-fitting suit jacket flapping around him comically from the gym's fans as he walks backward to the door.

"Fuck off and don't come back," Brady yells to him, and I hear sniggers from the other men around the gym. We are all cut from the same cloth here. Grew up with nothing, and still don't have much. But I am trying to change. That's why I started Fortress with Brady and Cody. Our new security company is only a few months old, but we're building. I just need it to build faster so I can get out of the ring and into a normal life.

"I hate that fucker," Cody mumbles, walking back over to the young kid he was training.

"You and me both," I say as I head back to the bag and try to refocus.

"You should just tell him to fuck off," Brady says, holding the bag for me again as I start to punch, my momentum now lost.

"I plan to. Just a few more fights. We need the money. Fortress has to bring in a few more clients before I can retire," I explain, not that he doesn't already know. We talk about this constantly. Our budget is tight, so my fight winnings and any profit we make go straight back into hiring more men and getting the business up and running. We pay our team fairly, all the while trying to get more gigs. It is a balancing act. One that has a time limit.

"Jimmy has us down for Club Vine on Saturday night," Brady says, and I nod.

"Club Vine, where the ladies are fine!" Cody yells out, and we scoff a laugh. Jimmy's slogan is so chauvinistic, but also very fucking catchy.

Club Vine, Baltimore's newest nightclub, is owned by Jimmy Sallon, an old school friend of ours who made a few dollars on a gamble and then invested in a club. He has done a good job too, fitting out an old warehouse and accepting our security contract immediately. It has only been open a few weeks, so the nights are slow. We are all hoping attendance increases and the club is a success, for Jimmy and for Fortress.

"Let's just hope we can get a few more clubs. Our boys are sick of hanging out at the local mall already." Manhandling shoplifting kids is not where I want Fortress to be focused, but it pays the bills. I feel bad every time I pick up a kid because that was me once upon a time. I had a mother who didn't give a shit, never had any idea who my father was, and there was never enough money for food. I stole my way through my teenage years until I found boxing, which became my only survival.

"We need to go premium," Brady says, and I stop punching to look at him.

"What the fuck are you talking about?" Cody asks from where he is training next to us. I squint at Brady like he has lost his mind.

"Just thinking, we should do the top end of town. You know, art galleries, luxury goods, the Porsche dealership. That kind of shit." I raise an eyebrow. That is the kind of money we could only dream of. And dreams don't pay my fucking bills. I hit the bag again, frustrated that at my age I still need to use my body to bring in a fucking paycheck.

"We are not exactly premium people, Brady," I deadpan, not sure I have ever heard him say a full sentence without a swear word.

"It's not a bad idea," Cody says, walking up to us, and I look at him sharply.

"Let's just focus on Club Vine, the mall, and getting this fucking fight done, and then we can look at the next steps." Now I am in a bad mood. Money problems combined with a visit from Marcus is not ideal. But one feeds the other. I need Marcus, because without him, I have no fight. Without this fight, I have no money. Without the money, I have no Fortress and no way out of this cycle of trying to get on my feet and failing. Every. Single. Time.

Marcus always tries to throw his weight around, get everyone to see him as a boss. Loves all us big guys to cower to him. I call it small dick syndrome. It does nothing but piss me off, and now I feel sorry for any patrons at Club Vine tonight because I know I will take my anger out on them.

I hear the door open and Levi walks in. The kid is full of attitude. Turned up here one day out of the blue, and it was like looking in a mirror. So I train him. Give him a way to get out his aggression and give him someone to talk to. Since then, a few other kids come in like the one Cody was just working with. Brady has a few he trains as well.

We know we aren't premium people. We have done some crazy, fucked-up, and illegal things in our time. But we are trying to make amends, and if helping a kid like Levi eases my conscience, then so be it.

3

VALERIE

"I swear, this is the most fun I have had in a long time. Thank you for bringing me out," I tell the girls as we get back to our private lounge in the VIP area. I'm hot from dancing but feeling good.

"Where did you find this place?" Chelsea asks Chloe as we all look around. My eyes survey the dance floor below. The crowd was smaller when we arrived, but now it is really pumping. I take in the busy bar, the few staff behind looking run off their feet.

"One of my best customers came into the store this week talking all about it. I thought it would be perfect for us tonight," Chloe says, looking at me with a worried smile. As a jewelry designer, she sees a lot of different people, all who love to give her the latest gossip and tell her about the trending places. Her pieces are very sought after, being one of the best designers in the country.

"It's great!" I say, giving my friends a small smile, and they all look at me with concern.

"You needed it. Let's be honest, the bomb Father Van

Cleef dropped on you this week... I can't believe you are not comatose somewhere, rocking yourself," Simone quips, taking a sip of her champagne.

"I'm fine. Everything is going to be fine," I tell her, trying way too hard to keep my smile in place. She looks at me like she doesn't believe a word I say. Neither do I.

"Seriously, can you just tell your father thanks but no thanks?" Chloe asks.

"I have no idea what I am going to do." Giving up on putting on a façade, my head drops to my hands. I haven't seen my father since I had dinner at his place earlier this week. I've spent my days working and trying to figure out how I can take my rightful place at the head of Van Cleef Corp and not get married to a man my father chooses.

"You're an adult. You can just not do it," Simone says, like it is the easiest decision.

"I know. But if I don't do it, then he will blacklist me from working anywhere in Baltimore. Probably the entire East Coast, actually. I would lose access to Van Cleef Corp entirely..." I fidget with my hands, the feeling of uncertainty crawling up my neck.

"And tell me again how that is any different to your current situation?" Chelsea asks, raising her perfectly shaped eyebrow at me. I balk then, because she is right; it is no different to my life now. My father has already told me I will never work again.

"I've never not done what my father has asked before. Plus, he is all I have left," I tell them, swallowing the uncomfortable feeling, pleading with them to understand. It sounds immature, but ever since Mom died, I have tried everything to be the perfect daughter. He always said he had enough to worry about and didn't want me to be one of them. So I made it my life's mission. Straight A student. I am not promiscuous, I keep my friends circle tight, I work hard, don't really party, and I've never stepped a foot out of place. But the real issue is, I have no one else. No other family. If I go against him and challenge him for the CEO position, then I will be on my own, an orphan.

"Of course you haven't. You have been the perfect daughter. Done everything asked of you. You work your ass off, you go to every charity function, and you are beautiful. Every man in this city wants you and every woman in this city wants to be you. You do it all in the hopes that your father will finally open his eyes and see how truly amazing you are and treat you like the beautiful daughter you are. Everyone else in this godforsaken city can see it but him. You need to stop doing everything he asks of you." I give Simone a small smile and nod, grateful to have such amazing girlfriends.

"It's not that easy..." I say, shaking my head a little. There is a lot to consider.

"We know it isn't. But just know you always have us," Chloe says, reaching out and grabbing my hand, offering me a small squeeze of support. I swallow as her words penetrate and remind me that I do have her and the girls. I have someone. They may not be blood, but they are more family than my father has been.

"Besides, you can't get married; there are too many hot guys here," Simone adds, lightening the mood, her eyes glued to a team of security men who stand at the front of the club. She isn't wrong.

"Don't you see enough hot guys during the week?" Chelsea asks, looking at her in question.

"I am a physiotherapist. I am a professional," Simone says sternly, sitting up straighter with a sparkle in her eye.

"A professional who has her hands all over the state's best NFL team," Chloe sniggers, and I cough a laugh.

"How is the Beauty Bar going? I need to come in this week," I ask Chelsea, both interested in her business and also trying to ascertain her availability to see if I can get in to see her for an eyebrow shape. My father's voice runs through my mind about losing a few pounds and fixing my appearance.

"Your brows are amazing, as always. You don't need to come in. But I am thinking of opening another store down on the water. Can you look over the legal contract for me?" she asks, and I smile.

"That is amazing. Of course. I am happy to." My cell vibrates in my bag, and I pull it out while the girls chatter. It's a notification from socials, so I click on it quickly and heave in a breath.

"What is it?" Chloe asks. She is eagle-eyed at the best of times, so I am not surprised she was watching me.

"Oh, nothing," I say with a forced smile, while my heart thuds in my chest and panic fills my veins.

"Seriously, you look a bit pale. Is everything okay?" Simone asks, and now all my friends are looking at me once again.

"I think... he's back..." I whisper, the words feeling like acid on my tongue.

"Who's ba—oh shit..." Simone's brain catches up with the situation.

"What did it say?" Chelsea demands, and I hand her my phone. I had a stalker situation back when I first left college. It was so frightening that for six months, I didn't leave the house. My father said it wouldn't matter how many security guards he put on me, that it wouldn't make a difference and I should remain hidden until he went away. So, as always, I did exactly what my father told me to and I stayed locked up in the house, going crazy for six months. Since then, nothing, and I forgot all about the vile messages I used to get from random usernames that no amount of blocking and reporting could fix.

"Oh, his username is *valimback*. How original," Chelsea says.

"It will be fine. Probably not him. Or her. Or whatever." I take a sip of champagne, noticing the small shake of my hands. It has been years, and I never did find out who was behind the messages. I left my father to take care of it all at the time. With a wave of my hand, I try to dismiss any worries. "It is probably just some kids playing around."

"Ahh, this is pretty descriptive..." Chelsea says, handing the phone to Simone as Chloe looks over her shoulder.

"Stop parading around like a little slut. You are nothing." Simone reads the message out loud, and I clear my throat and grab my cell phone back.

"You know what? Tonight is about shaking off the bad vibes and having fun, so let's forget about this stupid thing and enjoy ourselves," I say, throwing my phone back into my bag and sitting forward with my glass raised high. "To a fun girls' night." I say, waiting for the girls to clink glasses.

"To a fun girls' night," they all say in unison, and we down our champagne and move on.

"You need to find a man..." Simone gives me a mischievous look.

"What are you talking about?" I frown at her, questioning what she is getting at.

"Well, if you do go through with your father's request, then you need to have one last hurrah," she says with a grin.

"I do not." I laugh, swatting her idea away with my hand. I had a bit of fun in college and have been on a few dates, but my love life is nonexistent. It just doesn't seem to click for me.

"It has been a long time since you went on a date, so we are all wondering what is going on. If you appease your father, you need to get a few more notches on your bedpost before you have no more choice in life." Chelsea stares at me accusingly, and I ignore the fear churning in my stomach.

"I went on a date a few weeks ago," I tell them, and they all look at me as though I am crazy.

"It was months ago. That guy from the bank," Simone says.

"Wasn't he a lawyer?" Chloe asks, confused.

"No, it was the doctor, wasn't it?" Chelsea says, all three of them glancing at each other, then at me, for clarification.

"It was Charles, the accountant," I tell them, taking another sip of champagne. My dating history is so bland,

I am in jeopardy of becoming stale. Maybe an arranged marriage is a good thing, after all.

"The accountant..." Chloe says, smiling and nodding before all three of my best friends crack up laughing at me.

"Clearly, I am just not a good catch!" I say with a groan, thinking back to that disaster of a date, where Charles didn't realize that the sauce on his steak had seafood in it and his face blew up like a balloon due to an allergic reaction.

"Not a *catch of the day* on that date anyway!" Simone jokes, and all four of us need to hold our stomachs, laughing at her poor attempt at a joke. At least my friends help me laugh at myself.

"Oh no..." Simone says, looking at her cell.

"What?" all three of us ask.

"*Society News*. Someone has told them you are here. Now you are trending on social media and so is this club," she says, and I sigh. I can't say I am surprised that Baltimore's society gossip website has news on my whereabouts. They often run an article about the who's who and where everyone is on the weekend. But I didn't think they would find me here. And I didn't think they would have something up so soon. We literally only arrived an hour or so ago, so I know a member of the public is no doubt being their *source* for their story.

"I am seriously not that interesting. I don't know why they would put me in a story." I cringe on the inside. My father isn't going to be happy to see that spread all over the gossip news.

"But you are a Van Cleef!" Chloe says proudly.

"I am beginning to see that name as more of a curse the older I get."

"Ladies... Good evening. Welcome to Club Vine," a man greets, walking up to us wearing a suit, his hair slicked back, full of confidence.

"Thank you," Simone speaks up for us all, and I see his smile widen when looking at her. *Interesting.*

"My name is Jimmy. I own Club Vine, and I wanted to say hello and welcome you all tonight," he says, his smile wide, eyes flicking over us before settling back on Simone.

"I'm Simone," my friend almost purrs, and my eyes widen. *Are they eye fucking each other at the table?* She extends her hand, and he shakes it.

"Chloe," Chloe says swiftly, extending her hand as well.

"I'm Chelsea." She follows the others, then his eyes land on me.

"Thank you, I'm—" I start, but he cuts me off.

"Valerie Van Cleef. Everyone knows who you are. Thank you for the article in *Society News* tonight; it has made a huge difference to our attendance already." His appreciation takes me by surprise, and I look over the edge of the top floor onto the dance floor below and see that it is now packed, with bodies everywhere.

"Of course. No problem," I tell him, shaking his hand, not disclosing that I had absolutely nothing to do with that article and don't endorse it at all. But if it has made a positive difference to his business, then I guess that is okay.

"Well, I will let you enjoy your evening. Please take

my card and call me should you need anything." Handing us each a card, he steps away and walks out the back.

"He seemed nice," I say, looking at Simone.

"Hmmmm, Simone, you seemed to like him?" Chloe teases.

"There are a lot of good-looking men in here tonight. Jimmy just moved to top spot for me, though," Simone says with a grin.

"I'm going to the bar. I think a round of cocktails is in order." Standing, I grab my bag.

"Hell yes, good idea!" Simone cheers as she finishes her champagne, and I smile at her as I head over to the bar.

Here in the VIP lounge, it is a little less crowded, and I get my order in for four margaritas quickly. I look around the space. It is nice and new, the lounges are plush, the music is pumping, and although it's not really my taste, I appreciate it all the same.

"Four cocktails, on the house," the barman says as he places the drinks on the bar in front of me, and I raise my eyebrows.

"I'm okay to pay." I don't want anyone to think I expect freebies.

"Nope, a table of pretty ladies needs free cocktails. It is written in the bar rule book," he says, smiling and giving me a wink. I plaster a well-practiced fake smile on my face. Clearly, he is flirting. He is an attractive guy, seems friendly, and I think about what Simone just said, about having one last hurrah. But I've never had a one-night stand before or even a sexual fling. All my interactions have been dinner dates. Three of them, usually, before lackluster sex in a bed, which is usually missionary style, with a fake orgasm from me, which turns into a month of dating, mostly being seen at charity functions and the like, before I want to deliberately put my finger in an electrical outlet out of boredom.

"Well, thank you. I appreciate it," I say with grace and internally cringe. I am a smart, successful woman, blessed with thick shiny hair and good genes, but my flirting repertoire is woeful. Giving him another small smile, I decide to get out of here before I embarrass myself. I grab the tray of drinks, managing to pull it from the bar without spilling a drop. I turn to take a step just as the tray slams into a hard body walking by. The lights are low, the music loud, but I am wide-eyed as I watch the drinks spilling onto a large man like they are moving in slow motion. The glasses crash onto the floor at our feet and the tray falls from my hands as I stand there stock-still.

"What the fuck?" A growl comes from the tall mass of a man looming above me, and I gasp. It feels like I look up forever until I see his dark eyes. This guy is huge, angry, tall, tattooed, scary like no one I have ever seen before.

"Oh, I am so sorr—" I start to say.

"Don't you watch where you are going?" he spits out, running his hand down his front, trying to wipe away the four margaritas that now adorn his shirt. His attitude pulls me from my stupor, if only slightly.

"I didn't see you. You came out of nowhere," I tell him as I grab some napkins from the bar behind me.

"Too busy making eyes at the barman," I hear him seethe perfectly over the loud music.

"I was not making eyes," I tell him, affronted, as I start to brush the napkins across the front of his shirt. My hand hitting his solid body has me sucking in a deep breath on impact. He is hard as a rock, and I have no idea what I am doing. He could be dangerous. Deadly. His deep scowl and his muscular, tattooed arms certainly scream danger. My heart rate skyrockets as he moves fast, his hand grabbing my wrist and holding my hand against his chest. When his eyes meet mine, I forget to breathe as I look at him. His hair is as dark as his eyes and cut short, his black jeans hug his thick thighs, and his black shirt is opened a little at the neck, now wet, and showing me more tattoos on his chest, no bare skin in sight. His hold is firm, but not too tight. And I can't help but notice how the skin of his hands is rough, like they are hardworking hands, and nothing like the soft hands of the many suited men that I shake at work constantly. No, his are large and strong and encompass mine with ease. I swallow audibly, my mouth dry.

"Have you had too much to drink?" he asks, the heavy scowl on his face making me match it. My eyes flick to the lanyard around his neck, noting he's one of the security guards. You would think they'd have better customer service than this.

"I've had one drink!" I spit out. Who the hell does this guy think he is?

"Maybe that's all it takes you. I think I need to show you the door." My hackles rise. Yet another man trying to tell me what to do.

"Maybe you need to find your manners." Not scared of him, I step forward, glaring up at him. I am so sick of men bossing me around.

"I have five more hours tonight and no change of clothes. Fuck manners." Nostrils flaring, his hold on my wrist remains as we now stand chest to chest.

"If you opened your eyes, you wouldn't run into a tray full of drinks," I argue. We are both clearly ready for a fight.

"If you rich chicks got your head out of your asses long enough to know other people existed in this world, you would be more careful," he seethes.

"*Rich chicks*? Seriously?" I ask, mocking him.

"Are you offering to sweep up this mess?" He eyes me, trying to prove a point, and I wonder why he has such a chip on his shoulder.

"Let me just get the broom that is stuck up *your ass* and maybe I will." My eyebrow quirks just as his jaw pops.

"Let me help you with this..." Catching on to what's transpiring, the barman walks to my side.

"Fuck off, Mickey," the security guy snaps, proving his issue isn't only with me. The barman does exactly what he is asked to do, scurrying off as quickly as he came, seemingly scared of this guy, and he should be, he is downright frightening... yet my limbs don't shake. I feel perfectly safe. When his eyes don't waver from mine, I think he is trying to intimidate me, but it isn't working. I work in corporate America; I deal with slimebags every day.

"Do you speak like that to all your colleagues?" I

snide before I lick my lips, trying to bring moisture to my mouth. His eyes flick down, watching the movement before looking at my eyes again.

"Ahhhh, everything alright here?" Chloe asks, coming up to my side. Only, neither of us breaks eye contact for long seconds.

"No, your friend here is out." My mouth falls open. *Is he seriously kicking me out of a club?*

"You can't be serious!" I almost screech in disbelief.

"Deadly. Let's go." With his hand still holding mine, he takes a few steps toward the back stairs.

"Wait. What?" Chloe tries to stop him, looking between us, completely bewildered.

"She has had too much to drink. Can't handle her liquor," he says as he starts pulling me along, and I nearly stumble in my Jimmy Choos.

"Wait! Stop! Have you lost your goddamn mind?" I hiss at him, trying to pull my hand away from his chest where it remains in his grip tight.

"If you don't come along willingly, I will carry you out," he deadpans, and my eyes widen before they narrow in challenge.

"You wouldn't dare."

"I warned you." Moving fast, his hands encase my waist, and he hoists me up, plastering me to his body like I weigh nothing.

"Arghhh! Put me down, you idiot!" I'm acutely aware that people are looking, never having been this embarrassed in my entire life.

"As soon as you are outside," he grits out as he starts to descend the stairs. His hands are wrapped tight around my middle, and the warmth that flows through my body is instant. I don't think a man has ever picked me up before.

"What! Stop!" I hear my friends following, but I can barely see them over his shoulders.

"At least take me out the back where no one can see me," I hiss into his ear so he hears me over the music as we reach the dance floor. I am thankful it is crowded and too busy for anyone to really notice us as he walks around the perimeter with ease.

"Babe, I'm calling to get the car!" I hear Simone yell, the three of them right behind us.

"You will go out the front like everyone else," he growls, not even giving me the courtesy of turning his head to look at me when he speaks to me.

"I cannot believe this," I mutter to myself, my anger rising. I don't bother kicking or punching him because there is no point. This guy is a brick wall with a personality to match. There is no fighting him.

"Here," he says once he pushes us through a door and plonks me on my feet in the front foyer.

"Oh, thank God!" Chelsea says dramatically behind me.

"Do you have any idea what you've just done?" Chloe says to him, her hands firmly planted on her hips, but he doesn't flinch. His eyes don't even move from where they now stare at my face. With his arms crossed against his chest, he stands tall, looking down his nose at me.

"Watch your step, ladies. I wouldn't want you to trip on your way out," he says sarcastically, his eyes burning into mine.

"*Now* you are chivalrous," I quip back to him, biting my tongue so hard it stings.

"Car is here, let's get out of here before cameras catch anything," Simone whispers to me, and I see the big guy's eye twitch a little, registering the words, but they still don't leave mine.

"Are you alright?" Chelsea grabs my hand as I turn to leave, breaking our stare and walking with her to the car. Our driver has the back door open, and I see a few people in the crowded line watching. Some already have their cell phone cameras out, and I internally cringe, wondering what they have captured. We all remain tight-lipped until the car door closes and we pull away from the curb.

"That was intense," Simone says, looking at all of us with wide eyes.

"I accidentally spilled drinks on him. I apologized, but he had an attitude," I explain, while swallowing down my adrenaline and trying to get my racing heart under control.

"He has got something..." Simone murmurs, looking out the rear window. I don't dare turn around. I still feel his eyes on me.

"That was the hottest thing I have ever seen," Chelsea admits, biting her lip. "He is so into you."

"He was sooo not. He is infuriating. He just kicked me out of a club for doing nothing!" I have never been manhandled like that before in my life. No man has ever picked me up before. But as furious as I am, it was... kind of hot.

"And if he didn't, he would have totally fucked you in

the middle of the VIP lounge," Simone says, then they all burst into laughter, and I roll my eyes.

"*Society News* is going to have a field day over this." I'm already thinking about what my father is going to say.

"Probably. But you are going to be old and married soon, so maybe it is time you listen to me and live a little?" Simone raises an eyebrow.

"If my father lets me live after this, anything is possible," I tell her with a moan. How do I get myself out of this mess?

4

AJ

I watch the car until it drives down the street and the red taillights turn the corner.

"What was that about?" Cody asks me, stepping up to my side.

"Too much to drink," I murmur, my jaw clenched.

"Those girls? They only got here, like, an hour ago," Cody says in disbelief.

"For some, it only takes one." I know the words are not true. She wasn't drunk. But she pissed me off. My anger hasn't subsided all day. My body feels sticky from the cocktails, and my lack of sex has me wound tight. I shouldn't have snapped at her. I shouldn't have thrown her out, and I sure as fuck shouldn't have touched her. I roll my head to try to get rid of the tension building and get myself under control. I have never been so irritated yet so attracted to a woman in my life.

She was hard to miss, but she was sitting up in the VIP section like it was her ivory fucking tower, drinking champagne that cost a small fortune. She was fucking sexy, and I wanted to argue some more, make her mad, and then fuck her hard against the wall. That is why she had to leave.

"How's the front door?" I ask him, ignoring my inner turmoil and focusing on how it has been tonight.

"We are pushing people through. We are almost to capacity and the line is growing. I'm not sure what is going on tonight, but it is the biggest crowd we have ever had here," Cody says.

"We need to keep the boys on alert, there are a lot of people here. It's hard for them to keep their eyes on the job." My eyes flick immediately back to the dark street.

"Boys. Jimmy needs us," Brady says, poking his head out the door.

"All of us?" I ask, curious.

"Yep. He isn't happy about something," Brady says, and my shitty night just got even shittier. Jimmy is a friend, but we are also in business together and Fortress really needs this job. If I can't do security, then there really isn't much else for me. Anxiety crawls along my skin at just the thought of failure. Now that I am getting older and fighting is not really a future moneymaker for me like it once was, I need to make Fortress a success. Failing isn't an option.

As Cody and I follow Brady inside, I think through what could be so important that he is dragging us to his office in the middle of a busy Saturday night. But I come up empty. Because all I can think about is the feisty brunette in the red dress that was too fucking short and too fucking tight, showing me every inch of her curves. A growl vibrates in my chest, and I shake my head to dislodge the wayward thoughts.

"Alright, we're here. What's happening?" I say the minute we push through the office doors and see Jimmy standing at his floor-to-ceiling windows, looking at his nightclub below. The glass is tinted and one way, meaning we can see out, but no one can see in.

"What the fuck just happened in the VIP area?" he spits out, looking at me sharply.

"What are you talking about?"

"Did you, or did you not, just throw Valerie Van Cleef out of my club?"

"Who the fuck is Valerie Van Cleef?" I huff out a laugh, having no idea what he is talking about.

"The woman you just *escorted* from the VIP lounge by picking her up and walking her out, dumping her at the door," he says, his nostrils flaring.

"Oh, the woman we kicked out?" Cody says, putting two and two together.

"She was drunk," I tell him simply, but I have a feeling that reason wouldn't be enough for Jimmy with how he's reacting.

"She only got here a fucking hour ago and had one glass of champagne!" Jimmy yells, and I straighten.

"What the hell is going on?" Brady asks, us three boys not understanding what the problem is.

"Fucking Valerie Van Cleef. Richest woman in Baltimore. Was just thrown out of my club by you! Didn't you see the line! The fact that she was here tonight almost tripled our custom! And you go and kick her out! Have you lost your fucking mind?" And... the penny drops.

"Fuck me, she looked like she bathed in money. Now I know why," Cody says, as Jimmy and I stare at each other. I can't say I have heard of her before, but Jimmy seems to know exactly who she is. She did look good. Different from all the other women in the club. Her dress was perfect, her hair was perfect, her lips, nails, shoes, body, everything about her was fucking perfect.

"Fuck. I didn't even get a photo for socials," he grumbles as he runs his hand through his hair. "She can literally make or break this club. If she puts it out on social media she was here, the lines next week will be double. Now, after you threw her out, the opposite will probably happen, and the club will go under, and we will all be without a job."

"Fuck," I murmur, as the last half an hour finally settles in.

"Fuck is right." Jimmy sighs.

"What can we do?" Brady asks, stepping forward, all three of us now knowing what is at stake.

"I'm not sure there is anything we can do. But I will try to call her or her friends this week, see if I can get them back so you can apologize to her," he says, looking at me.

"I am not fucking apologizing," I mutter. I don't want to see her again. I can't see her again. The vision of her is now permanently burned into my eyes and the feeling of her in my arms felt too fucking good.

"If you want this fucking gig, you will. Now get out of here," Jimmy dismisses us, and I don't wait before I bolt out the door. Angry at myself. Angry at Jimmy and angry at Little Miss Perfect.

But I know I don’t need to worry because she won't be back. Women like her never come back.

As I step onto the main floor, the music is louder and the people appear drunker. It is past midnight and nothing good ever happens after midnight. Rolling my shoulders, I crunch my knuckles. Four more hours until I can call it a night, then sleep for a few hours before heading back to the gym. Because when you come from nothing, you work for everything.

There is no driver coming to take me home. I need to look after myself.

5

VALERIE

"Valerie dear, it was so lovely to see you," Mrs. Alderman says, shaking my hand limply and giving me her pursed-lipped smile.

"Lovely to see you as well. Please drive safely," I tell her as she glides around me and out the door. I take a breath. This fundraising luncheon on behalf of Van Cleef Corp is now almost over, and I can't wait to head home and kick off my heels. It has been a long week. I had meeting after meeting, signed a new deal for office space, reviewed the contracts on a new property development the company is looking into, and prepared some reports for the next board meeting. I have also spoken to George. He had no idea of my father's plans to marry me off and he didn't like it at all. We have agreed to meet to discuss things further.

"Thanks, Val. A great event, as always," Lucy Hamilton, owner of Bloomers Books, says, walking up to me, and I grab her in for a hug.

"Lucy, tell me something good..." I whisper to her, and she chuckles. She knows how draining these luncheons are. We have become firm friends over the past year. Ever since I started helping her with raising money for the literacy programs at Bloomers Books.

"You looked hot getting thrown out of that nightclub on the weekend." She giggles, and I huff a laugh as I pull away from her but don't let her go.

"Well, trust *Society News* to ensure all the latest Valerie Van Cleef news is widely available."

"Are you okay? What happened?" Lucy asks, looking mildly amused and slightly concerned.

"It was a misunderstanding. Nothing too dramatic." I wave off her question. For this entire luncheon, I have had people talking to me and behind my back about the photos of me that *Society News* published, being escorted from Club Vine. I've been mortified. I thought about sending a legal letter, threatening them with slander, but I know it won't do any good. They would probably report on that as well and the whole thing would blow up again.

"I got invited to Chloe's new showing. Please tell me you will be there?" she asks me.

"I will be. It has been too long since I saw you, though. We should catch up properly soon."

"Why don't you come by the bookshop?" her brother, Ben Rothschild, says as he approaches us.

"She is always at the bookshop!" Lucy says, grinning. It's true, I am there a lot.

"Hey, Ben. How's the firm?" I greet him with a smile. Ben runs Rothschild Law, one of the biggest law firms in the country. He mainly manages all the legal for their other businesses, but it is still a huge firm, nonetheless.

"The firm is great. Growing. I wanted to talk to you about business, actually," he says, and I tilt my head, intrigued. It isn't often opportunities like working with the Rothschilds come up, and it is something I would love to explore. I realize in this moment that this is what I will miss if I am married off. This business networking, collaborating with other like-minded people.

"Hmmm, you want to talk to the competitor? Really?" I tease, raising an eyebrow. I get along well with all the Rothschilds, but our parents never did. My father hated their parents, and Mrs. Rothschild was well known for her diabolical choices when it came to her boys. Our parents were always competing. It is something all us kids now hate.

"We are wanting to collaborate locally, and we were wondering if Van Cleef Corp would be interested?" he says with his trademark smirk. I would personally love to collaborate with the Rothschilds, but just standing here talking to Ben will make my father angry. At the thought, my eyes dart around the room, looking for him. Ben is vague, but I get the bubble of excitement in my stomach that tells me this could be something good. This is soon met with the new feeling of dread when I think that this could all be taken away from me in an instant. I don't have the weight of a ring on my finger, but it feels heavy just the same.

"I'm absolutely interested, although my father..." I start to say.

"I get it. My parents were the same. But perhaps we can have a confidential chat. Just you, me, and my brothers.?" His smile is genuine. I still haven't seen or spoken to my father. The voicemail he left me after the *Society News* photos went live made it very clear he was displeased, and he outlined exactly how much of a shameful embarrassment I am to him. I can almost feel his animosity from where I spot him standing at the other end of the room. I look at Ben. I want to lead Van Cleef Corp and maybe working with the Rothschilds is how I can make the business a success instead of this marriage idea my father has.

"You have my number," I say, my smile matching his as I watch him. I am good at what I do. I know Van Cleef Corp like the back of my hand. I know almost every employee. Throughout college, I worked in all divisions. Something my father has never experienced. When you start from the bottom like I did, you truly work your way up, and while everyone knew who I was, I don't believe they treated me with kid gloves. I am endlessly grateful for that. It has made me better than my father could ever be.

"We have to run now, but I'll call you and set up some time." Clearly happy with our discussion, he says his goodbyes and heads out.

"See you at Chloe's showing, if not before," Lucy says, giving me another hug before she follows him out.

I feel like I float lost in thought as I walk around the room for the next thirty minutes, saying goodbye to everyone until there are just a few people left.

"That went well. I think we raised close to half a

million, which is astounding," Abigail says as she grabs her bag. This was the first charity event that my father put on my new schedule. I have a million things I need to do at work as the Senior VP, Bordeaux needing some attention, and Chloe's showing coming up, so adding this to my to-do list has my mind in a mess.

"It is great, but that was what we were expecting?" I ask her, still a little preoccupied thinking about Ben's offer.

"Yes, of course, but after having you splashed across *Society News* this week at the front of that horrible club on the outskirts of town, I am surprised anyone turned up at all," Abigail says, and I pause.

"Seriously?" My frown's obvious.

"Your father was upset." she whispers to me, and I take a deep breath. "He is going to be even more so after seeing you talking with Ben Rothschild." She gives me a warning look, and my hackles start to rise.

"Well, Ben Rothschild just offered us an opportunity," I tell her, straightening my shoulders.

"What for?" She pulls back like I offended her.

"What do you mean, what for? For Van Cleef Corp," I tell her, squinting at her in confusion.

"Oh, don't be silly, Valerie. You won't be working there soon. Your father already discussed this with you." Abigail scoffs at me.

"He didn't discuss anything with me. He threatened and somewhat blackmailed me." I only just register my words as I speak them, causing me to pause. *My own father blackmailing me?*

"Here are the two most beautiful women in the country," my father says, walking up to us with a manipulative look of love on his face, with an even older man right next to him. My smile is instant, well practiced, and as fake as my stepmother's breasts. My fists clench, nails biting into my palm. I swallow roughly before I take a big breath.

"Hello, dear," Abigail purrs, as my father makes an act of curving his hand around her slim waist and pulling her tight, leaving the man standing next to me.

"Ladies, this is William Schmidt. William, my beautiful wife, Abigail, and my daughter, Valerie." My father makes the introductions. I know without even needing Dad to say it that this is the man. This is who he has chosen for me to marry.

"Pleasure to meet you." William shakes Abigail's hand, then turns to me. "Pleasure to meet you, Valerie." His voice lowers an octave, and his eyes roam across my body like he is assessing his new possession. I get a sick feeling in my stomach, but I put out my hand to shake his. My body stills when he grabs my hand and twists it in his, lifting it to his lips. Leaning over slightly, he kisses my hand in an old-world greeting that tells me everything I need to know about William Schmidt.

He is an older man, a little overweight, with not a lot of hair on his head. But none of that matters as much as the look in his eyes or the sleazy smile on his lips. We haven't met before, but his name rings a bell. The Rolex on his wrist shines brightly, almost matching the silver at his temples.

"Schmidt? As in the oil baron?" Abigail asks not so subtly, and I'm thankful she asked because now I remember. William Schmidt is one of the wealthiest men in all of the country. Married twice already, I think he has children my age, perhaps a bit older. How he ended up here at our little charity luncheon in Baltimore with my father, I don't know. But I don't like it.

"Yes, oil has been my family's interest for years. Just got back from Dubai, actually," he brags, and I try hard to focus. This all makes so much sense now.

Ever since the Rothschilds started taking their business global through their move into Singapore, Dad has been jealous. We have always had a healthy business rivalry with the Rothschilds. One, in my opinion, that isn't warranted. We work in different fields, have different specializations. I would rather work collaboratively like Ben just suggested than push against each other. But Dad obviously thinks marrying me off to an oil magnet with interests in the United Arab Emirates is the kind of business expansion we need, and to get it, he is offering me up like a pig to a slaughter.

"Ever been?" His gaze lands on me, and I push my thoughts to the back of my mind and come back to the conversation.

"To Dubai? No. I have heard it is nice," I say diplomatically, tamping down the urge to punch someone or something. It is one thing to suggest a marriage for business success. If he suggested I spend time with a man who was more my age, who I maybe had some things in common, then I probably could have looked at it from a different angle. But meeting William Schmidt solidifies exactly what my father thinks of me. There is absolutely nothing about this arrangement that is even remotely beneficial to me. Not one thing. My father doesn't care about my well-being. My life. My future. He doesn't care about me at all.

"We should go sometime?" His tone is laced with innuendo, and I still.

"Oh. There you are!" Simone's voice rings out behind me, and I have never been more grateful for my friend.

"Heeeyyy!" I turn to face her, giving her a look of *thank you*, and she nods in understanding.

"I have been looking for you everywhere. I am just going to steal our little charity bunny away. Nice to see you, Mr. Van Cleef," Simone says diplomatically, already pulling me away and I ignore Mr. Schmidt's scowl.

"Bye, nice to meet you, Mr. Schmidt," I say quickly, remembering my manners, then leaving them all before anyone can say anything more. But they don't need to. The look on my father's face says a million words, none of them good.

"Your timing is impeccable," I whisper to Simone as I grab my bag and coat and we walk out of the Four Seasons like it is on fire.

"Yes, well, I saw the moment your father brought the old guy over and knew I had to get you out of there. Who was he?" She waves to her driver.

"He was an oil guy. Just back from Dubai. I think he might be the one," I tell her, feeling suffocated and like I want to vomit.

"Your father sure knows how to pick them," she growls.

"Surely, he wouldn't try to match me to a man like

that?" I ask her, almost pleading with her to tell me not to be so silly.

"From where I was watching, that is exactly what he was trying to do," she says, as we both slip into her waiting car.

"But he is older than my father?" I shriek as soon as we are in the back seat and the doors close, giving us privacy.

"Your father has always been money hungry. You always told me that." She looks as angry as I feel. "Let's forget about him and old man oil baron too." I look out the window at the passing city and try to control my breathing.

My cell vibrates in my purse, and I pull it out, my nerves running wild as I look at it. My father's name lights up the screen, and I swallow. I go to answer, but my finger hovers over the button. Apart from this week, I have always answered him. I never ignore my father. I do everything he asks, and I do it all with a smile.

"Was that another stalker message?" Simone looks at me with concern.

With everything going on, I totally forgot about that. "No. Not at all. I haven't had another one. I told you, that was just kids mucking around. My father is calling me, no doubt to scold me for our little stunt back there," I tell her, and she rolls her eyes.

Deep down, I know that William Schmidt is the man my father wants me to marry. A man who will be on to his third wife, with kids my own age. A man who will cheat on me at every opportunity, a man who will expect me to be silent, not work, not have an opinion, and just open my legs whenever he feels like it. So I ignore his call and place my cell back in my bag.

I have had enough. My decision is made. I am not going to marry him. I am going to go against my father's wishes for the first time in my life. As I think about the decision, my chest already feels lighter, my shoulders lowering, and I start to think about what my next steps should be.

"We are going out tonight," Simone states, breaking me from my thoughts, and I lay my head on the back of the seat, looking at her.

"I don't really feel like it tonight," I say, feeling battered from the week already. The gossip from *Society News* doesn't help.

"We are going back to Club Vine," she says and I sit up quickly at that.

"Have you lost your mind?" I ask, looking at her like she is crazy.

"Well... the owner Jimmy called. Apologized, of course, and I thought he was kind of cute..." With a sigh, I sink into my seat.

"Ohh, he left me a very apologetic message. I haven't had a chance to return his call yet," I tell her, and she gives me a small smile.

"So I told him we would be there tonight..." Simone says, giving me her puppy dog eyes.

"But why do I need to go? Can't you girls just go?" I ask. I'm not in the mood to dance or be kicked out of a club again.

"You need to let your hair down. *Society News* was shit, but if you go back tonight, then you are just proving their horrible gossip wrong. Jimmy has given me his word that you won't get kicked out again. We will all be left alone, and we'll have free drinks all night. Plus, you worked hard putting today together. I heard Abigail. You raised close to half a million dollars today and that is all because of you. Now it is time to dance the night away, look at hot men, and drink champagne."

"I might have something else worth celebrating..."

I proceed to tell her all about my conversation with Ben Rothschild, and I need to cover my ears from her screams of delight at the prospect of me collaborating with the Rothschilds.

"That's three things we can celebrate!" she says with an excited clap as the car pulls up to my apartment building.

"Three? What's the other one?" I ask as we step out of her car and cross the sidewalk to my apartment complex, my doorman Victor opening the large glass door for us.

"You seeing that sexy security guy again?" When she wiggles her eyebrows, I shake my head at her. I won't lie. I have thought about him this week. His deep scowl, his strong hands on my waist, and his tattoos.

"I think I should stay well away from him," I murmur. "Hey, Victor." I greet my older doorman as we walk through the doors.

"Maybe we will enact operation: Get Val Laid Tonight," Simone says too loudly, and I hear Victor cough.

"At least we now know that even Victor thinks that is ridiculous," I whisper to her as I grab her elbow and we walk swiftly to the elevator banks. Simone cackles a laugh so large it rolls around the entire marble foyer.

But she is right. Maybe I need to go out, dance away this funk, and, if nothing else, prove the gossip hounds that everything is alright with Valerie Van Cleef. Even though inside I am crumbling.

6

AJ

Brady and I make our rounds throughout the club. The crowd tonight is noticeably bigger than last week. Maybe Jimmy was right; this Valerie Van Cleef woman does make a difference.

"We just need Jimmy to pay us, and then we should be okay for the next couple of weeks," Brady says to me as we take stock of the club.

"I need to win this fucking fight," I growl, feeling stressed. Brady, Cody, and I went through our financials earlier today. It's still too tight. We are surviving from job to job, the money not stretching as far as we need it to. We just need a little wriggle room to allow us to hire more guys to pitch for more clients. Without the men, we can't service new clients, and without new clients, we can't pay for more men. The cycle is a hard one to break and the thought of how we might succeed keeps me up at night.

"You will. That will give us some breathing room until

we can pick up some new clients. We are on the cusp of something big. I can feel it," Brady says, and I shake my head.

"We need more than a fucking feeling, Brady. We need cash. We need new clients. What about that small shopping mall on the other side of town?" I ask him, and he gives me a look that tells me I'm not going to like his answer.

"I went over there last week, chatted to the management team. They are locked in with the security company they have for at least the next six months and not looking at changing." I sigh, remembering we have already spoken about this.

"AJ!" Jimmy yells for me, and I leave Brady to it, heading over to the main bar where Jimmy is currently perched, having a drink.

"All good, Jimmy?" I ask, because he is fidgeting, appearing to be on edge. I can feel it.

"She is coming back tonight," he says, his eyes piercing mine. And I know exactly who he is talking about. *Fuck.* I clench my jaw. This was not what I was expecting.

"Seriously?" After I threw her out last week, she must have balls of steel to come back here.

"Her and her friends will be in the VIP lounge. Ensure you and your team don't fuck it up this time." That's my warning before he throws back his whiskey and stalks away.

"Got it," I murmur, mostly to myself, rubbing my jaw. We are a few men down tonight; otherwise, I would take off and leave Brady and Cody to manage on their own.

The crowd is also much bigger than we have ever had before so there is no chance of any of us not being front and center. I stalk to the front of the club to monitor the door, seeing everyone in place and nodding to Cody, where he stands at the beginning of the line, assessing everyone who wants to come in.

"Excuse me?" a small woman says from the corner, and I look at her.

"Line is over there," I say, nodding to the far right.

"Oh, I'm not coming in, but I wanted to talk to you." I remain quiet. "I'm Rena from *Society News*. I wanted to ask you a few questions."

"No," I say, keeping my eyes on the line. I had no idea that *Society News* even existed before this week, Jimmy highlighting it all to us boys, happy to see his club and Valerie's face together, even if it did paint her in a terrible light.

"I can pay. One hundred bucks if you can confirm you kicked out Valerie Van Cleef last week," she asks, and my body jolts. *What the fuck did she just say?*

"Step away from the security team, or you will be escorted down the street," I say firmly.

"Okay, two hundred bucks for a direct quote about her that I can use in a story tomorrow. Was she drunk?" She pushes again, and I unfurl my hands from where they are crossed at my chest and stand tall.

"I will call the police if you don't remove yourself from this side of the street in the next thirty seconds," I say in a growl, my teeth clenched.

"Oh. Shit, okay. No problem." Quickly putting her hands up in surrender, she walks away backward, realizing she has overstepped. I watch her run to the other side of the street to a small late-night diner and go inside, positioning herself on a stool in the window, watching who is coming and going. No doubt with her cell phone at the ready.

It's dark, almost eleven, and the night is cool, with a nice crispness to the air. It's refreshing after being inside all night. I should go back inside. I should be walking around the dance floor perimeter, but I don't want to leave.

I pace out in front of the club, monitoring the team who all look at me like it is odd that I am out here. Because it is. I watch each car as it pulls up to the curb. We have had a lot of people coming in tonight. The line for the door is the longest it has ever been. There are more glamorous women than we have ever had before stepping through our ropes, yet not the one I want to see.

Jimmy was right. The gossip that Valerie Van Cleef was here last week has obviously spread. I have read that small article more times than I would ever admit. Valerie Van Cleef is indeed one of the richest women in the city, all due to being an heir of Rose Van Cleef. From what I read, Rose was a ruthless woman who somehow built the family fortune that Valerie's father now runs. But that wasn't the most shocking thing in the article. It was the fact that Valerie is single and has been for some time. That is a thought that I have been ruminating on all week, how a woman who is rich, sexy as fuck, polite, and sassy is single. There must be something else wrong with her.

I look at the street and I know it is her from the

moment the car pulls up. The sleek black design of the Mercedes G-Wagon, almost comically expensive on this side of town. She steps out, her long sun-kissed legs first, and my eyes feast on the sight. Waiting on the rest of her, she slides out of the black leather interior like only a well-to-do woman can in those come-fuck-me heels she is wearing, the sparkly gold straps matching a short glittery gold dress that almost has my knees buckling.

"Fuck me," Tommy, one of my new guys, says from in front of me.

"Eyes off her and onto the job," I growl, not sure where my possessiveness is coming from. But I stand even taller where I am in the shadows, letting my eyes trail up her body and to her face. Her smile is wide, but I see the slightly unsure look in her eye. Especially when flashes go off from people's cells, including a few photogs that have appeared.

"Get them in, Tommy," I bark, wanting her removed from the open where anyone can see her. She and her friends didn't appear to want the cameras last week, and now I can understand why. I feel a little bad for putting her through it all last weekend.

I grind my teeth as I watch a few of my boys push the photogs out of the way, and Valerie's face contains a little more fear. It shouldn't be there. She has nothing to fear. She fucking owns everyone around her, including the three blond women who fall out from her car after her, the same ones who were with her last week. They all hold hands, and I watch her some more. She doesn't have a hair out of place. Her lips are glossy, her low-cut dress teasing me, with her tits looking too perky, too perfect.

"Ladies, welcome to Club Vine," Cody says, giving them direct access inside. "No need to wait in line when you're looking this fine." Her friends giggle as I watch Cody wink at the tall blonde. Valerie smiles, but her eyes search the landscape, looking for something.

A camera flashes, and on instinct, I step forward, ready to stop anyone who hassles her. Ironic, really, since last week, I couldn't wait to kick her out. She hasn't seen me yet, but I watch her like a hawk and notice every other motherfucker doing the same. My men all stand aside and let her group through the crowd. It is like she is parting the seas as the line into the club that is almost a block long gawks at her.

Valerie Van Cleef.

Her smile is small and gracious, but then she looks up. Her big blue eyes hit mine, and her smile falters a little as she swallows.

"Hey," she says breathily as she steps toward where I am standing near the entrance. I didn't realize that I had moved and walked right up to meet her. I grit my teeth as her sweet floral scent digs into my chest, and I clench my hands, giving her a small nod but offering nothing else. "Are we going to have any issues tonight? Because if so, I would rather just leave again now," she asks with her eyes locked on mine. Her friends stand around her, all of them now waiting for my answer.

"We're good," I murmur. That is as close to an apology from me as she is going to get.

"Great. Let's go, then," she says, breathing out what I think is a sigh of relief. I open the door for her and watch her walk in, looking at her fucking fantastic ass in the skintight dress.

Fuck. Me. Right the fuck now.

I am obviously so hard up for her because I haven't been with a woman in months. She is nothing but a rich, perfect little princess who wouldn't know a day's work or the resilience needed to fight for survival. She is a guest of Jimmy's and nothing more.

Only, my body is moving before my head catches up, and I follow her and her friends from a safe distance. Her group walks in like they own the place, straight to the stairs to go to the small VIP area that is reserved for people like her. Jimmy obviously got ready for them, because I notice we now do full bottle services in the VIP lounge and there are champagne coolers that reflect the light positioned on a large table, lounge chairs all around. Just for them.

"So your lady came back, huh?" Brady says as he steps up to me.

"Let's keep an eye on this crowd," I murmur, ignoring his comment as I look around.

"There are a lot of people tonight," he says as the two of us canvass the crowd.

"A lot of people and too much liquor." I look at the dance floor, seeing a lot of single men and not enough women. The ratio is a little out of balance.

I look back at Valerie as she climbs the last few stairs, leading her posse, and I don't miss when she turns her head, her eyes finding mine again. She raises her eyebrow in challenge, and I grit my teeth and force myself to walk away.

I can't go touching someone like Valerie. She is not a woman for a man like me. The thought reminds me of the signs I used to see in the gift shops as a kid. *Breakages need to be paid for.*

I will break her and I can't afford to fix her when I do.

7

VALERIE

After a few drinks in the VIP lounge, I start to relax. When I saw the big guy out the front as we arrived, I didn't know whether to ignore him, smile, or slap him. But I offered a small smile, a peace treaty, one he ignored and has all night. No apology, although I wasn't expecting one. A man like him doesn't apologize. He also isn't going to get one from me. I look over the balcony to see if I can spot him, but he is an enigma. Sometimes you see him, sometimes you don't.

"He was looking right at you when we walked up here," Chloe says.

"Who?" I ask, pretending I don't know what she is talking about.

"The big, burly security guard who looked like he wanted to fling you over his shoulder and take you straight to bed." I splutter on my champagne as she sends me a wicked grin.

"She isn't lying. I noticed," Simone quips, taking a sip of her drink and giving me a naughty wink.

"Oh, stop it. It is his job," I tell them, dabbing my lips with a napkin.

"It's his job to look you up and down like he wants to eat you whole? I wonder what that job pays these days..." Chelsea teases and wiggles her perfect eyebrows at me.

"Oh, stop! He kicked me out last week, remember?" I whine, thinking about the horrible photos in *Society News*. "Why is it always pick on Val night at this place?" I ask them all as I smile, trying to get my racing heart under control. The minute I saw him tonight, my body was vibrating. He makes me equal parts frustrated and flustered.

"Well, cheers to our amazing friend, Val, who in one day manages to raise half a million dollars for heart disease, get a kick-ass opportunity with the Rothschilds, and eye fucks the sexiest man we have ever seen," Simone says, smiling, raising her glass.

"Cheers!" we all say, giggling, clinking our glasses as we survey the room.

"There are a lot of people here tonight," Chloe murmurs.

"Let's dance before it gets too busy," Chelsea says, and we all nod before following her down to the dance floor.

As soon as we start to dance, I know it was a mistake. My smile leaves my face as the crowd piles around us like we are a magnet. I blame Chloe. She is super popular on socials, so everyone obviously knows her.

I try to get into the beat, hoping the crowd thins a little, and I see the other three girls laughing and twirling so I decide to just go with it. As my body sways, I feel hands on me and move in the opposite direction. A few dance steps to my left, and I think I am safe, until I feel more hands grabbing at my hips and grazing my butt.

Shit. I look up to the girls and see a few guys now positioned in between us. I don't know any of them, and I don't feel safe now that my friends are just out of reach. A man sidles up, his hips moving, gyrating against me. I try hard not to grimace, not wanting to be impolite, but he is seriously too close. It is hot. Sweaty. Loud.

I put up my hands, palms facing out to try and show I am not interested and step away from him. Dancing back toward the girls, I realize they have all partnered up with some men I am positive they have never met before. *It's just dancing, Val. Just go with it.* I roll out my shoulders and take a deep breath. The music changes to something more up-tempo and people start jumping. I feel like I am getting swallowed up, and the heat of bodies is almost overwhelming. Needing air, I push my way to the bathrooms on the other side of the dance floor and feel relief when I finally break through the crowd. I don't try to find my friends, knowing they are okay, and instead walk down the dark corridor and push inside the bathroom to freshen up.

Rinsing my wrists under cold water to cool off, I take a moment to fix my hair. The sweat is already making it puff up, and I try to tame it with no luck. The bathroom is empty so I apply some fresh gloss and decide that I will ignore the dance floor and go straight back up to our lounge to wait for the girls there. I probably should also have some water, my father's words about losing a few pounds ringing in my ear as I look at my side profile in the mirror. I'm wearing a new designer, a gold dress that shimmers and is tight over my curves. My stomach protrudes a little, and I suck it in, but with a few glasses of champagne already consumed, there is no hope of looking any slimmer.

I sigh at my reflection, knowing my father would be less than impressed if he saw me now. As I throw my gloss back in my bag, I feel my cell vibrate and pull it out. It is a notification from my social media, and I click to open it. It's a message from a user called *Valisawhore*. I sigh. I should just ignore these, but with some time to kill and the bathroom being nice and quiet, I take a look.

Valisawhore: Dressed like a little whore tonight, you're asking for trouble.

My breath gets caught as I look at the message. *Is someone following me?* I look at my reflection and pull at my dress before I shake my head. This is exactly what they want. Me to be scared, have doubts. What an asshole. My fear turns into anger as I quickly delete and block the user from contacting me again. It is nothing new. I have dealt with these things in the past, and I am not going to let them get to me this time. I try to not give them much thought, but as I look at my reflection again, this time with a more critical eye, I try to pull my dress down a little. *Is it too short?*

I huff at myself and take a breath to steady my shaking hands. I hate those messages even more than the lies that *Society News* prints. Gathering my things, I push out the door and walk back down the hallway, resigned to the fact that I am just not good enough for my father and now a member of the public has nothing better to do on a Friday night than troll me on the internet. Lost in my thoughts, I only make it a few steps down the hallway when an arm grabs me from behind.

"Hey, sugar." A man who looks a little unstable on his feet almost walks right into me.

"Excuse me." I try to be polite, even now as I wrench my arm out of his tight grip and away from him.

"Where are you going?" he growls and grabs my arm again, even tighter. I wince because it is painful and my heart races in fear. His eyes are red. It is the same guy who was trying to grind on me on the dance floor.

"I'm not interested," I grit out, fear and anger both starting to well as I try to pull out of his grip again.

"Oh, baby, but I am very interested." I smell the sour aroma of alcohol and sweat as he steps closer to me. Panic takes over. I've been propositioned before. Touched, grabbed, and groped. But a new terror runs through me tonight at this man, because I am alone in a hallway where no one can hear me if I scream.

"How about we go down the end of the hall here..." he groans in my ear, pushing his hips into my body, telling me exactly what he wants us to do. I try to turn away, not wanting him anywhere near me, before I feel a gust of wind across my skin and the man is no longer there. The grip on my arm is gone, and I gasp as I look up to see the infuriating security guard slamming his body against the wall.

"Get your fucking hands off her before I break every one of your fucking fingers, asshole," he growls, and I push myself back against the opposite wall as I watch in anticipation. My senses are overloaded at how strong he is. His stance is tall and broad, veins running thick in his forearms, the look on his face deadly, and I swallow as heat consumes my body. His gaze is hard, not looking at me, but looking directly at my attacker. I have never had anyone step in for me before. Not like this.

He grips the guy's shirt at his neck and slams him back against the wall again. I jolt, the sound loud and the action done with such force, I am sure the drywall cracks behind him. I remain quiet, too scared to talk or move, my heart racing, my stomach clenching, wondering what he is going to do.

Because he looks livid, and fighting him, I am almost positive would be deadly.

8

AJ

I slam his body against the wall with so much force I think I break the drywall. I will take great pleasure in ripping each of his fingers from his body. Every piece of skin that touched her, I want gone.

"Hey, man, she was asking for it," he pleads, and I pull his body back toward me to slam his back into the wall again, the movement quick, the noise of it loud, his wail sounding like a two-year-old. I hope I broke his ribs.

"Just fucking open your mouth again and see exactly how angry I am. Do it." I feel murderous. I hate men who put their hands on women like that. I saw my mom taken advantage of a lot as a kid, men always coming past our house to see what they could get away with. Eventually, it wore her down, and she gave up every time a man came to the trailer, almost like her life left her body and she didn't care anymore. My teeth grit together as I eye him, about to throw a punch in his fat, reddened cheek as I hear the thumping steps of my team from behind me.

I was watching her. All this time while she was being

mauled on the dance floor. My jaw is sore from how hard I clenched my teeth, watching all these fucking assholes grab at her when she clearly didn't want them to. I felt relief when I saw her get off the dance floor and go to the bathroom, and I watched her from the dark spot at the end of the hall. I saw him grab her; I saw him try to take what isn't his to take. My skin feels like it is on fire. With only a few weeks to go before my fight, there is no other AJ in me other than the fighting machine. I am a danger to be around and certainly bad for this idiot's health.

"What happened?" Brady asks as I step back, not taking my eyes off this asshole, even as my men grab him on either side and start pulling him down the hall.

"Get him out of here. And all his friends. Banned. Forever," I growl, and my team drags him away.

"You can't do that!" he yells.

When I take a step toward him, I feel a small hand on my forearm. I spin around quickly, ready to face off again, but it is her, standing there, looking wide-eyed. Her breathing is rapid, as is mine.

"Are you alright here?" Brady asks. I totally forgot he was still standing there. He is talking to me, and I feel his gaze on my face, but my eyes are glued to Valerie. I don't want to move them.

"We're fine," she answers for us, her voice quiet and in complete contrast to her sass from last week. I take a breath, hearing that she is okay seemingly enough to lower my anger level a little. I watch her as I see Brady walk down the hall in my peripheral vision, and she swallows and I trail the movement down her bare neck, my heightened emotions now running to my cock, which has been rock-hard since she walked in tonight.

I move toward her another step, making her look up at me.

"Are you alright?" My voice is low, and I hear her gasp of breath as her chest brushes against mine slightly. I have no idea what I am doing, but my senses are high, my natural protective instincts in overdrive. Leaning in, I settle my hand against the wall behind her head. I pull back from her but remain close. It's like she is the only thing that is calming me down. Keeping my anger at bay.

"No one has stuck up for me like that before. Ever." When the words fall from her glossy lips, I have the urge to run my tongue across them.

"Did he hurt you?" I ask as my eyes wander over her body, from her head down to her legs and back again. I ask because it is protocol. I need to know if she was injured. I feel a little panicked at the thought. I also want any excuse to go punch that fucker again for touching her in the first place. She shouldn't be here in the club. The men are animals, and she is too pretty and too fucking fancy to be anywhere on this side of town. My frustration rises at her audacity. Someone like her can go anywhere, Vegas, a country club, a fine-dining restaurant. Anywhere but here.

Her cheeks are flushed pink, and I bite on my back molars to hold myself back from cupping them in my hands. Instead, I grab her wrist and hold out her arm, looking at the red marks that now adorn her due to that asshole touching her. I treat her with a gentleness unheard of for me. I hear her release a small whimper that has my eyes shooting back to meet hers.

"Are you okay?" I repeat, realizing she hasn't answered me yet. Her eyes flick to my hand holding her wrist, so I let her go and put my finger under her chin and lift her face to meet mine.

"I'm fine," she whispers delicately, and my nostrils flare. I need to get myself under control because seeing her right in front of me is testing my need for abstinence at this point. *Why am I not having sex at the moment?* That's right, because I need to fight to financially secure my life. Something the woman in front of me has no idea about.

"You shouldn't be here," I grit out. I'm trying to remain professional. She just had a sleazebag all over her; she doesn't need another one.

"On the dance floor? I love to dance; I love live music and DJs. This place is perfect for that," she rambles, not understanding what I mean.

"No *here*. This club is not a place for someone like you," I tell her as my fingers graze her upper arm, her skin soft and warm, the red finger marks making my jaw pop. Her chest rises and falls a little quicker. I shouldn't be here with her. I shouldn't be touching her. But I can't step away.

"Someone like me?" she asks. Her demeanor changes, eyes thinning, and I tamp down the small smirk that threatens to appear on my face as she juts out her hip and her hand finds her waist. Her eyes flame in defiance and I'm starting to understand that Little Miss Perfect hates being told what to do. And I love a challenge; I love a fight. And when she starts morphing into a woman with a bit of attitude, my body temperature goes up a hundred degrees.

"Yeah, someone like you. Someone who should be at dinner parties looking all pretty. Someone who doesn't know a hard day's work if it bit her in the ass." Her eyebrows rise at my comment.

"Maybe your patrons need to just keep their hands to themselves," she quips, and I swallow harshly, hating her for thinking about him at all. My fingers grip into the wall behind her as I think about the asshole who is now on my kill list.

"That guy is being thrown out as we speak," I tell her, hoping to ease her concerns.

"How did you even see me?" she asks.

"It's my job." I don't share I have been watching her like a fucking stalker from the moment she arrived. She didn't breathe tonight without me noticing. She nods in understanding before we both turn to the sounds of high heels clicking on the tiled floor.

"Oh my God, are you okay?" Her friend with pixie-short blond hair rushes toward her. It's the same one who rescued her from the bar last week. Good to know someone is looking out for her.

"It is a meat market here. Wait until I tell all the girls from Pilates; they will be dying to come next weekend," a taller woman with long blond hair says mischievously, and I growl a little before pulling back, putting distance between us. I don't miss the pixie one's eyes as they home in on the movement, widening in surprise at how close we were.

"What happened? Are you okay?" the third woman, also blond but with curly hair, asks, and I feel a little more settled, knowing they are all with her now.

"You should go back upstairs," I say gruffly. The three blondes wrap around my brunette, making her even more noticeable to me.

"Do you ever smile?" Valerie asks, looking at me with intrigue. I love her eyes on me like this. Like she is actually interested in a guy like me.

"Never." With my facial expressions unmoving, I keep my asshole features in full effect. Because I am an asshole, and she needs to know that. I leave them all as I back away and strut down the hall, ready for blood.

"Oh, hey?" she yells, and I look over my shoulder at her. "I didn't get your name?"

"I didn't give it, sweetheart." Then I turn and walk away to get back to work.

Leaving Little Miss Perfect and her friends behind.

9

VALERIE

It has been a few days since I was at Club Vine. Since the security guy rescued me. And although I have been busy at work, and with the Rothschild opportunity circling in my mind, I have been constantly thinking of the big guy and his contradicting qualities.

How strong and tough he is with others, yet how gentle he was as he held my hand. How gruff he is in tone when others are around, but how soft he was when it was just us. My skin heats even now thinking about his hands on my body and the way my heart races every time I see him. I must be certifiably crazy to think that about a man I don't even know. I don't even know his name. In my limited dating experience, though, no man has had this effect on me ever. And that must mean something.

I feel flustered as I open my apartment door with my elbow and rush in to dump my bags on my kitchen counter before I pull out my ringing cell. The number is not familiar, but I answer it anyway.

"Hello? This is Valerie." I singsong, trying not to

sound flustered, even though I am. But I must uphold the perfect appearance, even on the phone.

"Valerie. This is Jimmy," a man's voice says on the other end as I balance the phone between my chin and my shoulder and open the red wine so it can breathe. "Jimmy Sallon from Club Vine." I pause at his clarification. I didn't call him back last week because I thought I would see him at the club. But after the situation I had with the guy in the hallway, I didn't stick around too much longer and forgot all about speaking to Jimmy.

"Ohh. Hi, Jimmy. How can I help you?" He is the last person I was expecting to call me. With only a few minutes before Chloe is due to arrive for dinner, I scramble across to my sideboard to find a vase for the flowers I just bought. Roses, of course, the namesake of my maternal grandmother. Rose Van Cleef herself.

"I hope I am not catching you at a bad time."

"No, not at all," I lie as I run the tap to fill the vase, multitasking my specialty. Bordeaux runs around my feet, his little nails rattling against my floorboards.

"I wanted to call and apologize for the incident this weekend. I can't believe that you were accosted like that in the hallway, and I want to assure you that security will be upped and more lights and cameras are being installed this week." This is unexpected. Most clubs don't care about these types of things. Women get unwelcome advances all the time. I've lost count of the number of times us girls have been out and experienced unwanted butt grabs and drunken men getting too close on the dance floor.

"Thank you, Jimmy. I appreciate that. I know it is hard

to keep a crowd like that under control, and you can't always know who you are letting into the venue. Thank you for making those changes."

"Well, your appearance at Club Vine, as you know, did the rounds on social media, and for that I am extremely thankful. It is hard to get a new business up and running in this city and having you and your friends in attendance made a big difference, not only that night, but the nights since as well. So if there is anything I can do in return, please let me know." My thoughts automatically go back to the security guard.

"Actually, there is. I was wondering, can you tell me the man's name who rescued me? The security guard? I would like to thank him," I ask, rolling my lips, trying to prevent the smile that threatens to spread on my face. I feel sneaky asking this, like I am going behind his back because he overtly didn't want to tell me his name when I asked at the club. Even though he is infuriating and totally frustrating, he did a nice thing. And while it was his job, the way his eyes pierced mine took my breath away and the way his nostrils flared as he looked me up and down has had me repeating the entire scenario in my mind since the weekend.

"That was AJ. He owns Fortress, the security company I use. He is an old friend of mine. During the day, you will find him at Joe's Gym down on Smith Street. He trains there for his fights," he says, giving me more information than I expected. *AJ.* His name is fitting. Simple, solid. No questions asked.

"Fights?" I wonder what he is talking about.

"He is a boxer. Has a fight coming up, actually." *Isn't he just a world of information?*

"A boxer?"

"Yeah, champion underground boxer. I got a good deal when he started his security firm with his friends, Brady and Cody. No one will mess with them. They are known as the Baltimore Boys. Grew up on the outskirts, still hard and angry, but they are damn good at what they do," Jimmy says proudly, and I make a mental note not to tell Jimmy anything because he seems to like to talk.

"Thank you, Jimmy," I say, my smile now wide, having gotten more information than I was expecting.

"No problem. So will we see you this Saturday? Maybe your friend Simone will come with you?" He fishes for the information I know he wants. Given he was so forthcoming on AJ, and I already know Simone likes him, I offer him a tidbit.

"Simone needs to work this weekend. She is a physio with the local NFL team, so she needs to be at the game this week. But we might be able to come afterward or perhaps next weekend." Now I need to tell Simone that I have spoken to Jimmy.

"I would welcome you all back anytime."

"I am sure we will see you again soon," I tell him, just as there is a knock at my door. "I need to run. Thanks for the call." I end the call quickly before running to the door.

"Hey," I breathe out, opening the door wide, seeing Chloe with her hands full of takeout bags.

"I'm stressed. I need to eat." She marches into my

apartment with what looks to be a week's worth of Chinese food. Bordeaux runs around her feet, growling.

"I still don't understand why your wino dog doesn't like anyone," she mumbles, clearly in a bad mood.

"Bordeaux loves you."

Like she's trying to prove me wrong, she leans over to pat him and nearly loses a finger in the process.

"Nope. Not going to happen," she says, pulling back sharply, and I pick up my little guard dog and put him in his bed. She is right. Bordeaux hates everyone. "I think he needs dog therapy or something."

"Is that even a thing?" I ask, surprised. I've never thought that Bordeaux needs any training, but she is right, he barks and growls at everyone and everything.

"No idea. I'll have my shrink talk to your shrink, and then we can sort it out," she says, throwing her bag on the table.

"What's happening?" I ask as we unpack our food containers on the kitchen counter, and I grab us two wineglasses.

"Everything *was* fine. I have the pieces ready. Catering, photography, my PR people have media coming, you girls will be there..." she says, and I push a glass of red wine to her. She takes a large gulp, and I raise my eyebrows.

"What happened?" I ask tentatively, knowing something with her jewelry showing is not working out for her.

"The security team I hired got a bigger and better gig somewhere else. I called them today to confirm numbers and they told me they double-booked and can no longer be at the event." Her shoulders slump slightly, the fight slowly leaving her.

"Really?" I ask, a smile coming to my face.

"Really. What assholes. I booked them months ago... Wait... Why are you smiling?" Her eyes thin at me over the top of her wineglass.

"We need to sit down for this discussion." Grabbing our food and wine, I walk into my living room and sit on my comfy sofa. I proceed to tell her all about the call I just had from Jimmy.

"Soooo, perhaps I can find AJ and ask if his company can do the job?" I ask her, to see if she is open to it. "Jimmy said they were new, so maybe they have room on their schedule?"

"That would be amazing. We've already seen them in action, so we know they are good. My store is small, so I will only need a few guys, and I really have no other contacts in the security business. I would be trawling through the internet to find someone tomorrow. Can you do it for me? Please?" she asks me, almost begging, and I laugh.

"Of course. Leave it with me. I will try to get in touch with AJ tomorrow and see if I can book them." I'm happy to take something off her plate because I know she is stressed. She shouldn't be. Her collection is fantastic, her craftsmanship is brilliant, and she already has amassed a good following of loyal customers.

"Have you seen this?" she asks me, her eyes looking at her cell.

"What?" I ask as I dig around in my food with the chopsticks. When she turns the phone to me, I almost choke on my noodle. There on her screen is a black-and-white photo of AJ, looking devilishly handsome with his trademark scowl.

"It's on the Fortress website. Says here his name is AJ Steele. Very fitting name since he looks as hard as steel." I grab her phone from her, my noodles now forgotten.

I scroll through, seeing a photo of the other guys, Brady and Cody too, but there isn't much more information. "Jimmy said he is a boxer..." I tell her, my fingers already flying over the search bar on the internet as I put in his name and hundreds of images come up.

"Holy shit..." I whisper, my eyes wide as I look at picture after picture of a half-naked AJ in a boxing ring.

"What? Show me?" Chloe says, leaning over and snatching the phone.

"Oh... My..." She sighs as the two of us crowd around her phone. "Look, there are videos." She clicks on one and the image comes to life as we watch AJ dance around the ring for a moment before he starts punching his opponent. He is hard, a wall of shiny muscle, and I swallow roughly as I look at his body. Not an inch of fat, his face focused, his eyes alight with fire, and his poor opponent absolutely no match as he goes down in a knockout, hitting the floor hard.

"Are you sure you want to have AJ as a contact?" Chloe asks me, sitting back on the sofa, looking at me warily. "You live a life of luxury, work with charities, went to an Ivy league school, have millions in the bank, not to mention you also have amazing friends. He just seems a little... rough. Different, dangerous."

"Boxing is a sport, and he works in security. I wouldn't

say that is dangerous." My body still hums from seeing him in action.

"That, honey, what we just watched, was not sport. That is anger, aggression, pain, blood. I am not even sure that they are following the true rules of boxing."

My eyes flick back to the video that has now finished. She is right, but there is something about him. His intensity, his commitment, his manner, he has absolutely no fear. The complete opposite of me, as I have lived in constant fear for most of my life and even more so lately. Fear of disappointing my father, fear of being married off to the old oil baron, fear of not ever taking my rightful place as head of Van Cleef Corp. The role both my mother and grandmother were able to hold. Fear of being too fat, not good enough, not friendly enough. Just not enough, and I am sick of it.

"Also, don't forget that little issue you have called *your father*. AJ Steele is not someone you can take home to meet the family, you know. Abigail would have a heart attack, and your father would have him sent to prison," she says as she takes a sip of wine, watching me to see if her words penetrate. And they do. She is right. My father would not like me associating with someone like AJ. He is not someone he would approve of. That thought alone makes me realize that I no longer want or need my father's approval. Not even a little bit.

My relationship with my father is deteriorating. Almost crumbling before my very eyes. There is nothing more I can do. I have done so much, and he still isn't happy. So no more. I like AJ, I want to get to know him, and I no longer care what my father thinks.

"To be fair, I am just asking him to do your security job, not running off into the future with him. Besides, boxing is aggressive, yes. But it also takes discipline. It keeps you healthy in body and mind, and to be as good as AJ seems to be, that also takes commitment."

"All true." She nods. "And I do need security," she confirms with a wink, and I smile.

"And he did rescue me from that guy at the club."

"Also true." She nods again. "Not to mention, he is the most good-looking man in this universe, and absolutely into you. I saw the way he stood next to you to make sure you were okay after that other asshole had his hands on you. You were both eye fucking each other. It was the hottest thing I have ever seen." I blush at her comment. His touch is burned in my brain.

"And I am an adult. I don't need my father to approve of all my choices," I tell her, straightening my spine.

"Again, this is all true. But Val, and I say this with love. You have never gone against your father's wishes before." That statement doesn't make me feel as good as it should. It makes me feel stupid. I am a strong, smart, successful woman. I can be strong on my own. I know I can.

I want to decide who I spend time with and who I eventually marry. I want to find my own hero. And I have a feeling I know just where to start.

10

VALERIE

I look around the boardroom and smile. This feels good. This feels right.

"Good to have you here, Valerie. About time we all got together," Tennyson says, taking a seat opposite me, next to his two brothers.

"Nice to see you too. I tend to agree, a meeting like this feels somewhat overdue," I say as I take everything in. Their offices are amazing. Not too different from Van Cleef, but just a little fresher.

"Well, I think we all know the choke hold our mother had on us for a long time. One I suspect might feel similar to that of you and your father?" Eddie broaches the elephant in the room.

"I assume he rejected your calls so you approached me?" I ask, not really thinking that, but trying to understand why they came to me instead of trying to work with my father. He is our CEO, and technically, they should be talking to him.

Tennyson barks out a laugh. “No offense, but the last person I want to talk to is your father,” he says honestly.

“Hmmm, he seems to have that effect on people,” I murmur, not giving anything away.

“We all know that you are next in line for CEO at Van Cleef Corp. We also know that you have what it takes. We’ve been watching you. We admire your tenacity, your work ethic. Which is why we are meeting with you instead of your father or anyone else.” Ben looks at me seriously, and I feel my chest swell with pride. I have worked hard. I am glad someone can see it.

“So what did you have in mind?” I ask the three men who sit before me, getting this meeting back on track. They look sharp, professional in their designer tailored suits, yet their smirks and grins put me at ease. We are friends. Not enemies.

“Well, now that Harrison is president, we want to invest in more local projects,” Eddie Rothschild starts, and I look at him and nod.

“We have a few of those,” I say with a grin, keeping my cards close.

“We really would be looking for something maybe in the South or Midwest. Somewhere that is the heartbeat of the country,” Ben says diplomatically.

“So you want something to show the American people that the presidential family is investing in them?” I clarify.

“Exactly,” Tennyson says with a shit-eating grin on his face. “We heard you are making moves in Montana. That may be something that we would like to get involved in.” He continues, and I pause. I keep my facial features schooled, but the comment surprises me. We have no business in Montana.

"I am working on Tennessee at the moment. A new hotel and retail precinct. I may have some options for you on that one?" I suggest.

"That would work," Ben says, nodding and sitting forward, clearly interested.

"Will your father be okay with that?" Eddie asks, and I take in a breath.

"My father wouldn't even like me being here today," I admit. The three nod. They understand. My father would kill me if he knew I was taking this meeting. But in their boardroom, where we sit high up in the sky, I know that this is exactly where I need to be. Talking business and making smart decisions with people like the Rothschilds.

"We are happy to remain a relatively silent partner. Keep the build and the management to you, while we promote that we are investing in the country, in jobs, and in the economy through our partnership," Eddie says, and I like the sound of his offer. It would be the first of its kind for our two families. The fact that we are even working together would make headline news.

"What kind of investment are you thinking?" I ask, wanting to know about the dollars.

"We would be willing to invest significantly, maybe something like thirty to forty percent." Tennyson lays their cards on the table. I think about the offer, mulling it over for a moment. Thirty to forty is well in the hundreds of millions and would allow us to speed up the build and also allow us to invest and step into a new project almost at the same time.

"Forty percent. We call it a collaboration. We mutually invest in the town, the people, the community. And..." I say, watching them all closely, "...I want you to bring me Whiteman's." Then I sit back and wait.

It is a bold move negotiating with the Rothschilds, asking for their money but also more. But I am feeling confident, and I know they are a safe space.

"Whiteman's?" Tennyson asks, his eyebrows pull together.

"Whiteman's is the country's biggest and best whiskey brand. We have been trying to get them on board for our hotels for years. I want them to be our exclusive whiskey supplier for the Tennessee project, and I know you can make that happen," I say, smiling, wondering just how far I can push these boys. I know they know Tanner and Connor Whiteman well. As do I. But I have never been able to get them over the line on a business deal. They are very strategic in their business partnerships and don't collaborate with many people. I also suspect that my father puts them off given he isn't the easiest person to negotiate with.

"It's not out of the question, but you might need to leave that with us for a few weeks..." Ben says, trailing off as he thinks.

"You got some balls, little Van Cleef." Tennyson looks at me with a broad smile, appreciating my somewhat ruthless business tactics. But if I can get two for one, my father won't be able to deny it. It is a smart and profitable decision, one that I brought into the business. It isn't every day that I sit in their boardroom, so I am going to make it count.

I smile back at him, feeling renewed confidence seep into my bones. This is the start of something big; I can feel it. This is how I can make Van Cleef Corp more successful and push us into the future. This is my legacy. Not William Schmidt and his oil. This is what I want to do. I want that CEO position that is rightfully mine and this meeting today has all but proved that I am capable.

As I look at the three men around the table, I feel like I have the upper hand. I clearly surprised them. They probably thought I was a pushover and that I wouldn't ask for more. It makes me think of AJ and what he said to me at the club. That I should just look pretty at dinner parties and that I wouldn't know a hard day's work if it bit me in the ass.

But as we wrap up the meeting, I watch Eddie, Ben, and Tennyson, all looking at me in what appears to be newfound appreciation and what I think is pride. Because while I don't do hard physical work like AJ, my hands still get dirty. I still fight for what I want, and I want to be CEO. As we say our goodbyes, and I leave the offer with the Rothschilds to discuss, I head out of the building and to my waiting car, knowing exactly who I want to see, and I think I will find him at Joe's Gym.

11

AJ

The smack of punches hitting bags fills the room, only dulled by the music thumping throughout the gym. I have been here most of the day, training this morning and now spending time with the younger kids. They need to know how to take care of themselves and they need an outlet for their rage.

"Hands up, protect your face at all times," I direct Levi. When he is not skipping school and doing petty crime, he usually has his head stuck in a laptop, gaming, or most likely hacking some business out of money, since his parents are too deadbeat to look after him. Like me, he has had a tough upbringing, but he seems to find solace here at Joe's Gym. Also like me.

"Is that how you got so pretty, AJ?" he teases. He is a smart kid, with a smart mouth. One that gets him into trouble. I smirk at him as I push the punching bag at him with force when he isn't paying attention, causing him to topple and fall onto the floor mats.

"If you are going to throw insults, be prepared for the

comeback." Everything around me stops as the gym suddenly goes quiet, and I look up and follow everyone's gazes to the front door. My heart and breathing both stutter as I watch Valerie Van Cleef walk in the door like she owns the place.

Her confidence is admirable. To enter a crappy gym on the outskirts of town that is full of testosterone and half-naked men takes guts. She looks like a boss, and I swallow as I take her in. Dressed in sky-high heels, tailored black trousers, and a crisp white shirt with the collar high and wide, giving me a great visual of her sun-kissed skin at her chest. As she struts right to me, my eyes settle on her cleavage, where I see golden layers of necklaces that shimmer in the light. As she gets closer, I take in her face, her brunette hair coiling softly around her face, and her blue eyes stare right at me, lips red and pouty and lit up in a smile.

"Fuck, I wouldn't mind tapping that," a guy says from behind me, and I growl deep in my chest.

"Hold five, kid," I tell Levi, who is still on his butt on the floor, his mouth agape, watching as I step away from the bag and walk to her. Presumptuous, maybe, but who the fuck else is she here to see?

Her eyes remain on me as she pays little attention to anyone or anything else, which makes me feel fucking possessive with all eyes clearly on her.

"Get back to work," I bark out to the gym harshly, and the guys at least now pretend not to watch and start hitting the bags or each other.

"What are you doing here?" I ask her as I cross my

arms over my chest and take the tough stance I am familiar with.

"Good afternoon to you too," she says with a wide smile, looking like I gave her the world.

"You shouldn't be here," I tell her, even though I want nothing more than Valerie Van Cleef right here with me.

"Ahhh, those familiar words again. I will let you educate me for a moment. Why not?" My eyes thin as my dick hardens. *Is she getting sassy with me?*

"This is not a place for a woman like you."

"Again, with the *woman like me*?" Oh yeah, she is getting sassy, and my fingers twitch on my biceps, itching to grab her. And I do. I grab on to her upper arm and lead her over to the side of the gym, away from prying eyes and open ears until her back flattens against the wall. I know I am being an asshole, but there are too many men in here looking at her and I need to fucking touch her. Need to show them she is mine.

"Every guy in this fucking place is staring at your ass. Shouldn't you be at one of your fancy country clubs or something?" She fucking smiles again.

"Are you?"

"Am I what?" I ask, lost in her eyes, her perfect lips, her sexy-as-hell body.

"Staring at my ass?" I can barely contain myself. She is the only person to question me or talk back to me and I fucking love it.

"Oh, sweetheart, I'm staring at all of you." It's a warning, my tone deep and low, not leaving any room for confusion. "But that doesn't mean I like everyone else doing the same thing." She bites her bottom lip. The move has my body burning. Swallowing, she considers her next words, and I follow the movement with my eyes, looking at her throat, her chest, her cleavage.

“Sweetheart?” She questions the nickname I just dropped, and my tongue burns with regret. I didn’t mean to let it slip again. I called her that in the club the other night, but with the loud music and her friends nearby, I didn’t think she heard it. Right here and now, she most certainly did.

“A sweet thing. I would bet some money that you are always doing the right thing. You know, Little Miss Perfect?” I smirk at her, then I see her eyes cloud over slightly and feel like I said the wrong thing.

“Why are you so dressed up?” I ask her, changing the subject, wondering if this is her everyday attire. It probably is, as she looks like a million bucks.

“I had a work meeting.” My eyebrows rise in surprise. I’ve done a little research on Valerie Van Cleef, and I know she doesn’t need to work. Her family are billionaires. One of the wealthiest in the country.

“How did it go?” I ask her, and her face lights up.

“Hmmm, better than expected, actually.” Her genuine grin is adorable and a weird feeling of pride runs through my chest.

“Well, good for you. Now what are you doing here?” I get back to the situation at hand.

“I came to find you.” I have absentmindedly moved even closer to her, now almost crowding her against the wall, her floral scent again encasing me.

“Who told you I was here?” I ask, her chin now tipped up to look at me.

"Jimmy," she says with a coy smile. I know why, because Jimmy runs his mouth off, and there is no doubt in my mind she now knows almost everything about me.

"Fucking Jimmy," I murmur, shaking my head. "Well, what can I do for you?" I don't know why I am asking. I need to end this conversation and get her out of this fucking gym.

"I need security," she says simply, and I straighten.

"Are you in trouble?" My senses are now on high alert.

"Oh, no, no, nothing like that." She chuckles as I relax and I feel off-kilter for a moment. "My friend Chloe, she has her own jewelry brand. She has a showing next Thursday for her new collection and her security company that she normally uses has just left her in the lurch. She needs a few guys to watch the shop while the event is going on."

"How many guys?" I ask, very interested in this opportunity. Anything that can bring in more money to ease our financial pressure is needed.

"She usually has two at the front door, two inside, and then two at the back. The event starts at seven and will finish up at nine. There will be media, celebrities, buyers, and about ten million in gold and diamonds on display." I grit my teeth. The million-dollar statement left her lips as easy as if she was saying it was mere cents.

"I can help you out." I nod to her while I run through the logistics in my mind. "Give me your number." I push my cell toward her. This is dangerous territory I am heading into, and I know I should walk away, but I am too far gone, her pearly whites, her button nose, her fucking smile every time she looks at me. It is like I hung the moon for her and all I have done is accept a job Fortress desperately needs. At least Brady will be happy, since this is the type of premium job he was referring to the other week. Looks like I may have just scored our first opportunity.

I watch her type in her details, and I grab the phone from her and send her a quick text so she has my number too.

"Text me the details, and I will put a quote together tonight and send it back," I explain and she nods, clearly happy with the formality.

"Anything else I can help you with?" I ask her as she remains where she is, me not letting her go yet either.

"I also wanted to say thank you. For saving me from that guy at the club." A light blush colors her cheeks.

"Just doing my job," I tell her, which is true in theory, but there was no way I was letting anyone touch her. All week, I have been murderous about the guy attempting to.

"I know, but you could have easily ignored it. Many security teams often do." That has my hackles rising.

"I don't ignore things. I am very attentive," I tell her, and I notice her chest rise and fall under the white shirt she has on. The movement has my skin prickling, giving me the urge to open a few buttons, just to see what's underneath. She breaks my gaze and looks around.

"What are you doing here?" she asks, and I step back and look at the gym. The guys in here are all still watching, although they're doing a bad job of pretending they aren't.

"Training."

"Training?" she asks, seemingly interested.

"Teaching."

"Teaching?" She's inquisitive. I usually remain tight-lipped about my life, but for some reason, I want to indulge her a little.

"I teach kids how to box. Self-defense, help them take care of themselves. It's important." I shrug, not expecting someone like her to understand.

"It is." Her eyes come back to look at mine. "It's very admirable." I huff out a breath at the awe on her face and shake my head in denial. "So, you box?" She continues her interrogation, and my body relaxes even more. It's a new feeling for me, especially when talking about myself. Her presence calms me as much as it lights me up. Like it did at the club the other night. It is weird because calm is not a word that I would use to describe me.

"A bit." I nod.

"Jimmy tells me you have a fight coming up?" she asks. *Fucking Jimmy, I'm going to kill him.*

"That's *certainly not* something you need to know about." My fights are mostly off the radar. I box sometimes fairly and other times not. There are also gallons of testosterone at fight nights, and I don't want her anywhere near that.

"Why not?" My eyes thin at the challenge in her tone.

"It's not a—" I start, but she cuts me off.

"A place for a woman like me?" she quips, and my lips thin as I nod. *Fuck, this woman drives me crazy.*

"You're too perfect for my world, sweetheart," I tell

her, trying to be sincere but giving her a warning. No good can come of us. This is fire we are playing with.

"You won't break me, AJ. I'm tougher than I look."

"Oh, sweetheart, I would ruin you." I watch her intently, waiting for her to step back and start retreating. But instead, she steps closer, pushing her chest against mine. We are a hair's breadth apart. Her lips are so fucking close, all I need to do is lower my mouth an inch and I could taste her.

"You don't scare me," she whispers, her breath coating my lips. I am officially getting hard in my gym shorts.

"You don't know what I am capable of," I tease her, fisting my hands, even though I am itching to grab her waist.

"I know you wouldn't hurt me." She is giving me everything back, and I am impressed. I thought for sure she would have run home to her father already. I don't have a comeback for that, because she is right, I wouldn't hurt her. I would kill any other man who tried.

"You two finished eye fucking each other or what?" Levi calls out. I had forgotten all about him as he sits waiting for me, and my jaw pops as the gym comes back into focus. Valerie steps back a little and clears her throat.

"See you around, AJ." My name falls from her lips again, and I stifle a moan, really fucking wanting to hear her scream it.

I nod to her, crossing my arms over my chest again, and watch her turn and walk away, my eyes on her perfect ass the entire time until she is out the door and across the street. Then the entire gym erupts into whistles, hollering, and crude remarks, all echoing around the testosterone-fueled space as I walk back to Levi.

"Seems like she likes your pretty face too, AJ," he quips, and I push the bag into him again, watching him topple for a second time.

"As I said, if you are going to throw the remark, be ready," I growl at him as he hops to his feet and we get back to work, my mind now only half on the job, the other half on Valerie fucking Van Cleef.

12

VALERIE

"The event is amazing," Chelsea says to Simone and me as we stand in a small group in Chloe's studio, her launch event now almost over.

My eyes canvass the room, but always come back to the same person. AJ. After a few brief text messages between us this past week, I locked in Fortress for the job and Chloe was able to relax. But my eyes have been glued to him all night. He's extremely well dressed in a black suit, a uniform that all his team are wearing and not something I briefed him on. But I am glad he had the foresight because they all look amazing. Better than the other security team Chloe usually hires.

"The security gives everyone something else to look at," Simone murmurs, following my gaze.

"Hey, you," Lucy Bloomer says, coming up to us with her man, Huxley, by her side. Those two are inseparable and have been since they met. They are a great couple. Down-to-earth and friendly, spending most of their time between Baltimore and their ranch in Whispers, a small town a few hours away.

"Heeeeyyyy. So good to see you," I say happily as I wrap my arms around her and hug her tight. "Hey, Huxe." I give him a kiss on the cheek in greeting as Simone and Chelsea move away to look at the jewelry nearby.

"This latest collection is so good," Lucy gushes, making me smile.

"I don't know how she does it, but every year she outdoes herself. There are so many nice pieces," I say.

"You know Connor Whiteman, right, Val?" Huxley says as another man walks up to his other side.

"Hi, Valerie, great to see you again," Connor says, and I give him a warm smile. I have only met him once or twice. He is a friend of Huxley's. His family owns Whiteman Whiskey, the best whiskey distillery in the country, the one I am trying to get a deal with. I wonder if the Rothschild men have spoken to him yet about our hospitality businesses and a potential collaboration.

"Great to see you, Connor." He leans over and gives me a peck on the cheek, and I hear a low growl behind me. Glancing behind me, I see AJ right next to us.

"No leaning on the display, please," he says formally, and I bite my smile away as he gives Connor a stern look. Connor steps to the side, not realizing that he had hold of the clear glass box that houses one of my favorite pieces tonight.

"Shit. Sure, no problem," Connor says as AJ's eyes flick to mine. We haven't had time to chat tonight, but I haven't missed the fact that he is already looking at me every time I look his way.

"Connor, I'm hoping we might be able to meet up soon. I want to chat to you about Whiteman's. We are opening a new hotel down in Tennessee, and I think having Whiteman's as our whiskey of choice would work really well," I say, planting a seed. Van Cleef Corp runs a few hotels in our empire and this next one I am hoping to make a little more exclusive than the others.

"I am always open for a chat, Valerie. Ben Rothschild mentioned something to me the other day in passing. Call me, let's discuss," he says, giving me a wink and a sexy-as-sin smile. If I didn't know better, I would say he is flirting, but this is his manner. Seductively sweet, like his liquor.

"We need to go, Luce. Car's out front, and I think I have spent enough money already," Huxley jokes with her. I see the love and light in their faces for each other and sigh. That's what I want. That connection. My eyes flick over Lucy's shoulder to AJ once again. He is looking right at me, so I quickly look away and say my goodbyes, watching all three walk out the door.

"Urgh, they are so perfect for each other," Chelsea says, passing me another glass of champagne.

"Aren't they just?" I say, smiling.

"How much longer do you think we will be here tonight?" Simone asks.

"Do you have somewhere else to be?" I raise my eyebrows.

"Maybe we should hit Club Vine again later tonight?" she suggests.

"Oh, I told Jimmy you work for the NFL team," I say quickly before taking a sip of champagne and looking away from Simone.

"You did what?" she almost shrieks, and I look back in surprise.

"Jimmy called, gave me intel on AJ. I had to give him something in return." I shrug, secretly hoping she doesn't mind. I see her face soften and a look of intrigue takes over.

"So what did he say about me?" she asks coyly.

"Nothing. He just hoped that you would be back in the club sometime soon," I tell her, and she smiles. I think I see a hint of blush to her cheeks.

"Do you seriously like him?" Chelsea asks, and I look around the floor for Chloe, but she is busy being interviewed with the last few media.

"Photo, ladies?" Chloe's photographer friend asks, and we all have our camera-ready smiles on high voltage tonight. I usually don't love the media attention and try to steer clear of anything gossipy. But tonight is Chloe's night, and anything we can do to bring awareness to her brand and increase her business is at the top of my agenda.

"Valerie, can we get a shot?" Once one starts, another approaches. I didn't realize Chloe would have so many influencers here tonight, but I smile and take photos with them all.

"Valerie, Rena from *Society News*, do you have a minute?" Simone rolls her eyes as she turns away, not wanting anything to do with it.

"Sure." I fake a smile this time and take a few steps away from the crowd.

"Just a few questions, if you don't mind?" Rena says, looking at me expectantly.

"Of course."

"Chloe's line, which one is your favorite piece tonight?" I immediately feel relief that the questions are on the event and not me personally.

"Oh, the rose. She designed that one in memory of my grandmother and it is my favorite piece. Designed with a pink diamond at the center and a dusting of white diamonds on the outside, it is by far the most amazing piece of jewelry I have seen." Chloe designing that necklace was the nicest thing anyone has ever done for me.

"And at the charity luncheon last week, you raised over half a million dollars for heart disease research. How is it that you can always manage these amazing events?" she asks.

"Oh, it was a fantastic cause, and we had some very generous donors that day."

"I heard that oil baron, William Schmidt, donated a high amount. Do you know him personally? Rumors say that he is personally interested in you?" I balk at the question because, one, I didn't know William Schmidt was our biggest donor—something Abigail failed to tell me—and two, I shiver hearing that man's name and do not want it connected to my own.

"He was in attendance, but I can't recall his donation. And no, I don't know him at all. I actually met him for the first time at the charity luncheon," I say, telling her the truth but feeling uncomfortable.

"Okay, enough questions. I need you to step back from the display," a rough voice says, and I feel the familiar warmth of AJ's hand on my lower back. Rena is not near the displays and wasn't doing anything that would affect the show or security, but I am thankful someone interrupted the interview. I lean back into AJ's hand, needing to feel his protective manner, even though he is only doing his job.

"Of course. Thank you, Valerie." Rena looks between me and AJ, then moves swiftly, straight out the door, obviously happy with whatever information she gleaned. I let out a sigh.

"You alright?" AJ asks, and I start to put on a fake smile before I stop. I don't need to be fake with him.

"I'm okay. I don't really like answering media questions that much." I admit, this life is getting more exhaustive by the minute.

"I can tell. You do this thing with your arm when you are uncomfortable," AJ says, moving his arm slightly, and my brow crumples in question.

"I do not." I have no idea what he is talking about.

"You do. You grab your elbow and pinch the skin. I noticed it every time someone came up for a photo or asked you a question." His eyes are full of concern, which makes my stomach do these weird flip-flops.

"Have you been watching me, AJ?" I tease.

"Little hard not to in this dress, sweetheart," he admits before walking away, and I swoon a little as I watch him saunter back to where he was standing near the rose necklace.

My palms sweat at hearing his compliment. The first

time we met, we were at each other's throats, but every meeting since, it is almost like we have thawed out a little more. He is still gruff, but I can see a tender side poking through his tough exterior.

"Here, I got you a napkin," Simone says, waving the white linen napery in front of my face.

"Thanks. What for?" I grab it, looking down at myself, thinking I must've spilled something on my clothes. I don't see anything. I wore a little black dress tonight, so even if I did, nothing should show up.

"To clean up that drool falling down your chin every time AJ is near you. Seriously, can you two just bang already? The sexual tension rolling off both of you is enough to make me want to run home to my battery-operated friend," Simone says, as Chelsea chokes on her champagne.

"Bang? You need to fix your locker room talk," I teasingly scold her, throwing the napkin back at her.

"I agree with her," Chelsea pipes up, looking over at AJ, who looks just as angry with the world as he did the first time I met him.

"Stop ganging up on me," I tell them both, doing everything I can to prevent my eyes from seeking out AJ and appearing more interested in watching Chloe on the other side of the room.

"Stop being a nun and just take him home tonight. Have a long, sweaty sex session before your father marries you off and your life is no longer your own," Simone says, and my lips thin.

"I am not getting married," I state with full conviction.

"Oh, how did your father dearest take the news?" Simone presses, her eyebrow rising in question.

"Notice that she didn't decline the sweaty sex session?" Chelsea murmurs to Simone as they both look at me.

"I wouldn't decline that man, either," Simone answers her in a low tone, the two of them talking about me like I am not even here.

"Seriously. I can't take him home," I tell them with a quick shake of my head.

"Why not?" Chelsea asks.

"Because... well... I am not that good..." I feel heat in my cheeks at my admission.

Simone scoffs. "You're good at everything."

"Just not that, apparently..." I close my eyes. This is so embarrassing. But if I can't talk to my friends about it, then who can I talk to?

"Are you talking about sex?" Chelsea whispers with a frown forming on her face.

"Sex. Flirting. Dating. Anything to do with the opposite sex," I blurt. "The last guy I dated ended up in the hospital from an allergic reaction, and the last guy I had sex with lasted less than five minutes, then rolled off me, said, 'Thanks, but I prefer bigger boobs,' got dressed, and left. Leaving me alone and with the hotel room bill." When it comes to men, I am a disaster.

"Clearly, the men you are dating are not the right ones. Let me guess, half of them are men who your father introduced you to?" Chelsea says, her eyes thinning as she thinks over her words. I pause because she is right. Most of the dates I have been on are with men whom I have met through work or my father. They have all been much older, clearly only trying to get closer to my father rather than sweep me off my feet.

"Bigger boobs? What a douche. I love your boobs," Simone says, and I feel movement to my side.

"Doesn't Val have great boobs, AJ?" My cheeks flame as I turn and see AJ standing only a few feet away. My eyes catch his and the burn in them is intense as they fall from my eyes to my chest and back again before he gives me a small nod and walks away to the other side of the store.

I wonder for a brief moment if one can die from embarrassment.

13

AJ

I have been watching her all night. In another figure-hugging dress, sky-high heels, and her hair in soft waves, long and glossy down her back. *Doesn't Val have great boobs, AJ?* All I can think about now is her perfect tits. They are perky, full, the kind that look like they would fit in my palms perfectly. I missed most of their conversation, but she has no reason to think her tits aren't perfect, because they are spectacular. She looks like a million dollars. Sure, the other women here are pretty, fancy, all made up. But Valerie... Valerie is...

"Last guests have now left," Cody interrupts my thoughts as he walks up to me where I stand at the back of the shop. It was a good event. Easy. Classy. We didn't have any issues, and everyone was well behaved.

"Goods are now all locked up in the safe. Back door locked. Chloe is happy," Brady says, walking to us from the back.

"Let's send the other boys home. The three of us can stay until Chloe locks up," I say, still watching Valerie talk with her friends, smile, and hug them, giving everyone her full attention. She has worked the room all night. I haven't seen the smile drop, but I know it is fake, her arm grabbing near constant. You wouldn't notice it because she has such confidence, but she doesn't appear truly happy. I wonder what she does for fun.

"Are you going to take your eyes away from her anytime soon?" Brady asks me, and I hear Cody snort in laughter from where he is a few steps away, sending the rest of the boys home.

"If you've got something to say, you should just say it," I mutter, sending him a glare.

"No. Nope. Nothing. Just an observation," Brady says, a sly smirk on his face, and I crack my neck. "Just never seen you look at a girl like that before."

"She isn't a girl. She's a woman." My eyes are back on her, catching her watching me. I clear my throat. "Let's finish up," I say to Brady, and we walk over to where Valerie and her friends are standing.

"Thank you so much, guys; it was perfect!" Chloe says, her grin wide, her face now relaxed in complete contrast to how she was before the night started.

"Thank you. We loved helping you out. If you ever need us again, we are more than happy to come and do any event." Brady talks for us as Cody comes to stand by my other side.

"Looking very dapper tonight, boys. Brilliant job," Simone says as she finishes her drink.

"We are all done here. We'll help you lock up and then be on our way." My voice contains a little more bite and annoyance than I intended.

"Of course!" Chloe says. "Girls, are your drivers here?" she asks the others, and I look at Brady, who rolls his eyes.

"Yep. Gotta go. I need to be up for early practice tomorrow. Kisses." Simone says her goodbyes.

"I'll get the door." Cody walks her out.

"My ride is here. I will talk to you guys later," the curly-haired one says. I think her name is Chelsea, and I watch her kiss both Chloe and Valerie before walking out the door.

"Let me help you grab your things and hopefully my car will be here by then," Valerie says, still smiling as she helps Chloe with a few bags, both of which I take off their hands as the two of them, along with Brady and I, walk out the door.

"Where's your car, Val?" Chloe asks her as Brady locks the front doors and hands her the keys. I look up and down the street, but it is pretty quiet. There is one black car here aside from our rides.

"I don't think he is coming. Something must have happened." I watch Valerie as her hands fly across the screen of her cell. "It's fine, I can grab a cab."

"I'll take you," I offer before I can think it through, and her head shoots up to look at me.

"Oh. It's okay, I don't want to be a bother. I am sure a cab will be here soon."

"I'll take you," I insist, my tone dominant. I watch her lips purse slightly as she looks at me.

"Okay. Thank you. That would be great," she agrees with a sweet smile, and I give her a nod before wondering what the fuck is wrong with me. I have a week left until my fight. I can't get close to this woman. Besides, I brought my bike tonight. That is going to make it even more painful for me. But knowing her, she probably lives around the corner. These rich people all live in the good part of town.

"Brady, help Chloe to the car with her things, then you and Cody take off. I'll drop Valerie off and talk to you later," I tell him, my eyes carrying weight, ensuring he doesn't have another smart-ass comment.

"Sure thing," he says, biting his tongue, his smirk threatening to break through, but we wait for the girls to say their goodbyes. Brady walks Chloe to the car and puts her inside, and as the car drives away, I see both Brady and Cody slip into the truck and drive off.

Val and I watch them leave. The street is so quiet at this time of night, to the point I hear her stomach growl.

"Hungry?" I ask her, raising an eyebrow. Her cheeks flush a little as her hand wraps around her stomach.

"I didn't get a chance to eat much tonight," she says, sounding a little embarrassed.

"I know a place." The words feel foreign as they fall out of my mouth. "They make the best burgers in the city." I follow up as she looks at me a little wide-eyed. I feel my jaw pop, waiting for her answer. I can't recall ever asking a woman out to eat. Now I stand here next to one of the wealthiest women in the country, asking if she wants a burger. It's like my sensible mind can't stop my mouth from talking.

"I can't remember the last time I had a burger..." she says softly, like she is almost talking to herself. I frown at the statement, because who doesn't eat burgers? She bites her bottom lip as she thinks, another little quirk of hers that I have noticed.

"Let's go," I say, making up her mind for her before I can talk myself out of it. Taking Little Miss Perfect out for burgers is one of the stupidest ideas I have ever had, but it's happening. I start walking toward the curb.

"So where's your car?" Valerie asks, and I hear her heels on the pavement behind me, so I know she is following.

"Just here," I say, stopping next to my bike.

"What? What is that?" she asks, her voice rising an octave as she comes to a sharp stop.

"It's a bike," I explain sarcastically.

"I know it is a bike, but I've never been on a bike before. I don't even know how to ride a bike." Her words tumble over each other.

"Just sit down and hang on to me," I tell her. "Here, put this on." Grabbing a spare helmet from my bag, I put it on her head. I don't ask her to tie it up, I just do it for her, looping the chin belt and pulling it tight to ensure it is nice and secure. I bite my tongue at the smirk that threatens at how cute she looks.

"But is it safe? I am not really dressed for the occasion," she says, and I look down at her body. She most certainly isn't. I let my eyes wander over her. I like the way she is tiny but still has curves. She could definitely do with a few burgers in her life, but she has enough to grab on to.

"Here," I say gruffly, trying to get these thoughts under control. Pulling out my leather jacket I wear when I ride, I hold it out for her to put on.

"I don't think that is going to fit me," she says, but I slide it on her anyway. I zip it up at the front and roll the sleeves a little. She is right, it swims on her small frame. It is almost longer than the dress she is wearing, but it at least will keep her warm.

"Fits just fine," I grumble. She looks ridiculous but so fucking hot at the same time.

"But I'm wearing Jimmy Choos, and my dress is too short..." She keeps going, and I don't give a shit about the heels, but the dress concerns me. It is too short.

"You will be fine," I assure as I straddle the bike and sit forward a little. "Put your foot here and then jump on." I guide her as my teeth clench, my body finally catching my mouth now that I realize her fucking fantastic legs are going to be wrapped around my middle. I wonder if I can actually ride with her behind me after all, because my cock is so fucking hard right now, I may not be able to ride in a straight line. She stands near me, glancing at both me and the bike, looking unsure.

"It's alright, sweet thing. Live a little," I tell her, almost in a challenge, and then hold out my hand. My words have the desired effect as I watch her swallow and take a breath.

"I can't believe I am doing this," she mumbles quietly to herself before she places her small, soft hand in mine, and I hold hers tight.

"Foot there, hands on my shoulders, and then throw your leg over and sit." She follows my instructions and sits behind me. Her legs curve around my thighs, and I look down, spotting only bare, silky skin and her long, luscious legs. Her dress has ridden up and barely covers her ass, and I swallow hard and start the bike. The roar rumbles out of my Harley, vibrating through my body. I love this bike. It is my one indulgence. Something I saved years for. It is literally the only asset to my name. The lunchbox-size apartment I live in is not far from the gym but is only a rental, one where the hot water doesn't even work on some days. But this bike, it is my pride and joy.

"What do I hang on to?" I hear her yell, her legs now settled around me, and I am itching to touch her.

"Here," I say, leaning back, grabbing her hands and pulling them around my middle. She holds me tentatively as I rev the engine and take off quickly. Letting out a small squeal, her grip on me tightens. I severely underestimated my need for discipline for this ride. I am not even sure why I offered. But after watching her all night, I couldn't not.

We ride to the end of the street and stop at the red light.

"You alright?" I ask her.

"This is insane," she says, half in fear and half in awe. I chuckle as the green light ignites, and I kick off down the street at speed.

"Aggghhhh!" I hear her mini scream, her hands gripping into my shirt at my chest, her legs now squeezing around my middle, holding on tight. Setting the pace down a little, I start to cruise. There is not a lot of traffic at this time of night, and as I ride around the streets, I feel her body soften, now enjoying the ride. We can't really talk, which is a good thing, because I can barely concentrate as it is. Her hands are on my chest, her fingers digging in. Her tight little body is pushed up against mine. I can feel her perfect tits pressing on my back, her body keeping me warm. But it is her legs that are teasing me the most. I see them out of the corners of my eyes. I can't take it any longer, so I let go with one hand and drop it to her bare knee that is at my side. Cupping my hand around her leg, I hold on to her, my thumb tracing a small pattern back and forth over her bare skin. I shouldn't be touching her, but the minute I do, I feel her soften even more and her hold turns into more of a hug. One that feels too fucking comfortable. I can't remember the last time someone hugged me. This feels... nice.

I drive through the streets to my side of town. The burger joint is still open at this time of night, but thankfully the crowd is thin and, by the looks of it, safe. I pull the bike up and park.

"Jump off the same way you got on," I tell her and I hold out my hand for her to take as she peels herself from me, her dress barely doing anything to cover her backside. I am glad no one is around to watch her.

Once she is off, I step off in front of her and remove her helmet.

"There, it wasn't so bad, was it?" I ask, waiting for her verdict as I slip the jacket from her shoulders.

"No. It wasn't," she says, fixing her hair. "I don't know much about bikes, but this one is nice. Pretty comfortable, actually." Pride swells in my chest.

"Comfortable?" I ask her.

"Yes. I have helmet hair now, don't I?" Her hands run through her long dark hair, her eyes alight with color. She is smiling, clearly happy, and warmth spreads through me.

"Not a thing wrong with it," I mumble, imagining seeing her hair ruffled on my bedsheets, looking thoroughly fucked and perfect.

"Mr. Burger..." she mumbles, taking in the shop signage.

"Best burgers in Baltimore," I tell her, and she smiles at me. "Let's go before your stomach growls again." Grabbing her hand automatically, I pull her along the sidewalk and inside. Her hand is small in mine, and it isn't until we are almost to the booth that I realize I have done it. It's a move I never make a habit of, yet here I am tugging her behind me, not wanting to let her go. Needing to have her close to me. As I walk us inside, I feel her other hand rest on my forearm, keeping me close, and my nerves settle a little. I feel like a king leading his queen, even though we are in a shitty diner about to eat burgers.

The place is quiet at this time of night, which I like. The traditional black-and-white tiles coat the floor, the booths red vinyl, and pictures of yesteryear scattered around the place.

"So, you come here a lot?" she asks as she ducks into the booth seat, and I sit opposite her. Mr. Burger is clean, but nothing like I am sure she is used to.

"Sometimes." Although, I do come here almost weekly. "I haven't been in a while. I need to keep fight fit." Burgers a week or so out from a fight is unheard of for me. Yet another thing I completely forgot about since seeing her tonight.

"Tell me about this fight you have coming up. Have you faced this opponent before?" she asks as her head tilts slightly, her hair falling subtly to the side. She looks genuinely interested.

"He is a new guy. I haven't seen much of him, to be honest," I tell her with a shrug, not sure how much detail to go into. I'm not used to sharing information about myself. No one has really ever asked me too much before.

"Rago something-or-other, isn't it?" My eyebrows hit my hairline.

"Sounds like someone has been doing their homework." I never told her about my opponent, and I smirk, calling her out on her internet sleuthing.

"Well, I am not agreeing to have burgers with just anyone," she teases as Betty, the waitress, comes up to us.

"Anthony James, it isn't like you to come in here on a weeknight," Betty greets us, and I give her a look as my full name leaves her. "Ohh, and aren't you a sweet thing." She ignores my scowl as her eyes sweep across to Valerie, placing a menu in front of her. Val picks up the menu and gives her a wide smile, her eyes almost sparkling under the dim lighting.

"Hi, I'm Valerie." She introduces herself with a big grin, and Betty almost swoons at how polite she is. I imagine she usually doesn't get more than a few grunts from the people who come here.

"Nice to meet you, Valerie. I'm Betty. I will be your server tonight." I have never heard Betty speak like that before in my life. And I have been coming here for years.

"The usual for me, please, Betty," I tell her, not entertaining her clear need for information on Valerie.

Valerie is looking at me with a small smirk on her

face. "And for your date...?" Betty asks, her head moving to look at Valerie. I remain silent, not correcting her.

"I'll have whatever he is having," Valerie says, putting down the menu.

"Coming right up. Nice to see you here with a friend, AJ," Betty says, then gives me a wink before she saunters off to pit in our order.

"So you *do* come here a lot?" Valerie asks, smiling like she has caught me on something.

"Seems like it," I tell her, pressing my lips together to prevent them from quirking up.

"I can't remember the last time I had a burger." She sighs as she looks around the diner. "I can't even remember the last time I was ever in a place like this."

"Why is that?" I ask, interested to learn more about her. She looks out of place here. We both do. I am still in the black suit and she's in her dress and heels. It almost looks like we stepped off a catwalk. I undo my shirt cuffs and roll the sleeves up to my elbows, then unbutton my shirt at the collar so I can breathe. Watching her at close range like this has me hot.

"To be honest, I really don't know. I guess burgers and diners are not really what my father would have thought was appropriate." She bites her bottom lip in thought.

"What do you eat, then?" I ask, wondering if she really is the type to have lobster and gold-leafed shit like I imagine all rich people eat.

"Urgh, fish and salad," she says with a groan. "I have had so much fish and salad in my life that I think I am growing gills." She rolls her eyes.

I lean over the table and put my hand on her chin,

eliciting a small gasp from her lips. My hold firm and possessive as I look deep into her eyes before I move her head one way and then the other slightly. "Nope. No gills," I confirm, letting her go and sitting back again. I watch her tongue dart out and wet her lips.

"You should see the fin that is growing out of my back, though. It is frightening." She's making fun of herself, but I'm still tempted to ask her to show me. When I notice her biting her lip, I realize I've been staring at her for too long.

"Do you always do as your father wants?" I ask, wondering exactly how close she and her father are because I am sure he wouldn't think I was appropriate for her either. Even I know I'm not.

"I used to. But not anymore." Her eyes alight with determination, and I nod.

"Sounds like I brought you to the right place, then."

"Well, if Mr. Burger doesn't live up to the hype now, I will be disappointed," she says with a laugh, her mouth wide, eyes bright. Fuck, she is stunning.

"I would only suggest the best. You will not be disappointed when you are with me." The words sound more seductive than I was planning, and I see her chest rise and fall a little faster as she looks at me.

"Two choc malt milkshakes for you," Betty says, cutting into our moment and putting our drinks down. "Burgers won't be long." Valerie clears her throat as Betty walks away.

"So, how did you get started in security?" she asks me, and I am momentarily silent as I watch her lean forward and take the straw in her mouth and suck. I have never been more jealous of an object in my entire life. I hear a small moan escape her lips as she tastes the chocolate, and I think I almost go into cardiac arrest. I swallow roughly as she sits back, oblivious to the fact that I am staring at her once again.

"We started Fortress about six months ago. Still trying to build it up, get some clients. We have each worked and trained in different parts of security before, though. I fight and have been a bouncer before. All three of us have trained in defensive driving and personal security somewhat." I watch her take in the information. "What about you?" I ask, still not really knowing exactly what she does.

"I'm a lawyer. I have worked in the family business my entire career. Straight out of college. I love it. It was always my dream to be the CEO, like my mother was and her mother before that." I can see it. The way she holds herself. Her quiet confidence, her sass. She has the guts and determination to make it.

"I can see it," I tell her honestly, and her eyes lock on to mine.

"You can?" she asks, like she is astounded that someone could see that in her.

"Yeah. As long as you survive Mr. Burger, you have no problems." My smirk shines through at seeing her look at me with her relaxed grin and sparkly eyes.

"At last, he smiles..." she murmurs, taking the straw in her mouth again before Betty delivers our burgers, and it is then I realize that this is the first date I have ever been on where I have actually smiled.

14

VALERIE

"I think I am going to explode," I murmur, never having eaten as much food in my entire life. Truth be told, I was full after the milkshake, and given I haven't had dairy in forever, I wonder if I will regret that decision later.

"You haven't even touched your burger," AJ says, looking at me as though I am crazy.

"It was delicious. But it was huge." I look at the half-eaten monster burger on the plate. He finished off his meal about ten minutes ago. I have never seen a man eat so fast, so I am guessing I wasn't the only one who was hungry.

"Too much for you, love?" Betty says, coming to our table.

"It was, but it was amazing!" I say to her as she chuckles.

"Told you," AJ says as he stands, and Betty clears the table. I grab my bag and scurry to find my purse to grab some cash, but I am too slow as he throws a few bills down. "Don't even think about it," he warns.

"I'll get the next one," I say, slipping out of the booth, catching a small scowl on his face at my comment. I raise my eyebrow in question.

"Never going to happen." I chuckle at his chivalry.

"Let's go." Grabbing my hand, he pulls me along with him. "See you next time, Betty."

"Thanks, Betty," I chime in as we walk out of the diner.

"See you soon," she says, getting back to work.

"I better get you home, Cinderella," he says as he lifts the helmet and jacket for me again.

"I feel like a pumpkin already." I seriously feel like I gained at least five pounds.

"You look as sexy as sin, sweetheart." He brushes the hair from my face, and the air leaves my lungs for a moment.

"I bet you say that to all the girls who jump on the back of your bike," I tease, smiling up at him.

"Never had any women on my bike before." My grin falters a little at his seriousness.

"Never?" I ask, astounded.

"Nope. Never. You're the first." There is a soft breeze that skirts across my shoulders, and I shiver.

"Here," he says, draping his jacket over me again. My heart is beating a million miles an hour as he stands close, dressing me as my mind remains stuck on the fact that a man like AJ has never had a woman on his bike. Except for me.

"If they haven't been on your bike, then how do you

take girls on dates?" I ask. Maybe he has another car or something. My breathing is shallow as I wait for his answer.

"I don't go on dates." I start to smile at his response when he looks at me.

"We just had a date," I say, grinning at him.

"We just had burgers," he confirms, not entertaining my teasing.

"I think you might like me, AJ..." I smile wider. This is so unlike me, but I find him so easy to be around, and I enjoy teasing this big, grumpy man. He looks at me like he is trying to decide what to say.

"Looks like that feeling might go both ways, sweetheart," he says with narrowed eyes and the slightest tilt of his head, like he doesn't know what to do with me. "Where's home?" he asks quickly, steering the conversation away from us.

"Harborside. The high-rise at the..." But he doesn't let me finish.

"I know it. Here." He puts on my helmet, tying the strap before he gets on the bike and holds out his hand to me. Butterflies dance in my stomach as the impact of being the only woman AJ has ever had on his bike settles in my mind, and I throw my leg over and snuggle into his back. As he kicks the bike into gear, we zoom down the street, and I hang on for dear life. Sparks fly up my leg as his large, warm hand rests on my knee, and I lean in closer. I never want this date to end.

All too soon, we pull up at my high-rise and he parks the bike at the curb, switching off the engine. The loud rumble is unfamiliar in these posh city streets.

"Miss Van Cleef, is everything alright?" Victor asks from the front of the apartment building, rushing out at hearing the noise as I lift the helmet from my head.

"Hi, Victor, yes, everything is fine. This is my friend, AJ. Please let him up anytime he is here," I tell him. That offer only extends to my friends. Even my father can't come into my apartment without Victor calling me first. I look at AJ, and his eyebrows rise.

"You sure about that, sweet thing?" he murmurs, looking at me curiously.

"No, but it could be interesting," I say with a smile. "Here is your jacket." I start to grab at the collar.

"I've got it." Stepping forward right into my space, he grabs the zipper. He lowers it slowly, like he is opening a gift, and I watch him as his eyes look over every inch of me. My breathing is rapid, and I can feel a light sheen of sweat across my bare skin as AJ pulls the zipper all the way down, then takes the jacket from my shoulders and throws it onto the bike behind me.

"Thank you," I say breathily. I don't move and neither does he. We stand close, his eyes searching mine, almost calling to me. I lose my senses for a minute.

"You have a pretty mouth," he says, his deep voice hitting me right in my core and giving me goosebumps.

"Are you asking if you can kiss me, big guy?" My lips curve into a smile.

"Maybe I am." His answer has my teasing smile almost faltering as my heart races. I didn't expect him to agree with me, but now that he has, my eyes flick to his, and I see the heat swirling there.

"Then I say yes." Leaning forward, I look up at him,

and my body moves before I even know what is happening. He grabs me around the neck and pulls me straight to him, our lips smashing together in a kiss that makes me whimper.

He is eager, possessive, his hold firm like he knows exactly what he wants and will not stop until he gets it. My body turns liquid in his hold, my limbs vibrating in need, so I wrap my hands around his middle, as his large hands cup my jaw, keeping each other close. I don't think I have ever kissed a man like this, so hungrily. I part my lips a little more and his tongue dives in, the sensation pulling a moan from my chest and a groan from his. I am lost, not strong enough to stop this, because I am enjoying kissing him way too much. Pulling back slightly, I whisper against his lips.

"I want more. We should go upstairs, for privacy." But like I can't be stopped, I keep kissing him as needily. My nerves tingle a little at this new confidence of mine, but the way his hands hold me is unlike anything I have experienced before, and I want more. I hear a throat clear, and AJ pulls away, growling.

"Ahhh, are you sure you are okay, Miss Van Cleef?" Victor says again. Pulling back, I notice AJ giving him the evil eye, and Victor balks a little. I move my hand to rest on AJ's chest, and I feel him relax under my touch.

"Thanks, Victor, I'm still fine," I say, not looking at him as he steps back, sliding inside the glass door before I giggle.

"Are you laughing?" AJ's eyes thin at me in mock anger.

"You were growling at him," I say, my grin now wide.

"I don't like being interrupted."

"We can go inside?" I suggest again and hold my breath. I have never had any men in my apartment. My dating history is so bad that I usually book hotels, never wanting to get personal enough to invite them into my space. But one burger with AJ and I am ready to give him a key. I see AJ's jaw clench and disappointment fills me.

"I can't. I have a fight next week. I don't fuck before I fight," he says, and my eyes widen. Even as my thighs clench.

"Oh. Seriously?" I ask, because I am not sure if he is joking or not.

"Seriously." He nods.

"How long do you, um... you know, train for?" I ask, intrigued.

"Too fucking long, and right now, I am finding it really hard to reject your offer," he mumbles, and I smile as he moves his thumb and brushes it across my lower lip. Before we can say anything else, his cell rings. I watch him look up at the sky in frustration. "Fuck."

"It's fine. Get it. We are one for one now. I have Victor's interruptions, and you have your phone." I laugh, trying not to act like a loved-up schoolgirl, but that is exactly how I am feeling.

He pulls out his cell, and I see him stiffen.

"This is AJ," he answers abruptly. I turn slightly, trying to give him some privacy, but his hand lands on my waist, keeping me close, like he is scared I will walk away from him.

"AJ. I'm in trouble. I need you to come and bail me

out." I hear the voice on the other end, and it sounds serious.

"What happened?" he barks out, and my brow furrows, but he won't meet my eye.

"They picked me up for robbery. I'm downtown," the other person says. I take in a breath because whoever it is sounds young.

"Fucking robbery? Levi!" AJ shouts, running a hand down his face. "I'll be there in twenty. Behave until I get there." Looking down at me, he releases a heavy breath. "I've got to go."

"Is everything alright?" I ask, concerned, and he shakes his head. I feel him pulling away, both physically and emotionally. Whatever moment we had tonight is now over. His hand that was on my waist drops, leaving me cold.

"Everything is fine, sweetheart. I just need to go and get my young training partner out of some trouble," he tells me as he packs away the jacket and helmet.

"Can I help?" I ask, stepping toward him.

"No," he says sharply, and I stop abruptly. "Look. You should go upstairs. I've got to run." Sitting on his bike, he starts it up, and before I know it, he has kicked up the stand and is roaring away without saying another word.

15

VALERIE

I watch his bike until it turns the corner, and even then, I remain standing on the curb, listening to the roar fade. I heard the phone call. I know where he is going.

"Victor!" I yell to my doorman, who has been too observant tonight.

"Yes, Miss Van Cleef?" he asks, appearing right behind me. I love Victor, and I trust him. We have known each other for years.

"I need a car," I say to him. "Now."

"Certainly. Donnie is right here, ma'am," he says, moving down the curb to the dark town car and opening the back door for me.

"Thank you," I tell him as he shuts me in.

"Where to, Miss Van Cleef?" Donnie asks.

"Police station downtown, please." I settle into the leather seat, grabbing my cell from my bag to do some quick research. Juvenile robbery charges are taken seriously, but depending on what he stole and from where, it may not stick. I don't know his age, and I don't know his history, but I am assuming this is the boy he was training with at the gym last week when I walked in there. If this isn't his first arrest, then it will be harder for him. Not impossible, but increasingly harder with every misdemeanor he commits. I am making a lot of assumptions, and I am hoping I am correct.

In no time, the car pulls up at the police headquarters, and Donnie jumps out to open my door for me.

"I will walk you up, Miss Van Cleef." He almost falls over himself to help me. It is ridiculous, and I have no idea how I never saw this all before. It is almost like I am seeing my life from the outside, and the more I see, the more I dislike.

"No need. Wait here for me; I don't think I will be long," I tell him, my words holding more confidence. But I am already halfway up the stairs, secretly glad for my weekly Pilates class now that I am running in my high heels. I spot AJ's Harley over to the side, so I know I am in the right place. I push through the double glass doors and make my way around to the desk.

"What do you mean, I can't see him?" I hear AJ's voice, and I look over to spot him talking to an officer at a desk at the side.

"I'm sorry, sir. Only family or his lawyer can see him," the officer says. I walk over slowly because I can tell AJ is angry.

"He doesn't have any family. His mother is a drunk. His dad is not around. I am all he has," AJ tries to explain calmly, but I know it won't make a difference.

"Sorry. Lawyer or family only," the police officer reiterates.

"What is his bail?" AJ asks.

"Bail hasn't been set," the officer says.

"What do you mean, it hasn't been set? He has been here all fucking night." AJ's voice rises, and I take a deep breath. "I need to see him. Make sure he is alright. He is just a kid."

"Family or lawyer only."

"I'm his lawyer," I say, walking forward, and AJ spins around. If looks could kill, I would be dead. "I am his lawyer, and I would like to see him right now." I slide my card across the desk.

"Miss Van Cleef... I'm sorry, I didn't realize..." the officer starts to say.

"Didn't realize that holding a juvenile overnight is in complete contrast to the new policies currently being discussed by your police chief with the government just this week? That the young boy you are holding is probably with adult males who are not meant to associate with young boys, but you have them all in the same holding cell? I don't have specifics, but I think we both know how these things work, so you have exactly five minutes to take me to my client or things will get extremely uncomfortable for you," I tell him, my voice strong, even though I can feel AJ's stare burning into the side of my face.

"Uncomfortable, ma'am?" The officer doesn't move from his spot.

"Well, it is a Thursday, and we both know the police chief would hate to be interrupted from his weekly chess game. I think he is probably sipping scotch with my father as we speak." I watch him carefully, seeing the moment the penny drops that I am not someone to be messed with. Not that I would call my father. I haven't answered any of his calls to me lately. I am surprised I haven't been summoned to his office at this point, but so far, I have been able to dodge him, giving me enough time to get my thoughts in order.

"Right this way, Miss Van Cleef," he says, walking to the side and opening the hallway door. I turn to AJ.

"Okay, I know you are angry, but just text me quickly what I need to know," I whisper to him as his eyes look deep into mine. His jaw is set, his shoulders high, but he grabs his cell from his pocket to text me before I turn and follow the police officer down the hall. I wait mere moments for Levi to be brought into the small office I am left in. Full of attitude, he saunters in before he looks at me, and I see clear surprise on his face.

"Hey, I remember you, you're AJ's girl." I try to tamp down the butterflies swirling at his observation.

"I'm getting you out of here. You will still have charges, but they can't hold you," I tell him, almost positive that the officer is out front, printing the release forms as we speak.

"So you are a bigwig lawyer... What are you doing with AJ?" he asks, trying to figure me out.

"You're a fourteen-year-old kid. What are you doing robbing a liquor store?" I ask, having quickly seen the text AJ sent me as I was waiting here for Levi.

"Touché." He sighs like the smart-ass kid he is.

"Let's go." Walking to the door and down the hall,

Levi follows me. I am not sure of his history, but I guess I will find out all of it soon enough.

I sign a few papers as AJ and Levi have words in the far corner. AJ looks mad as hell, so I sure wouldn't like to be Levi right now. Maybe a prison cell would be a better option for him.

"All done," I say to them, handing some paperwork to AJ. "He needs to come back tomorrow, talk through some things. Second offense is not ideal. I suggest not doing that again, Levi." All Levi does is smile and give me a wink.

"Manners, asshole," AJ mumbles, hitting his shoulder.

"Thanks, Miss Van Cleef," Levi says sarcastically, and we all turn and walk out.

"Go wait by the bike," AJ says sternly, and I watch Levi saunter off to the side.

"He seems like a handful," I comment, taking a deep breath.

"You shouldn't have done that," AJ says, looking at me with his jaw clenched. I swallow harshly, trying to not feel slightly hurt by his tone.

"I was just trying to help." I have stuck my nose in his business, but I got a good result. Can't he see that?

"I don't need you coming in and threatening to call your daddy whenever you need to throw your weight around." His words sting. I am quiet for a beat as I look at him. I did drop my father's name, and I think about what that must have sounded like, and he is right. Even though they knew exactly who I was anyway. I feel sick. I am stronger than that; I am good without my father. If I am to become CEO, I need to start remembering that fact.

"Well, we are even now. You saved me at the club, and now I saved your friend," I say, hoping we can broker a peace treaty.

"Didn't know we were keeping score," AJ huffs, looking everywhere but at me.

"Maybe not. But people help people they care about." That has his gaze settling on mine. His eyes burn into me, holding a mountain of emotion.

"You're a pretty little rich girl who has daddy's billions to fight her battles. I've barely twenty bucks to my name and couldn't even tell you who my father is," he grits out, and my heart sinks, taking in the information. "We can't be anything, sweetheart."

"But that's the thing, AJ... I think we already are," I say, stepping away from him and walking to my car where Donnie waits, the back door open, allowing me to slip inside and into the secure back seat. Once the door closes, I release the breath I was holding, along with all the bravado, and my hands start to shake. I have never done anything like that before. I am a corporate lawyer. I've barely ever set foot in a police station. I have no real idea exactly what Levi has done or what he is capable of, but because AJ believes in him, so do I.

I am not sure how such a fun and perfect night could end in ruins. Maybe I was wrong to help, but eating burgers with AJ and getting to know him more, kissing him like that, there was never a chance I wasn't going to help.

As we drive away, AJ stands on the steps, watching the

car leave. Anger, confusion, and stress are evident in his gaze, and I have no idea what to think or where this leaves us. He is right, we are completely different, yet I feel drawn to him like no other.

It is then I come to the conclusion that over the years I have raised millions of dollars for charity, but never once have I actually stepped in their shoes. Levi is a kid, with no one else to call besides AJ, his boxing teacher. A real person who needs help. Not a fancy luncheon, where the rich donate purely for show and to help their tax situation, with no real idea where their money is going and how it is going to help. No idea of the grassroots issues within our city.

Maybe it is time I get my hands dirty. Maybe spending time with AJ will help open my eyes a little more. Van Cleef Corp will still be mine, but I don't need to run it how my father does. Maybe the difference I can make will be me focusing on the people, our staff, customers, and associates, rather than thinking about our bottom line like my father does.

Money isn't everything. People matter too.

16

AJ

"We got paid from Chloe," Brady says as I hit the bag over and over. I don't stop to look at him; in fact, I don't acknowledge him at all. My mind and body are both confused and angry, and right now, I am taking it all out on this bag. What the hell was I thinking putting Little Miss Perfect on the back of my bike and kissing her at her door? That isn't my life. That isn't what she needs.

"That was fast," Cody says. Since the event was only last night, full payment was quick. A lot quicker than some of our other clients. Chloe paid a deposit, which was how we managed to buy the suits we wore, knowing full well that this opportunity would be our best shot of breaking into those types of security gigs. The high-end stores, events, and businesses that Brady was talking about. We looked good too, and *so did she in that little black dress...* I start to think, before I shake my head and hit the bag harder, trying to erase her from my mind.

"We got a tip. A big one," Brady says, and I stop and look at him.

"How much?" I ask, feeling a bitter taste on my tongue.

"Five grand," Brady says with a big shit-eating grin.

"What the fuck?" Cody stands in shock.

"I know, right. These rich people sure know how to tip." Brady laughs.

"Refund it," I spit out.

"What?" they both question, looking at me like I have lost my mind, and they wouldn't be wrong. I have no idea where my head is at.

"I said return it. We are not a fucking charity case." I feel like after Val waltzed into the police station last night, waving her rich privilege in our faces, that I am now nothing but a charity case to them all.

"Fuck you, I am not retuning anything. Chloe called me herself this morning to explain that the tip was for services that went over and beyond. Apparently, the previous security team never waited for her to clean up. They never helped her out of the shop at the end of the night; they never helped her lock up or secure the premises. They never even wore fucking suits. She wants to book us again already for her next showing, which is in three months, since she does one every season," Brady explains, and my anger subsides a little. The tip now makes a little more sense.

"Whomever she had before must have been shit operators," Cody says.

"We should find out who they were and start targeting their customers," I say, deep in thought.

"Great idea. Can you ask your girlfriend?" Cody asks me, and I look at him swiftly. Both Brady and Cody have matching knowing looks on their faces.

"Not my girlfriend." My previous anger is now back.

"What? You put her on the back of your bike and took her home. No one else has ever been on your bike before. It is your pride and fucking joy," Brady says.

"Just forget it ever happened." Throwing a half-assed punch to the bag, I try to move the conversation on. I couldn't sleep last night thinking about everything. I met this woman weeks ago and already she is in a police station in the middle of the night, bailing out a kid for stealing three bottles of whiskey from a liquor store. It took nothing for me to drag her down to my level, and I feel sick over it.

"No way. Spill it." Cody pushes, and I take a deep breath and grind my molars.

"She got Levi out of jail last night," I tell them quietly.

"Fucking Levi. What did he do this time?" Brady asks.

"Robbed a fucking liquor store." Of all the stupid things that kid has done, this is one of the dumbest. Liquor stores are known to have cameras everywhere, hidden emergency buttons, and are notoriously hard to rob these days. Five or ten years ago, it was easy money, but now, not so much.

"Jesus," Cody murmurs, running his hand through his hair.

"How did she get him out of jail, then?" Brady asks, confused.

"She is a fucking lawyer and has a rich father that she

name-dropped. All she had to do was walk in and drop her card and the doors opened. I spoke to them for fifteen minutes and couldn't even get any answers. She got everything in under five," I spit out, thumping the bag again for good measure.

"Well, she got him out. That is all that matters, right? Who cares how she did it? It is obvious she did it for you," Cody says.

"I didn't ask her for anything. She shouldn't even be at the fucking police station at night. This is the kind of shit she shouldn't be involved in." I punch the bag in between my words.

"What's it about this girl that has you so flustered?" Brady quizzes, looking at me like he is trying to figure me out.

"She doesn't have me flustered. She is a fucking rich princess who lives off her father's money and lives a life many people can only dream about." *That I can't stop thinking about. Who I imagine underneath me, naked, moaning my name.*

"No doubt she is rich, but she and her friends seem nice. Down-to-earth. Friendly. Sure, it is obvious they have a fuckton of money, but they don't act like spoiled brats," Cody offers with a shrug.

"So what if she is a lawyer? Law is hard, and those fuckers have to study for years, work their way up the ladder. She may have a bit of help, considering who she is, but she can't just parade around as a lawyer and not know the law. She worked for it," Brady says, giving me a pointed look.

"She can't change where she came from any more than you can," Cody finishes, and I look at them both as my anger simmers down. He is right. I can't help my history, and neither can she. I rub my eyes with my gloves, thinking about how good it was to just talk with her last night. She is funny, teases me, and the conversation flowed. Then the kiss. Having her in my arms, the feeling of her body melting into mine. I have never felt like this about someone before, and I have no idea how to navigate any of it.

"There's something else about her. There is something you're not telling us," Brady says, always the fucking observant one.

"Can we not fucking talk about it? Let's talk about the fight. I have less than a week, and I need to fucking win this one. The winnings coupled with the tip we got will put Fortress in a really good position for the next quarter. With our regular Club Vine gig and maybe a few others, we should be able to move away from the shopping centers," I say to them, needing to get my head in the game.

"Okay. Let's talk strategy," Brady starts. "Cody and I will walk down to the ring with you."

"We will bring some boys with us. It is always good to have more guys than not enough in case shit happens," Cody says, and I nod. We have had a few fights that I won that went pear-shaped afterward. Men who bet a lot of money and lose, many who are so desperate they jump in the ring or attempt to take their frustrations out on me or those closest to me by following me to my training room or jumping on me as I leave the ring.

"We just need to be mindful of Marcus. No doubt he will be strutting around the place, being his usual asshole self. But don't look at him or acknowledge him; otherwise, you will lose focus. Keep your eyes on the ring and your opponent, that is it," Cody continues.

"I need to really focus on this one. I can't have distractions," I tell them. I can't lose. We need this money. But my mind is a battlefield. I have so much pent-up energy rattling around in my body. I am quick to anger, quick to judge, and I feel like such a loose cannon that I will probably forget to go the entire three rounds with the guy like Marcus requested.

"Three rounds. We will remind you at the top of each round," Brady says, like he can read my mind.

"You will need to let him get a few punches in. We don't want to look like we are deliberately stringing him along. Even though we all know you could knock him out in the first few minutes," Cody says. He is great for my ego.

"Then afterward, we can go out, find some women, and celebrate," Brady says with a smile. My nostrils flare, and just like that, my mind is back on Valerie, her long hair, pretty smile, perfect tits, and smart mouth. And those fucking long legs that I want wrapped around my face.

"I'm taking five," I say to them as I throw off my gloves and grab my drink. They get back to their own workout, and I walk to my bag and dig out my cell. I look at it, rolling it in my hand before I pull up her contact and type in a text.

AJ: Thanks for your help with Levi last night.

I hit send, then cringe to myself. Taking a sip of my drink, I watch the screen, waiting. My heart thumps in my chest, never having been this involved with a woman before. I hold my breath as I see the dots dancing as she types a reply before they stop, and no text comes through. But then her name flashes on my screen, and I hit answer immediately.

"Is this your way of saying sorry for being an ass?" Val says before I even have a chance to say hello. I laugh, because she calls me out on my behavior, and I like it.

"You are the one with the good ass, sweetheart... but, yeah, thanks. I appreciate you stepping in and helping," I tell her as I take in a breath.

"You're welcome. I truly didn't mean to step on your toes, AJ. I just wanted to help." I can hear her walking as she talks.

"I know. Are you busy?" I ask, thinking she must be at the office.

"Just pulling together my paperwork for world domination. You?" she asks, making me laugh again.

"Training," I tell her.

"Ohh, yes, the fight is this week, isn't it? Saturday night, right?"

"Yeah. Not that you need to know anything about that."

"Hmmm. So, I owe you a burger?" I swallow as I feel the heavy weight I was carrying earlier leave my shoulders. The fact that I was a bit of an asshole to her last night and she is still wanting to meet up with me again makes me happy. I look over to the boys where they train.

We are days away from the fight, so I don't go out, but we have a tradition the night before. Nothing late and no drinking for me, but it is a tradition.

"The boys and I go to shoot pool the night before my fights. We will be at Jordie's on the west side at seven on Friday night if you want to come." I am sure playing pool with the boys in a rough bar is not her idea of a good time, but I wait with bated breath just the same.

"Sounds fun. I'll see you there." My eyebrows shoot to my hairline.

"Text me when you are close, and I will meet you at the front. Some of the patrons are a little unsavory," I tell her, and she laughs.

"Okay, big guy, I will text you. I'll bring the girls too."

"I'll let you get back to world domination," I say, unable to stop the corners of my mouth rising.

"I'll let you get back to being all sweaty and macho." She giggles before the line goes dead, and I throw my cell back into my bag.

"Yeah, I knew there was something else about her..." I turn quickly in surprise and see Brady standing right at my back with a grin. He obviously overhead my entire conversation.

"Don't start," I warn him.

"What, that you invited girls to our traditional pool night?" he teases but does so from a small distance so I can't throw my fist in his face.

"Shut it."

"You've got it bad, AJ." I take a step forward, and my fist connects with his cheek lightly. He stumbles back and folds himself in half, laughing like he has heard the best joke ever.

"My boy is in loveeee," he says between chuckles, and I jump on him, wrestling him to the mats, where we roll around on the floor and rumble together like kids. It is the most fun I have had in a long time.

17

VALERIE

I look at the reports in front of me, wondering if I can make sense of them all. I have immersed myself in work these past days, so much so, the numbers I am looking at are all starting to merge. I have read every report, every strategy, and have had meetings with key people across finance, marketing, and sales to ensure I am well-versed. I have reviewed our HR policies, seen the reports from our employee hotline, did a pulse check on our team's mental and physical health, tried to gauge the culture, what it is like, what we can improve. I have even spent more time with our team who run the Van Cleef Foundation, a department that my mother started and one I have worked with a lot. I have tasked them with looking at more grassroots charities and ways we can help the local community, particularly kids. After the incident with Levi, I know that is an issue the city has, and if Van Cleef can put some money together to help, then that is what I want to do.

But regardless of how much work I am doing, my

mind still wanders to AJ. His body, his strong hands, the way we rode his bike together. His protective nature, his dislike of accepting my help, the way he kissed me. Actually, mostly the way he kissed me. I have never been kissed like that. Ever. With so much possessive want, the tight grip he had on my face like he couldn't let me go for a second.

It's been a few days since that night. I made calls the next morning and managed to get Levi off with a fine and a final warning. If he breaks the law again, he will be looking at jail time. I was surprised to get the text from AJ, and I wasn't sure how the call would go when I rang him, but he invited me for another date. I can't say I have heard of Jordie's before, but I have talked the girls into coming with me tonight, and I desperately want to see him again. Now as I sit here with George, discussing the business and my situation, my confidence rises as does my confusion and anger.

"So George, you're telling me that my father is trying to secure the entire foothold of this region of Montana?" I ask, wide-eyed. I have been looking at the map on my screen for mere minutes, but I can already see that something isn't right. *Who needs that much land in Montana?*

"That's what he wants..." George says hesitantly.

"But if he does this, he will effectively be pushing people out of their homes, to what? Build a resort? Construct some office and retail spaces?" I look at him like this is ludicrous, because it makes no sense. George has worked for Van Cleef Corp for years and was my mother's right-hand man. He and my father don't see eye to eye, but my mother made the instructions clear when she passed. George was to stay on, no matter what, and for that, I am glad. He is my closest confidant in the business.

"He doesn't care. He wants to buy the property and build." George nods in confirmation.

"But that makes no sense. Sure, we build properties all the time, but we have never gone into a new region with the idea to flatten homes, take over an entire portion of a neighborhood, and kick people out. What is he even thinking?" I almost shriek. This makes me really unsettled. "My mother wouldn't have wanted this."

"She always said we build for the success of everyone," George states.

"She did, didn't she?" I murmur, her words now coming back to me. Van Cleef Corp has been highly successful over the years. That's not to say that we haven't made some questionable decisions, but for the most part, we have been successful in building our wealth and that of others where we can.

"Your father doesn't care. He wants to own that parcel of land," George confirms.

"But we have Tennessee to focus on?" I question. While we run multiple projects at a time, buying businesses, merging them, building new ones, focusing on a new hotel build in Tennessee while also managing something nearly identical in Montana doesn't make a lot of sense to me.

"Tennessee is good, but your father can't get a collaborator and he is chasing the dollars."

"I understand that. But we have run the numbers. Tennessee will be fantastic for us. It will increase employment, provide much-needed infrastructure, and we are using all local builders and suppliers. Not to mention, it is right near Whispers. We both know how that town has grown to become a billionaire hotspot. But this?" I taper off, not seeing any additional benefit aside from our bottom line. It feels icky.

"We need a partner in Tennessee to make it marketable, though," George says, looking at me.

"I've got us one." I know I can trust George. He hates my father.

"Who?" he fires back. He might be close to seventy in age, but he is quick as a fox.

"Well, maybe two, actually..." I tease, my smile small but there. "Whiteman's and the Rothschilds." His eyebrows shoot to his hairline.

"Well, shit. Your father tried to get Whiteman's and they wouldn't take his call. But the Rothschilds?" he says, leaning back in his office chair, not looking convinced.

"I had a meeting with the Rothschild boys. It's early days, just starting conversations, but they are keen to reinvest in more local projects now that Harrison is president. While their overseas expansion into Singapore has been fantastic for them, they now need to refocus domestically and they would like to collaborate, to again show the people they are investing in America. They want in on our Tennessee project and anywhere else we might have our sights on," I say, my mind racing with the possibilities.

"And in return?" George asks, deep in thought.

"They invest, Whiteman's will get naming rights of the bar area, as well as exclusive whiskey supplier across our hospitality businesses, and we retain complete control, keeping us majority shareholder." My smile widens as he looks at me in wonder. I have been on the phone all week, but I managed to get verbal agreements from everyone on this, and I am proud to have gotten that far.

"Well, my dear, your mother would be smiling about now." His eyes become glassy.

"We just need to get it past my father..." I murmur, and George takes a big breath as his lips thin. "Why is my father so adamant about Montana?" I ask, knowing there has to be more.

"Ownership. If he purchases this area, then he will own a large portion of the town and outskirts. Then the governor will be in our pocket," George highlights.

"Why does he want the governor?" My eyes thin, hating the sound of this entirely.

"Because the Rothschilds have solid political connections, so he wants Van Cleef to as well," George says, his jaw set.

"You cannot be serious? He is investing in a business decision, not based on strategy, financial outcome, or community benefit, but because he wants the same connections as the Rothschilds?" I say the words that seem so crazy, yet I already know they are true.

"Your father always wanted to be bigger, better, have more, look smarter, be more popular..." George says.

"That doesn't sound ethical at all," I quip.

"Where your father's concerned, nothing ever is," George comments, and I swallow, finally seeing it all now.

I take a breath and ask the question that plays on my mind.

"Why is he the CEO, then?" Over the years, I haven't been privy to all of my father's decisions, and I have come to the conclusion that he, no doubt, is unethical and borderline almost criminal in some of his decisions. Ever since my mom died, his standards and his ethics have completely been erased. I ignored it before, because I always thought that my ascension into the CEO position would happen naturally and that I could fix everything when I was in the role. But now that he wants me to marry and get out of the business, I need to make the moves myself.

"Who else?" he asks, eyeing me suspiciously. We have talked briefly, but I haven't gone over my entire plan with him yet.

"Me," I say firmly, and he looks at me. "I'm ready. I have attended every board meeting for the last two years. I have worked in every department. I know everyone in this building from you, as our VP, through to David in the mailroom and Theresa who delivers our catering. I know our profit and loss for the past three years. I am aware of everything we do in this business." Nervous voicing my idea, the words rush out of me.

"Your father always said you weren't interested. Said you prefer fashion and shopping, not the business," George says, sitting forward.

"My father is a liar." George nods in understanding. Sure, I love fashion. I like to have nice clothes; I enjoy wearing designers, but being a fashion influencer is not my job, merely a hobby when I have the time.

"Your mom would be proud of the woman you have become," George says, and the air leaves my lungs momentarily. I swallow down the tears that sting my eyes because that's what I want.

"But my father is not." The familiar feeling of anxiety and dread settles in my stomach.

"With all due respect, your father is an asshole," he says, and I huff a laugh.

"So do I have your support?" I ask, looking at him, waiting on edge to hear the words that could either make or break my future.

"To be CEO? To overthrow your father?" he clarifies, because that is exactly what we are talking about. He gives nothing away as he watches me. I nod, waiting for his answer.

A broad smile spreads across his face. "I have been waiting for this day since the moment you were born." My grin widens, matching his.

"Let's put together a plan, because he is not going down without a fight," George says, sitting forward, and I swallow harshly, my anxiety growing, yet I know this is what needs to be done.

After George and I strategize for another hour, I feel renewed as I walk to my office, excited about the plan going forward and George's help. I know the business development team likes my ideas; I have worked in the legal team for years, so they all know me well, and I wasn't lying to George when I said I know every staff member here in our office. All 256 of them.

"Valerie!" my father's voice barks at me, and I stop short, heart thumping. It shouldn't be like this. I shouldn't experience immediate fear as soon as my father calls my name. I turn to face him, and as I do, I plaster on the fake smile I have mastered over the years. I need to remain innocent and appear as though I am doing what he asks. He can't know my plan to overthrow him until I need him to.

"My office. Now!" I jump slightly at his tone as I watch him turn and walk into his office, not even waiting to see if I follow his command, because he knows I will. I always do. I balk for a moment, wondering what it would be like to walk in the other direction. I imagine him sitting at his desk waiting and then the anger that would overtake him knowing that I wasn't coming. But we are at the office, his assistant is watching, and those nearby heard his command. I give them all a small smile that I know doesn't reassure them at all, and they all look at me with a healthy mix of nerves and pity. I never noticed it before, but that is exactly what it is. I roll my shoulders back and strut to his office. If I am going to be CEO, I need to get used to uncomfortable conversations, and my father's office provides a perfect training ground.

As I walk in, he isn't looking at me, but he barks, "Close the door."

I do as he commands and close the door, standing in front of it, waiting.

"What in the world do you think you are playing at?" he seethes, and my muscles tense. I only just talked with George, so surely he didn't say anything.

"I have no idea what you mean." I feign confusion.

"Valerie! I told you that you are to be married. You are not taking any of my calls, and then I see this!" he yells, throwing photos onto his desk. I don't move, but my eyes lower, and I see images of me getting off the back of AJ's bike in front of my apartment. Of us kissing. It is dark, they are blurry, but there is no mistaking it is AJ and me. At first, I think it must be Victor who has taken them, and I feel the familiar sense of betrayal from a man I consider a close ally, but no, they are photos taken from the other side of the street. I can see Victor in the background of a few.

My eyes flick back to my father, whose hands are on his hips. I keep my features schooled, not wanting to give him anything. The number of calls that my father has made to me has been astronomical, and I have ignored each and every one. I did make the mistake of listening to his voicemail. He never leaves a message and his seething tone at me ignoring him was chilling as I listened, enough to almost have me run to the bathroom and empty the contents of my stomach.

"I am not playing at anything," I answer his original question.

He stares at me, his nostrils wide. "You are on the back of a fucking motorcycle. You are kissing a nightclub bouncer on the curb."

"He is not a nightclub bouncer," I say, even though, yes, technically, he is, but he is so much more.

"Oh, I know everything there is to know about AJ Steele." I start to panic a little. "And let me tell you, if you keep up this fucking charade, there will be consequences." I remain silent, biting my tongue. Now is the time to be smart. Not emotional.

"It's just one last fling before I get married. You told

me I have a few months. After I am wed, my life changes forever." The lies on my tongue taste bitter, but I need to play the game. The fact that he already knows who AJ is concerns me. AJ is big and tough enough to fight anyone, but I know my father. He wouldn't play fair.

My father's shoulders lower, and he takes a big breath. "Just stop acting like a slut in public. I will be moving up the timeline. William Schmidt is going to be back in town soon and expects a better greeting from you when he is here. I had to practically grovel to get him to come back and you will not act indifferent to him again. Until then, pull yourself together. Stop eating carbs and stop liaising with the poor people in town. You might catch something," he says, sitting at his desk and picking up his phone, signifying the end of the conversation.

I turn and walk out the door, strutting to my office, my nails digging into my palms. I thought I disliked my father before. I thought he was being irrational and demeaning, and I didn't like the way he treated me or others. But now, with the way he talks about AJ, my blood boils. I don't care where AJ lives. I don't care that he works in security and is not some Wall Street finance guy or oil baron. AJ has already treated me better than all the other men in my life and that has to count for something.

18

AJ

Her text comes through, and I throw my cue stick to Cody so he can finish the game of pool with Brady.

"Girls are here," I tell them as I walk away and make my way to the front door. Jordie's is packed tonight. I see some regulars, but it's mostly full of people kick-starting their weekend with too much liquor and not enough class.

"Look at him running..." Brady comments, and I flick him a scowl, which turns into a smirk as I see the black eye he sports from where I hit him at the gym.

I nod to the bouncers and push open the door as I see her pull up. She is hard to miss in her blacked-out Mercedes G-Wagon, and I watch as she and her friends spill out of the car. Last time I saw them all together was at Chloe's store event, where they were all in dresses, high heels, and full of glamour. Tonight, as they all walk toward me, they are still too overdressed for this place, but in jeans and jackets, they are somewhat more subdued.

"Hey, big guy," Val says, her smile wide as she looks up at me. Fuck, she takes my breath away. Her long hair is all slicked back into a long, straight, glossy ponytail flowing down her back.

"Hey, sweetheart," I murmur, kissing her on the forehead as my hand automatically finds her waist.

"Ohhh, look, they even have pet names for each other already!" Simone jokes as the other two grin.

"Girls." I pull Val behind me and into the bar, the three of them following.

The music is loud, and I lead them through the crowd to where the boys are sitting by the pool table we have commandeered.

"Now the party is starting!" Cody says, smiling at the girls.

"Beer?" Brady asks, and the girls nod.

"I'll help," Chloe says, and the two of them walk off to the bar. I see Simone is already chatting with Jimmy, which looks interesting. Any usual Friday night, we would all be at Club Vine, and Jimmy and the boys will go there later. But I will be going straight home to bed after a few hours to prepare for the fight.

"What happened to Brady's eye?" Val asks.

"He ran into my fist," I tell her, and she looks shocked before she laughs.

"I don't need to know, right?" she asks, and I shake my head.

"Nope. Not at all." I take a swig of my drink.

"What a place," Val says, looking around.

"Let me guess, your father wouldn't approve of this place either?" I tease.

"Not one bit. But I love it regardless of what he thinks." She smiles, looking up at me. She looks good when she is happy. Relaxed and at ease. She is glowing.

"So, your girls all came?" I comment, seeing them all hanging with my boys over to the side, leaving me and Val to talk.

"They are more my family now. They are great. What about you? Family?"

I grit my teeth. This is why I don't date. I hate talking about my past.

"Just my mom. She lives in a trailer out of town. Same one I grew up in." I take another sip of my drink, trying to push down the feelings of shame that arise.

"So we are alike with that too, then? Our friends are our family?" she asks, not pushing me for more answers. Even though I pretty much told her I have nothing, grew up with nothing, and am worth nothing, she still finds a silver lining to the dark cloud of me.

"Seems like it." I admire her. She doesn't care. She could buy this entire bar—hell, this entire block we are on—yet she doesn't care where I came from.

"So what were you like growing up?" she asks, and I swallow. Might as well lay it out for her.

"Trouble. Didn't go to college. Got in trouble with the law a few times…" I say, leaving it out for her to digest. Her eyes move from my face, down my front, and back up again, like she is checking me out.

"What for?" she asks, and I don't blame her. She is a lawyer; she needs to know these things.

"Petty crime. Bit of stealing when I was a kid. Much like Levi," I tell her, and she nods. She bites her bottom lip, so I know what she is thinking. "You can trust me, Val. I won't hurt you." I mean it. She needs to know that I am a good guy now, even though my history leaves little to be desired.

She smirks at me. "I know that already, AJ. It just makes me admire you even more."

"What?" I ask, almost shocked.

"Well, you obviously had it hard growing up, but look at you. You have your own business, amazing friends, you're fit and healthy. You train young kids and give back to the community. We can't let our history define us. We can only change the path we are on for the future." I wonder where the hell this woman has been all my life. She fits right into my soul like she is part of it.

"You give me too much credit," I say, because it can't be that simple. She should be back in her car now and halfway home, running from me. The lifestyle I lead is nothing like she is accustomed to.

"Sounds like you don't give yourself enough." Continuing, she changes the subject. "So, big fight tomorrow?" she asks, as Brady and Chloe come back with their beers, and she grabs one.

"Yep. A few hours here, then I need to tuck myself into bed to try to get eight hours." My hand drapes around her waist, feeling a little off-kilter but happy at the same time as I keep her close to me. I can feel her body heat, smell her floral scent. She drives me crazy. I can't not touch her.

"No time to waste, then," she says, looking at me like she knows something I don't.

"On what?" I ask, my eyes thinning.

"Twenty bucks I can beat you at pool?" she challenges, her eyes flashing wicked in delight. There is no way this pretty little thing from the good side of town will even be able to compete. I grew up in pool halls. I know how to win at pool.

"You're on," I growl, putting down my drink and grabbing hers to do the same. She laughs as I take her hand and lead her over to the pool table and we select some cues.

"Ohhhh, this is going to be good," Simone says as she jumps up on a stool with her beer and gets ready to watch.

"You got this, AJ," Cody yells, leaning back and chatting with Chelsea.

We have all our friends watching us and it feels good. Feels right. Our friends are getting along, and Val and her girls look comfortable in this bar, even though it is not where I would imagine them to be. I watch as Val takes off her jacket, revealing a tight singlet, her jeans sticking to her legs, showcasing the curves of her body, and I internally groan. This is going to be harder than I first thought.

"You sure about this, sweetheart? No one will think any less of you if you pull out now," I tease, knowing that my girl will never back down.

"Are you scared, AJ?" She tilts her head, her hair flicking behind her. That fucking long ponytail is doing something to my insides. I want to wrap it in my hand and pull her head back, watch her body arch.

I clear my throat and refocus. "Not scared, just concerned, wondering how you will deal with defeat," I say as I chalk the tip of my cue, smirking.

"You know what. I will give you an advantage. You can go first," she offers, and I will admit, she does a great job of talking herself up.

"You got it, babe." Giving her a wink, I lean over the table, ready to get this game going. I hit with force, and the balls scatter, but none drop into the holes yet. I step back and give her the table.

She leans over the table and takes her shot, pocketing two balls with one hit and doesn't let up. Our game is over in about two minutes as I stand shocked, mouth agape, as Val totally wipes the floor with me.

"Where the hell did you learn to play like that?" I ask, still rooted to the ground. Apart from the first shot, I didn't get a chance to take another. She pocketed every ball she tapped.

"What a shark!" Brady laughs, as do all our friends. The girls holler and hoot at Val, and the boys are either in shock or laughing as well.

"I didn't spend *all* my time at college studying..." She smiles like the cat that got the canary.

"If you tell me some rich dude from Yale taught you how to play pool and had his hands all over you in the process, this night is not going to end well," I murmur, feeling jealous of a dude I don't even know exists.

She laughs. "No. I worked in a pool hall in my senior year," she says, and I balk.

"You worked while at college?" I ask.

"Yep. I didn't need to, obviously, but I wanted to." She totally surprises me.

"Okay, out of the way. It's our turn, lovebirds," Simone teases as she jumps down from her stool and pulls Jimmy over.

I grab Val by the waist and maneuver her over to the leather lounge chair that Jimmy vacated, and I take a seat, pulling her on top of me to sit on my knee.

"You know I can sit on the stool," Val says, looking over my shoulder as I pull her back to sit on me properly. My hands curve around her waist, and I rub my thumb up and down her lower back.

"I know, but I want you here," I mumble, feeling my dick thicken in my jeans. Maybe this wasn't a good idea.

She gives me a playful smile, her lips glossy and shining in the lights as her hand rests on one of mine. She relaxes on me a little, still sitting up straight as we both look over at the game, watching Simone and Jimmy. My eyes home in on her ponytail that is right in front of me, and I lift my hand, grabbing it lightly at the top and running my hands all the way down the length. It is so fucking soft, I can't even believe it is hair. I do it again, but this time, I roll my hand so it wraps around the hair and pull through it slowly. Her head falls back a little in the process, and I see my dream come to life as her body arches a little, her ass pressing into my hips, and I run my other hand up her side, following her curves.

Fuck me. I want this. I want her. I clear my throat as I let go of her hair, and her head rightens to look back at me.

"You like the ponytail," she murmurs.

"Oh, I like it all, sweetheart," I grit out.

"I like you too, AJ." She leans back, her body hitting my chest, and I wrap my hands around her waist again, keeping her close. My lips meet her soft skin on her shoulder, and we sit together like a couple as our friends banter.

Val chuckles at something her friends do, and I notice Brady looking at me. He stares at me seriously and nods, giving me his best friend approval. I take a deep breath and let the stress dissipate, wondering briefly if I could be lucky enough to have Val in my life.

19

VALERIE

"You're all sharks," Brady says as we step outside. Each of us girls beat the boys at pool, and they aren't happy about it.

"We won, fair and square," I tell him.

"Yeah, don't blame us because you don't know how to handle a stick," Simone quips.

"Alright, time to go," AJ says, breaking up the debate as we walk out into the cool night air.

"Party pooper." I pout, and he squeezes my waist where his hand has rested all night. I have enjoyed myself here at Jordie's. It isn't a place I ever thought I would come to, but AJ is taking me out of my comfort zone more and more. I love it.

"Give Simone your keys," he growls, and I look up at him and frown.

"I can drive. I only had one beer," I tell him, seeing his eyes shimmer with something that looks like adoration.

"I know you can, but I want to drive you home on my bike." My frown lifts into a small smile. We have been together all night. If anyone was to look at us, they would automatically think we are a couple. AJ had his hand on me the entire time and didn't once let me go. The feeling is mutual. I enjoy being with him, having him hold me. From the kiss to my forehead in greeting when I arrived to the kisses he sprinkled on my bare shoulder, I'm almost melting into a puddle at his feet.

"Not ready to get rid of me yet, huh?" I tease.

"Keys," he demands, and I grab them from my purse.

"Simone. You okay to drive the beast? I'm going with AJ," I ask her, and she smiles.

"Sure. Just don't be out too long, you two... You have a fight tomorrow, remember?" She smirks, taking my keys, and I kiss my friends goodbye as they jump into my car.

"Don't be late," Brady says to AJ as I watch the boys shake hands and backslap.

"No problem, boss," AJ says in jest, and we watch them go.

"That black eye really doesn't look good," I murmur, which only makes AJ's smirk grow.

"His fault, he brought it on himself," he says, grabbing my hand and leading me to the bike. I feel better equipped to ride tonight. With jeans and boots, I will be warmer and more comfortable.

"You know the drill," he says, handing me the helmet.

"Where are you taking me?" I ask. I know he won't take me straight home. It is only ten, and while he needs his sleep, I have a feeling AJ isn't ready to drop me off yet.

"I have a place I want to show you," he says cryptically, and I smile as he secures the strap under my chin.

I get on the bike, and as we start to ride, I relax

around him. It is only my second time, but it feels nice. The breeze is fresh, and I wrap my arms around his waist. The way he drops his hand to my knee and rubs his thumb across makes butterflies swirl in my stomach. The vibrations from the engine run up my legs and around my body. My already heightened arousal from all his touches tonight skyrockets even more, my fingers digging into his chest. He squeezes my knee like he knows exactly what I am feeling, and I am grateful that I have a helmet on to cover the flush that I feel on my cheeks.

We wind up a small mountain, and the area looks familiar. It is an exclusive part, out of town, with massive homes obscured by large gates and hedges lining the streets. I look around, knowing that both Ben and Eddie Rothschild live up here somewhere. I am confused for a moment when he takes the bike down a small path that looks more like a sidewalk rather than a road through a small park. He drives down between trees and stops right at the edge of an embankment, turning off the engine.

I pull off my helmet where I sit.

"Where are we?" I ask in awe. The view of the city from here is amazing. The lights twinkle below us. We are at a lookout or something.

"It's just a place I come to. When I need to think." Taking my helmet from my head, he hangs it on the handlebar. I hold on to his shoulders and stand, stepping off the bike and looking around.

"It is so beautiful," I say, my eyes wide. I have seen a similar view at a party I was at a few months ago up here somewhere, but because we are in the pure black of night, surrounded by trees, the lights are all much brighter than I remember.

"It is nice and quiet," he murmurs low, almost a growl, and I turn to look at him. He is still sitting on the bike, having moved back on the seat with his large legs flat on the ground on either side. He looks like one of those big men in a Harley commercial.

"Between Mr. Burger, Jordie's, and now this, I am starting to think you know all the good places around town," I tease as I walk back to him.

"Well, it's not the Four Seasons, but..." He shrugs, and I smile.

"The Four Seasons isn't all that great, to be honest," I say. "Besides, a view like this is a million times better." I sigh, looking back out at it again.

"You continue to surprise me, sweetheart."

I look back at him with a small smile.

"Oh, why is that?"

"You are just nothing like I guessed."

"Let me guess..." I say as I move closer. "Stuck-up rich girl. Never worked a day in her life. Gets everything handed to her on a silver platter..."

"I sure as shit never thought you would work at a pool hall in college," he says, shaking his head, and I bark out a laugh, thinking about our night. "Fuck, you are pretty when you smile." His words catch me off guard, and I pause, our eyes connecting. "Come here," he commands, and I take a few more steps toward him before his hands shoot out, and he grabs me at the waist. Standing, he picks me up.

"Ahh, AJ!" I squeal in delight, grabbing on to his forearms as he lifts me to where he is and saddles me on his bike. This time, though, I face him, my back to the handlebars, my legs over his thighs.

It is intimate. Sure, I was sitting on his knee back at Jordie's. His hands skirted across my waist and my body a few times throughout the night. I felt him harden underneath me, so I know he was turned on. But this, facing each other, nothing between us, it is new. I feel open, exposed, vulnerable.

"This alright with you?" he asks, his voice gravelly as his hands run up and down my thighs. I swallow my nerves down and nod as my hands rest on his knees.

"As long as I don't fall," I say, smiling. The bike is sturdy and so is he, but I could topple at any moment.

"I won't ever let you fall. Don't worry." His promise hits me right in the chest. My heart thumps, palms sweating a little.

"Kiss me, AJ..." I whisper. We haven't kissed since he dropped me off after our burger date, and the way he is looking at me now makes me grateful that I am sitting down because my knees are wobbly.

His hand cups my face, and he pulls me to him. I slide down the seat, sitting right on his lap, as his other hand circles my lower back, pressing me to him. Our lips meet, and my body melts to his almost immediately. As I grab on to his biceps, they flex under my touch, his tongue swooping across my lips. A growl comes from his throat as we devour each other.

My body arches into him when the hand on my back pulls me in tighter, and he swallows my moan. He is relentless as he kisses me, the heat from his hand moving from my back upward to grab my ponytail. With a tug, my head falls back. His lips don't move from me as he kisses down my jaw to my neck.

"AJ..." I whimper, feeling out of control, my nipples pebbling, clit throbbing, and goosebumps littering my skin. This is the hottest thing I have ever done. He tugs my hair more, and I arch further, my breasts pushing out. His lips continue to go lower, across my shoulder. My bare skin aches for more of his touch.

"You smell so fucking good," he murmurs as my head rests in his palm, while his other still tugs on my hair. I move my hands, running them up to his neck and digging my fingers into his hair. He moans as I massage his scalp, and I feel him hard underneath my ass. My hips automatically rock, needing some friction.

"My body feels like it is on fire..." I breathe out as his lips continue to suck and bite, kissing me down my shoulder and back up again.

"You make me so fucking hard..." he groans, his voice sounding pained. His hand falls to my hip, and he grips on to my side as I grind onto him, our jeans giving me a little more friction.

"Fuck. What are you doing to me?" Our kiss becomes more urgent.

"The same thing you are doing to me..." I moan as I kiss him some more. His hand travels to the front of my jeans, and I feel him pop the button. My heart races. I have never done anything remotely like this before, not even in private, but we are under the cover of darkness, with no one around.

"I am hard as a rock, but I can't do anything about

that because of my fight tomorrow. Let me help ease your burn, sweetheart," he growls into my neck as he kisses and sucks my skin. His hand pulls down my zipper, and I lift, creating some space, desperate for his touch.

"Yes... please. God, yes," I moan, feeling so needy it is almost embarrassing. His hand delves into my jeans and beneath my underwear.

"Shit... you're so wet," he growls as his finger glides through me, and I lift my hips, wanting more.

"It's your fault, all your fault." My eyes close as I continue to wither on top of him, his hands holding me exactly where he wants me. His face still buried in my neck, my arms anchor around him. I feel his finger slip inside, and I moan instantly.

"Jesus, give me strength," he murmurs as the heel of his hand rocks against my clit, and he pushes his finger in and out.

"Oh, AJ..." I moan, biting my bottom lip, feeling my arousal grow.

"Keep rocking like that... grind on my hand... Good girl." I whimper at his words. My hips move faster, his hand and fingers matching my speed. I feel my body temperature rise even more, my fingers gripping his hair tighter, and I am right on the cusp of coming.

His lips suck on my shoulder and neck as his other hand splays across my lower back, holding me tight, rocking me back and forth over his rock-hard length beneath me.

"AJ..." I warn. "I'm going to come." I'm already out of breath and in mild panic because I can feel the pressure rising and I am not sure I am ready for it.

"That's it, fuck my fingers, sweet thing. Give it to me." He growls some more before he pulls back and takes my lips with his. He bites my lip as the pace of his hand increases and the feeling is overwhelming.

"AJ, AJ, AJ." I breathe out his name over and over, my hips now rocking uncontrollably. Pulling back from his lips a little, I rest my forehead to his.

"Come, baby, let go. I want to watch you when you come on my fingers..." And I let go. My entire body quivers, like it has never orgasmed before. I feel like I was wound tight forever and someone let go of the string, and I am finally uncoiling.

"Ahhhhh! Ajaaayyyyy!" I can't help it, I cry out. His pace slows as my clit throbs under his palm, and he rocks my hips more, dragging the entire orgasm straight from me like he is a magician.

I drop my forehead to his chest as I come down from the high, and he removes his hand from my jeans. Lifting my head up with one hand, I watch as he sucks his finger, cleaning me from his skin.

"Wow," I say, still feeling a little out of it but so ready for more of him.

"You are a little addictive, sweetheart. I want to do that all over again already." He murmurs.

"I didn't realize that a bike was so... multi-purpose," I say, wondering if my words are making sense. I am still floating on cloud nine.

"Neither did I. I've never done that on my bike before," he murmurs, looking at me, watching for my response.

"I like being your first, AJ," I say with a smile. "But you

know, maybe we should do that again some other time just to... you know... double-check the safety of the kick-stand." My face breaks into a smile. He huffs a laugh and gives me a big grin, and my heart almost bursts. He looks hot with his grumpy scowls, but AJ with a full-blown smile... that is an image for the history books.

"Tonight, I will take you home. But after the fight, you are all mine, sweetheart."

I have never been more ready for anything in my life.

20

VALERIE

"I for one am thoroughly enjoying this little crush you got going on with the security guy. There is so much testosterone in here, I can no longer find my feminism," Chelsea quips as we walk into the massive space.

"I think mine flew out of me the minute we walked in the door and the buff doorman with tattoos up his neck winked at me," Simone says, flicking her long blond hair over her shoulders and giving eyes to every man walking past us.

"Is that Leonardo over there?" Chloe's looking through the crowd, always spotting the celebrities, while I ignore my friends and look straight ahead.

Chelsea is right. I have never been anywhere like this before. It's a large warehouse room full of men which is loud and crowded, and although I walk with full confidence, I am starting to wonder if this was a bad idea. I got tickets to AJ's fight. I don't know how. It was completely sold out. But I called some people and got four, close to the front, with good views of the ring.

"It's a wonder the paps aren't here, since the *Society News* article this week," Chelsea says, and I bite my tongue. I have no idea what is happening in my life at the moment, but *Society News* is taking more of an interest in me than usual. Of course they caught me on the back of AJ's bike after Chloe's showing. The photos were all over the web this week.

"Well, it's not like *Society News* would be somewhere like this. This isn't the usual place you expect Valeria Van Cleef to be," Chloe says in jest.

"So, what's the protocol? I've never been to a fight before," Simone asks as we walk toward our seats, many pairs of eyes looking us up and down.

"I did some research this week. Apparently, there are fifteen rounds, three minutes per round. Unless there is a knockout, then the fight finishes earlier," I tell them as we reach our seats.

"Oh, I think I see Tennyson Rothschild..." Chloe says, clearly happy we are in good company, and I immediately raise my gaze in the direction she is looking. Tennyson waves at me, so I smile and wave back. And cameras promptly click in my face. *Shit.*

"You know, now *we will* be on the front page of *Society News* tomorrow right," Chelsea comments, and the short-lived relief I had earlier now dissipates.

"What's new?" I murmur, frustrated I can't do anything in this town without the whole of Baltimore society knowing about it.

"What is Father Van Cleef going to say?" Chelsea asks,

and I bristle a little at that statement. Of course, he is not going to be happy.

"He doesn't get a say in what I do in my spare time or who I choose to do it with," I tell her, feeling confident in my decision. The girls take a seat as I remain standing, glancing around the room.

"Didn't picture you as a fighting girl." Tennyson grins at me, walking over to stand next to me.

"First time," I share. "But I know one of the fighters, and I wanted to support him." His eyebrows rise.

"You have friends in this scene?" Tennyson fishes for more information, so I decide to be transparent. If we go into business together, I appreciate honesty, and I can't expect it from him and his brothers if I don't give it to them.

"AJ and I are getting to know each other." A small smile reaches my face while the butterflies in my stomach take flight.

"He's tough. But from what I've heard, he is fair."

"I know. He is also a good man," I say, nodding, and Tennyson smiles.

"Nice to see you spreading your wings, little Van Cleef." He sends me a knowing smile and a wink before stepping backward. "It feels good, doesn't it?" I know he speaks from experience. His family has gone through so much with their late mother.

"Feels great," I tell him as I feel my shoulders lowering.

"Good to see you ladies," Tennyson says to my friends, giving them all a sexy smirk before he turns and heads back to his seat.

"Now *that* is a man..." Simone murmurs, and we laugh, breaking any nervous tension. I blow out a breath.

George and I are moving chess pieces at work, getting things ready for me to challenge my father. We have meetings lined up over the next week with board members. I have no idea exactly what is going to happen when I start to make my moves, but I know it isn't going to go smoothly. The small feeling of joy that shines inside of me at the excitement of starting my life anew is almost pushing aside the nerves I have of seeing AJ. I know he won't be happy I am here.

The lights dim and the announcer starts talking over a loud microphone, causing the crowd to settle down. There is a warm-up fight before the main event, and I watch as each fighter is announced. Us girls get comfortable, and so far, the theatrics are somewhat entertaining, but when the bell rings and the two fighters start dancing around each other, my stomach plummets. It is brutal.

"Shit," Chelsea whisper-yells.

"This is crazy!" Simone gasps, watching wide-eyed.

Chloe and I remain quiet, and my fingernails dig into my palms as I hear the thwack of gloves hitting skin and fear crawls up my spine.

The fight goes nine rounds, and I was on the edge of my seat for each of them and I don't even know these men. The fighters leave the ring, looking bloody and sweaty, while the announcer talks about the main event. People jump into the ring and start wiping the floor, mopping up the blood and sweat that remains, and new equipment is brought to the ringside. I slowly look around the room again. There is not a spare seat anywhere. Men are standing, talking and shouting, beer is being sloshed, and I take another deep breath. *What the hell am I doing here?*

"Are you sure you want to watch this?" Chloe asks, her eyes searching mine, Simone the only one of us seemingly enjoying the display of testosterone. I want to see AJ. But I don't want to see him hurt. I should leave, but I can't move.

"I'm sure." I nod as the lights lower and loud music starts. Rago Ragatonio is announced. I don't know anything about him other than he is AJ's opponent tonight, and he dances around down the aisle, making his way to the ring. He is big, with bushy dark eyebrows, broad shoulders, and bulky arms. The applause for him is lackluster; he is clearly not the fan favorite. That makes me feel a little better.

He steps through the ropes and into the ring, shuffling around as the lights dim again and the announcer grabs the microphone.

"Ladies and gentlemen..." The announcer's booming voice makes my body jolt, and I swallow harshly. "He is the man, he is the machine, he is AJ Steeleeeeee!" His voice carries the *E* for a long time as loud thumping music comes on, and I think I might faint.

"Holy Mother of God." I barely hear Simone as the audience is on its feet, grown men screaming. Thunderous applause radiates around the room as the deep base of the music pumps through my feet via the floor.

"Wow," Chloe says, her mouth dropped open, her eyes even wider.

I can't yet see what they can, so I turn my head and

poke around the shoulders of the men in front of me to get a look, and when I do, my breath catches. He is beautiful. His skin is shiny from oil, tattoos on full display, which are dark and cover most of his torso. He is wearing a pair of shimmery red shorts, his thick thighs looking solid. I thought his opponent was large, but AJ is bigger. Everywhere. His arms, thighs, he is taller, broader, there is just more of him, more than I ever realized. Bouncing on his toes, he ducks under the rope and into the ring, and as the bright lights finally reach his face, I take in his heavy scowl. He looks dangerous. Deadly. Every inch a frightening fighter that he is, and it makes my mouth dry and my belly flutter. I feel unsteady with admiration.

"I can't believe that is what is underneath all those black security clothes." Chelsea giggles.

"No wonder you have been lusting after him for weeks," Simone quips as we all sit down with the rest of the crowd and wait for the formalities to finish and the fight to start.

"I have not," I refute with absolutely no conviction in my tone. I haven't told them about last night other than that we went for a ride. I am not exactly sure what we are or if I should even label us.

"The drool coming from your mouth says differently," Chloe says, grinning.

On instinct, I wipe my chin, and the girls cackle at me. I roll my eyes and look back up at the ring, and my smile disappears as I meet his icy-blue stare. He has spotted me, and as expected, he does not look happy.

I have no idea where I get the courage, but I don't move my gaze, and instead, I place my fingers to my mouth and blow him a kiss. His jaw clenches, and he turns, saying something to his team, who all look in our direction.

"Ooohhhh, he is not happy..." Simone singsongs, and now all four of us watch as AJ, Brady, and his other friend, Cody, all stare at us, then turn away.

They whisper something to their security guys behind them, and while AJ is getting his mouthguard pushed in and a final drink of water sprayed into his mouth, two large security guys walk toward where we sit and stand next to us, like our own personal bodyguards.

"Oh shit, he just sent us security," Simone says, looking them up and down.

"Shit, do we need security?" Chloe asks.

"I have no idea..." I say quietly, feeling out of my depth as a few men around us now look our way. I glance around and spot Tennyson's eyebrows quirking up at me. I can only shrug. My heart is beating faster as I realize that AJ is protecting me, and I feel bad for a second because I know he didn't want me coming here.

The ring of the bell pulls me from my thoughts, and I sit forward on the edge of my seat. My heart feels like it is going to leap out of my chest as the two men dance around each other. Then the punches start, and I feel physically ill. My arms immediately circle my waist as I lean forward and watch every step AJ takes, trying not to vomit.

I am captivated as AJ takes a few punches and gives a few, and before I realize it, we are two rounds in.

"This is intense..." I say to the girls, my eyes still on AJ where he sits in the corner of the ring, Brady yelling at him, and Cody squirting water into his mouth.

"This is hot," Simone comments, still looking around at all the men in the crowd.

"I feel like I am going to throw up," I tell them, wishing this was all over already.

"Not yet, the next round is about to start," Chloe says, and my eyes immediately look back at the ring. The familiar bell signifies the start of the third round.

My eyes don't leave AJ, and when a hard punch hits him right in the side, my body is up off the seat in a flash, as is everyone around him.

"No!" I yell as my friends grip my arms on either side. His blues find mine again. "Hit him!" I yell, scared that if he doesn't, the other guy will get another one in. Fear creeps up my throat, and I watch with bated breath, and then I see it in his eyes. Fire.

He jumps around again, shaking his head and getting busy. He lands punch after punch, and the entire place is on their feet. There is yelling and screaming as AJ pummels his opponent, landing every punch as Rago wobbles. I can't move, holding my breath, looking at every move as the crowd around us yells louder. We all watch as Rago's barely able to stand from AJ's punches, and then it's like the whole place holds their breath as AJ pulls his arm back and slams it into Rago's chin. His eyes roll back as his back hits the floor, and he doesn't move. He is out cold.

I'm jumping up and down, cheering my head off, a mix of relief taking over at him winning and not getting hurt and a feeling of pride that he succeeded at his sport.

My smile is wide as I clap and us girls do high fives, laughing at each other, and as I look around, I see that absolute pandemonium has broken out. The crowd erupts, the men around us stand and shout, some jumping, whistling, fist-bumping, and us four women are immediately engulfed with what can only be described as pure masculine energy that we have no way of battling.

The two burley men AJ sent over round us up and move us immediately, and I start to get nervous. We are sandwiched between them both, and as we start walking, it's almost as if we move as one. I turn to look for AJ, but I can't see the ring anymore as people push us, clamoring to get closer. I can't even see where we are going as the people around us push from all directions, the music deafening. But the four of us huddle together and walk holding hands with our heads down, rushing along an aisle and past another wall of security into the bowels of the warehouse. They are not escorting us outside, which means they are taking me to meet AJ. My body simmers in desire to see him, but my hands shake a little at being so out of my comfort zone. I am nervous because I don't know what to expect.

"Through here." one of the men says gruffly as he pushes us inside a huge room. Those are the first and the last words they say as they close the door behind them and leave the four of us girls inside. We look around and take in the room, the yelling from outside now muffled.

"That was intense," Chloe says, looking at each of us.

"That blond security guy can grab me anytime he likes," Simone murmurs as she looks around the room.

"What room is this?" Chelsea asks.

"I think it is AJ's room," I say, trying to swallow the thick feeling that is forming in my throat as I, too, look around. There is a bathroom to the side, but in this main room, there is a massage bed set up. I see skipping ropes, towels, and a change area as well as a small kitchenette, the counters covered in energy drinks, water, and ice. We stand in a small lounge with a fridge beside us and what looks to be a large medical bag filled with all sorts of things.

We all jolt as the door opens. The roar of the crowd gets louder as men pile in, and the four of us walk backward, out of the way. Then I see AJ. His eyes are on me the moment he steps inside. His face is murderous as Brady takes his gloves from his hands.

"Leave! Now!" he barks out to the room, and everyone looks at him before they look at me, then start to walk back out the door. As the men all move around him and out the door, he glances at my friends. "Brady, take the girls into the main lounge." I nod to them that I am okay, and they follow Brady out the door.

It closes behind them, and the room is silent again. I look at this large, sweaty, rugged man in front of me, in nothing but his shiny red shorts and white tape on his hands, and I hold my breath, tamping down the butterflies that fly around my body every time I am in the same room as him. The very butterflies that have been absent from my body with every other man I have ever met. The ones that are multiplying every second he looks at me so intensely.

21

AJ

My body is sore, but the relief at winning this fight fuels me. I am so fucking happy. But when I spotted Little Miss Perfect, the woman who must do everything I tell her not to do, sitting in the crowd, my world moved on its axis. Now in my changing room, my eyes don't leave hers. When I saw her in the stands tonight, I was in disbelief before frustration and overwhelming need took over. She shouldn't be here. It is dangerous, and when I am in the ring, I can't protect her. But looking at her now, my body is on edge, and I am ready for her.

"What are you doing here?" I bark. I might be livid to see her here, but I'm also more than pleased my eyes get to feast on her again so soon. This is the consistent feeling I get with her. Angry she puts herself in danger, happy that she comes to me, and frustrated because I want to fuck her. It is a wonder I won the fight because my mind is a fucking blur.

"I came to see you. To watch you," she says, her hands

landing on her hips, obviously ready for what I am about to say and to battle me on it. Her lips are bright red, and she is wearing sky-high black heels, fitted black jeans, a tight black top, and a leather jacket. She looks badass, and I want her.

"This isn't a place for you," I tell her, fisting my hands. *What the hell was she thinking coming here?*

"But you're here?" She says it like a question, like she is confused as to why I can be here and she can't. I swear this woman drives me fucking insane.

"The fights can be dangerous, sweetheart. This world is not for you." I shake my head. She continues to surprise me as well as frustrate me.

"Why not?" she fires back, and I run my hand through my hair, my swollen knuckles catching a little.

"Because when I am in that ring, I can't protect you if shit goes down. And believe me, shit always goes down in a place like this." My fingers thump in pain. I need to get this tape off my hands, but I can't focus on that right now when this sexy woman stands right in front of me. I haven't yet decided if I want to yell at her or fuck her senseless. Maybe both.

"I just wanted to..." she starts to say, but I stalk toward her, cutting her off.

"Wanted to what, sweetheart?" I grit out. She is fucking too much, and I am about to implode.

"I just... I want you," she admits seductively, and although she looks full of confidence, I see her hesitate a little as she bites her bottom lip. I push down the growls about to rumble from my chest.

"Are you sure you want me? Because we're different,

you and me. You don't know what you are getting yourself into..." I look her over, eyeing her like prey, because I am about to fucking devour her right here, right now. My cock is heavy, my balls full. But I am giving her one last chance to walk away, because I know I can't. Not now. I want her more than the air I breathe.

"No?" she asks in challenge, her chest rising and falling quickly, her lips glossy and fuckable. She steps into me, and I feel her fingers skirt around the skin at my waistband, teasingly so. "Then show me." Looking up at me from under her lashes, she knows exactly what she is doing to me. Sassy Valerie is my favorite, and any hesitations I had fly directly out of my body.

"Get on your knees and put those fucking fantastic red lips on my cock." This is not how I want to treat her, and I wouldn't be surprised if she slapped me, but she needs to know that a man like me is never going to be the country club polo-wearing type. A girl like Valerie Van Cleef would never get on her knees for any man. Especially in a shithole stinking training room, where the floor is concrete, and I have my entire team standing on the other side of the door.

She doesn't balk, doesn't misstep, doesn't even hesitate as her hands connect with my chest. I am covered in oil and sweat, and I wait for her to cringe, but she doesn't. Instead, she traces my ridges with her perfectly manicured fingers, leaving flames of arousal across my chest that lead directly to my dick and make it throb. I growl as her hands run down my chest to the waistband of my fighting shorts, and she pushes them down at the same time she falls to her knees.

"Fuck," is all I can say because it is now game on. I get a new visual of Valerie fucking Van Cleef on her knees in front of me, and my body stills. I'm in shock. I didn't expect this. I want it, damn, I do, but I was expecting her to push me some more. This woman continually surprises me.

My dick is heavy and hard, and when her hand wraps around me, my length twitches in her firm hold.

"You're big..." she murmurs, more to herself than to me. "Much bigger than I have ever seen." She pumps me a little, her small palm no match for my rock-hard cock, and I see her swallow.

I lower my hand, placing my finger under her chin and lifting her head so her eyes look at me. "Rule number one, never talk about another man when we are naked." I am a fucking jealous territorial type, and I don't want her thinking about anyone else when we are together. My eyes don't fall from her gaze. "Don't be shy, sweetheart. Put me in your mouth, show me what you got." I challenge her, knowing she will react, and I hold my breath as she leans forward and her pretty red lips take me in.

"Fuck..." I groan. I just went three rounds, my body is battered and bruised, and I should be in an ice bath about now, but I grip the wall at my side so I don't topple as her warm, wet mouth takes me deep.

"Jesus, sweetheart." She is taking her time, her movements slow, borderline unsure, but the minute she got on her knees, I didn't care. And now as I watch her take me deeper and deeper, sucking on me, the lipstick she is wearing coating my cock like she is marking me as hers, smiling around my length, I know she is enjoying this as much as I am. If that is possible.

"You look so good on your knees for me, sweetheart. Yeah, like that. You look good with my cock sliding in and out of your pretty little mouth," I grit out as her nails run up and down my upper thighs. My skin zings from the contact as I grind my teeth together, savoring the moment. I am going to come too soon. It has been months since I had a woman, and it has been almost a month since I met Valerie and started daydreaming about her in exactly this position.

She moans then, the vibration sending shock waves to my balls, and I see her squirming, her hips moving. She is turned on as well, and that makes me even harder. My dick throbs in her mouth, but she continues to take me deeper with every suck.

"I am going to come down your throat, and then I'm going to fuck your wet pussy with my tongue… I need to taste you," I rasp, my stomach muscles tightening as she hums and nods in agreement, but she doesn't let up on the suction that she is now expertly applying. My hands fall to either side of her head, and I sink my fingers into her soft hair. As I pull it tight, her head falls back slightly, and her jaw automatically opens a little more, allowing me to piston in her mouth.

She again moans at my manhandling, and I bite my lower lip, gripping her hair tighter, moving my hips faster. Her moans set me on a path of no return. She looks up at me, right into my eyes, and my torso muscles clench right before I come with a roar. My hips jerk faster as my orgasm coats her throat, a low growl emitting from deep within my chest. *Fuck, she is too good at that.*

I loosen my hold on her hair, letting it fall, and I cup my hand around her face, rubbing her jaw with my thumb.

"Good girl," I purr, pulling out of her mouth slowly. Her lips suck me dry like a lollipop, and I am still semi-hard. One time is never going to satisfy me. She remains on her knees, panting, her lips still cherry red, looking wide-eyed and full of desire.

Bending down, I pull up my shorts, then grab her under the arms, lifting her from the floor. Her legs dangle in the air as I slam my lips onto hers. Wrapping her hands around my neck, her legs circle my waist as I palm her ass, liking the feel of her in my arms. She weighs nothing as I pull her to my chest, her perfect tits squished against my bare skin as our tongues fight frantically. I walk her over to the massage bed that we set up for my warm-up and soon-to-be cooldown.

"Lie back..." I tell her, not sounding soft or caring, but needy and impatient, because I am. Putting her ass on the bed, my hands are already opening her jeans as she lies back. I roughly pull her jeans down, spotting her red lace underwear, and I grit my teeth, my cock immediately rock-hard again. Red is my favorite color, so now not only will I have the vision of her red lips on my cock, but also of her in nothing but red lace underwear. She is killing me and doesn't even know it.

"AJ, I want you so bad." she says, and my dick twitches, already thinking about round two. I look up at her face briefly. She is flushed, her hair splayed out, her chest rising and falling rapidly. The urge I have to rip all her clothes off and fuck her every which way I know, pushes to the front of my mind, but now is not the time. Now is just to take the edge off, just to have a little taste, see how far she is willing to go for me.

"Spread your legs, sweetheart. Show me how wet you are from sucking my cock." I am not sure if she is hot or affected by my dirty talk, but either way, I watch as her legs part. My hands land on her knees, and I spread them as wide as they'll go.

"I would rip this lace from your body, but red is my favorite color so they can stay on for now," I tell her, my large fingers running up and down the apex of her thighs, the lace wet under my touch. Slipping my fingers beneath her panties, I feel her again. What I've thought about every hour since touching her last. She is bare, soft, and I groan at how wet she is. Pulling the fabric to the side, I look at her, how perfect she is.

"AJ, stop teasing me," she begs, her hips wiggling.

"Just taking it all in, sweetheart. I've never seen anything so fucking good in my entire life." My finger trails up her wetness, circling her clit slowly. When I push in a finger, I see her take in a deep breath, pushing her tits out like they are taunting me. I pull out a little before I push in again, fucking her slowly with my finger, before lifting it to my mouth to suck.

Once my fingers hit my mouth, I groan at getting a taste of her again, and I can't wait any longer. Leaning over, my mouth hits her core so fast and hungry, her hips buck up from the bed.

"Oh... that feels so good." Her hands whip to the top

of her head, then grip the side of the massage bed as she arches her perfect body, making me wonder how flexible she is and how many different positions I want to try with her. *Fuck me.* She tastes exactly how I thought she would. Sweet, like fucking honey, and I am famished. I can't get enough. I lick and suck like I will die without her on my tongue. My hands grip around her ass, hard, my fingers digging into her flesh, pulling her to me, not wanting an inch to spare between us.

"AJ... AJ... Oh my..." She says my name over and over again as her body withers underneath me. I will fight a thousand battles over and over again if I get to touch her like this after every one of them.

"That's it. You're gonna come so nicely, sweetheart, aren't you?" I push a finger inside her tight, wet center again. She moans long and loud as her back arches again, her body jolting. There is nothing sweet about the way I am touching her, nothing tender and sultry about it. That is not me. She got a taste of that last night on my bike. But the way she is reacting to me tells me she is enjoying every minute of it, and my eyes take in how fucking beautiful she is.

"Yes... oh God, yes... I want this... I want you..." Hearing her say the words gives me a renewed sense of longing. I fuck a lot of women, but none of them say they want me, not like this. They may want my cock, may want my tongue, but none ever said they wanted me. I lean over and suck on her clit again as I move my finger slowly, curling it to that special spot, and her body responds immediately.

"AJ! AJ... that feels good... Don't stop... don't stop."

Crying out for me, her hand flies down and lands in my hair. Her fingers spread and dig into my scalp, holding me to her, and I love it. I continue my assault until she is convulsing underneath me, sucking on her clit and looking up to watch her come.

And it is the prettiest damn thing I have ever seen.

22

VALERIE

I can barely breathe as I come down from the high. AJ kisses my inner thighs as I pant, and I move my hands from his hair, wondering what the hell we just did.

I have never done anything like that before in my life. I have never gotten on my knees for a man; I have never had such an experience where I wanted someone so much I would drop my pants in a place like this. But that is exactly what I have done. Two nights in a row. I am becoming a hussy and I love it. I laugh at myself, at how in less than two days AJ has already surpassed every man that has come before him. Literally and figuratively.

AJ looks up and is about to say something when there is a loud thump at the door. I jolt in surprise, and AJ scowls before kissing my thigh again and lifting me from the bed, pulling my jeans up.

"Sweetest damn pussy I ever tasted, sweetheart. Bathroom is in the back. Go make yourself decent, because I don't want any other fucker looking at you like this but me," AJ says roughly, his eyes a little less intense. I swallow harshly and give him a nod as I walk past him, grabbing my handbag and shutting the bathroom door behind me.

In the small space, I am able to take a breath and gather my thoughts. My body still hums in a post-orgasmic swoon, my legs weak, my heart racing, and yet I have never felt better. His hands on my body felt like they were always meant to be there. He is strong, possessive, and takes what he wants. I've never felt so desired, so sexy, so needy. I look at myself in the mirror and stare at my reflection. My hair is everywhere, my lipstick smudged a little, but considering what we just did, it is surprisingly not too bad. I get busy trying to look presentable again, not needing anyone with a cell phone camera to be taking shots of me like this. I tie my hair into a loose, messy ponytail with the hair band I keep for emergencies, and I grab a wet wipe in the room to delicately clean up my lip line before adding fresh lipstick and a bit of powder. Checking my cell in case the girls have texted me, I see the flash of a notification from socials. I hesitate before deciding to get it over with and click on it.

Hanging on the rough side of town with losers is where you belong, such a trashy dirty whore. This time, the message is from *valisaslut*. I take a deep breath. These messages seem to know where I am and who I am with, and I don't like it. But there is not much I can do at this stage, so I delete and block, steadying my nerves. The noise from AJ opening the main door and what sounds like scores of people now walking in and talking pulls me back to reality. I quickly spray some perfume and put everything back in my bag, before opening the door and walking out, trying not to look like I had the most insane sexual experience of my life. I stop short. There are people everywhere.

His friends and mine are on the lounge talking, AJ is sitting on the massage bed where we just were, and a man who looks to be a trainer stands behind him, massaging his shoulders. His eyes meet mine, and he flicks his head at me, calling me his way. I walk over, not wanting to be anywhere else, and his eyes don't leave mine the entire way. The way he looks at me has immediate flames licking my skin and my underwear grows wet again.

"You alright?"' His voice is low and gravelly as his large hands find my hips, and he pulls me to stand between his legs as the masseuse continues to work his shoulder. My hands land on his thighs, my fingers lightly scratching his skin.

"Never better," I say with a smile, and his lips quirk in return.

"Good. How did you get here?" he asks.

"I drove," I tell him. It isn't usual that I drive myself places anymore, but last night and tonight have been exceptions.

"You drove?" he clarifies, his eyebrows rising.

"Yeah, my car is out front."

"Jesus. You drove to this shit end of town, to a boxing match, in your G-Wagon?" He looks at me like I am crazy. Maybe I am. "You and I are going to need to have words about that," he mumbles.

"Believe it or not, but I am capable of driving myself places. Besides, I like the beast," I say, thinking about my car and rolling my shoulders back.

"You drive me crazy, that is for sure. So, your place or mine tonight, sweetheart?" he says, and I suck in a sharp intake of breath. His hands flex on my hips, like he is holding me from running, but I don't move. Instead, I lean more into his hold, not wanting to leave at all.

"Excuse me?" I ask, raising my eyebrow. A smile threatens to form on my face as I look at him.

"You didn't think that was all we had for tonight, did you? The fight is over now." His face is serious, his eyes challenging, reminding me that his rule of staying away from sex before a fight is no longer valid.

"But you just were in a boxing ring! You're sore, aren't you?" I ask, looking at his shoulder, at the masseuse who is doing a good job of ignoring our conversation. I see the bruises on AJ's face, the redness of his knuckles. He may have won, but his body is still beaten.

"Not that sore." His hands flex again. I feel like this is a test. Like he is pushing me to the edge again to see if I am, in fact, all in or if I will crumble and run home to my father.

"I need to drop the girls off," I tell him simply.

"I'll meet you at your place, then," he says. "Text me when you are on your way home, and I'll head over." He looks for any hesitation on my face, but there is none.

"Okay," I say, smiling. I like his self-assuredness. He knows what he wants.

"Okay." His hand grabs my neck, and he brings me to his lips. I kiss him slowly, and I almost melt at how sensual this kiss is. It is different from before. His hold on my neck is possessive but not tight. *But I want it to be.* It is like he is wanting everyone to see, to show everyone that I am his. As he pulls back a little, his hold on me remains firm, our foreheads nearly touching. "You like it when I grab you like this?" he asks quietly, his eyes thinning, looking at me with interest.

"I do. A lot," I tell him as I swallow, my throat moving under his fingers. I hear a deep rumble of satisfaction from him as the crowd behind me comes back into focus.

"Okay, we get it! You two are so fucking hot I want to join in, but can we go now, please!" Simone yells, and I pull away, laughing. AJ growls, and as I step away from him, he slaps my ass, making me jump.

"Drive safe," he says as the girls grab my hands and we all walk out, leaving all the sweat and testosterone behind us, along with my good girl image.

But I don't care because the stupid grin on my face is the most genuine I have ever had in my life.

23

AJ

As I pull into the garage and punch in the code she texted me into the keypad, I don't even think about driving away. I should. I should remove myself from this situation. I shouldn't have touched her. Tasted her.

But I'm too far gone.

My balls are still heavy, encased in my jeans, my zipper so tight against my permanently hard cock that I am pretty sure my skin will be indented by the time I get upstairs. My libido is on fire and ready to go all night. And that is exactly my plan as I drive down underneath this high-rise to the parking garage, following her directions, to get to *her*.

The bright lights of my Harley showcase the cleanest garage I have ever seen. Polished concrete floors, white walls without a hint of graffiti. I ride past luxury cars, all with high-shine polish, and I take it all in. There must be at least a few million in cars down here alone. I see numbers painted on the floor and pull my bike in, parking in the spot she mentioned. Right next to a blacked-out Mercedes G-Wagon, which I already know is hers.

This woman lives in complete security, yet has given me one hundred percent access to her. I am equal parts mad and pleased. She trusts me. And she can. But she needs to be more careful with her security, and not hand out those details to just anyone.

You're a good man, AJ. Her voice repeats in my mind, and I like to think now that I am older, with life experience, I make better decisions. I'm smarter, healthier, and more in control of my life than I ever have been before. *Except for now.* Right now, my body is humming to be inside hers, and as I turn off my bike and step away from it, my legs take me to the elevator, and my finger presses the buttons almost on autopilot. Nothing and no one will keep me away from having her tonight.

The ride is quick, and I step out, spotting her door and knocking. I look around at the polished decor as I wait. There is no mistaking that this apartment building is the best in the city. You can't live here for less than a few million. Up here, on the top floor, I'm guessing that Valerie paid a pretty fortune. I catch my reflection in the black shiny marble coating the walls and grit my teeth. Everything is so clean and perfect; I am the only thing out of place. The door sweeps open, and my head whips around to see her standing before me, her chest moving rapidly like she is breathless. My dick throbs as I take her in, and I fist my hands, ensuring I remain where I am and don't barge into her apartment and fuck her against the wall, which is what I really want to do.

"You made it!" she says, chewing her lip. She seems a little nervous. I let my eyes drop over her again. She has taken off the leather jacket, her black singlet top the only thing hiding her upper body and doing a poor job of it, as I see a slither of red lace peeking out. *She is wearing matching underwear.* I swallow thickly. My eyes lower to her bare feet, noticing she's a few inches shorter than usual, and I can see her toes are painted red. *Matching her underwear.* Her hair looks freshly brushed, her lips glossy, her eyes wide.

"Letting me in, sweetheart, or am I going to stand out here all night?" I ask when neither of us moves. My voice is a little hoarse because I haven't spoken since she left the training room. I couldn't. My mind has been focused on nothing but the fight for months, and now I am only focused on one thing. *Her.*

"Come in," she says, reaching forward. My hand immediately takes hers, entwining our fingers. I haven't held hands with a girl as much as I do with Val, ever. I clearly remember the last girl I held hands with. Her name was Stacey, and it was in sixth grade. Back at a time when I still attended school. We held hands for merely a second during gym class for some activity before she sharply pulled away and told me I was disgusting. I watched as she wiped her hand on her top and looked mortified. I was still living with my mom at the trailer. We didn't have any money, so I often wore the same clothes. Quick cold showers were all I could muster at that age, and even then, they weren't daily. I don't blame Stacey for not wanting to touch me. But the entire class laughed at me, and I have never held hands with a woman since.

Until now. It should feel strange, but her hand is small, delicate, soft, and my hand totally engulfs hers. And I like it.

"Are you sore?" Her brows crumple, looking at me with concern, yet another thing I don't see often, as I step into her space and close the door behind me.

"My mind is on other things," I say, looking at her, before taking in her apartment. It is nice. Real nice. Floor-to-ceiling windows overlook most of the city. Creams and whites, everything fluffy, plush and soft. No blacks or grays. A few pops of pink, enough to make it girly. Fresh flowers on most surfaces, all roses. Feminine decor and amazing artwork on the walls. It is luxurious and like nothing I have ever seen before. And in complete contrast to my living arrangements.

"You took some hard hits." She continues, pulling me into her kitchen where a large island counter sits with what looks to be a marble countertop, again perfectly clean and polished.

"We are going to have a stern talk about why you were at my boxing match and what the hell you were thinking coming, but that is going to happen after I make you scream my name so loud your prissy neighbors complain." Her cheeks flush a little as she sucks in a breath. But I don't wait a moment longer.

I pull her by the hand to me quickly, wrapping my other hand around her waist, my hand settling firmly on her lower back as my lips meet hers. Her body softens in my hold immediately, leaning into me, her hands running up my body and resting on my chest. As her lips open slightly, I sweep my tongue across hers, and she lets out a whimper that shoots me directly in my balls. I want to make this woman beg. Whimper, pant, moan, mewl. All of it. I want to make her do it all.

My hands roam her body, and as fucking hard as I am right now, I am trying to take my time because I didn't get to earlier. In the training room, I had to be quick. I had to get my taste of her before I exploded. Now the urge to have her is just as strong, but I want my lips on every last inch of her skin. Tracing her curves, my hands find her ass and squeeze. I grind her hips hard against mine, rubbing my hard length against her. She has a great fucking body.

Her hands run up my neck, and her fingers dig into my hair. I lift her by the ass and place her on top of her kitchen counter so we are eye level. Stepping into her open legs, our mouths don't come off each other. My hands move around her front, and I cup her tits, molding them in my palms.

"You've got incredible tits," I murmur against her lips, remembering the question Simone asked me at Chloe's showing. I sweep my hands lower and grab the hem of her top and pull it straight up her body and over her head, letting her hair fall back down around her shoulders, and I get my first glimpse of her in her red lace bra. Grazing my fingers down the strap and around the cup, I leave a trail of goosebumps on her skin. As I move lower, down her body, her soft skin taunts me until I reach her jeans. I want to see her in nothing but her matching red lace underwear.

"Your turn," she says, grabbing at my t-shirt, and I let her pull it off, happy to have her touching my bare skin again. As I pop the button of her jeans and pull down her zipper, her hands smooth over my shoulders, tracing my tattoos.

"Down," I say as I grab her from the counter and put her back on her feet, as I pull her jeans down in one shove. She steps out of them as her hands hit my belt, and once she undoes my jeans, I push them down as well. Going commando helps the situation, as my dick springs up, hitting my stomach, and a little gasp leaves her mouth.

"As much as I loved your mouth earlier, this time I am fucking your pussy, sweetheart."

Her eyes meet mine, and I watch her throat bob on a swallow. I give her a wink, and she grins. I like making her smile. Her smile with me is genuine, nothing at all like the smile I see her give almost everyone else. Another thing that does something to my insides.

I grab a condom from my pocket and rip it open, precum already forming on my tip.

"I have never been with someone so..." she trails off, a little nervous about my size.

"You can take it," I tell her, cutting her off as I sheath myself. Picking her up by the ass, I kiss her again. Her legs wrap around my waist and her hands circle my neck as I start to walk slowly with her in my arms. We are glued to each other, me totally naked apart from the latex on my cock and her in her matching red lace underwear, looking like a model from one of those fancy magazines. I lower my mouth, lifting her slightly, and put my lips on her tit, sucking her nipple from the outside of the lace.

"Oh... AJ," she moans, her head falling back, hair tickling my fingers as her nipple pebbles in my mouth. I move a hand, bringing it to her front and pulling down her bra cup, watching in pure lust as her tit pops out, and I take it in my mouth again. My mouth is greedy as my lips suck and my teeth nip. Her back hits the wall, and I push her against it, securing her body as I pull down the other bra cup and give the other breast the same treatment.

"Hmmm, God, that feels good..." she murmurs as I lap at her nipple, my hand now moving lower.

"Is your pussy weeping as I suck on your perfect tits?"

Her body automatically responds. Fingers digging into my flesh at my shoulders, she grinds her hips into me some more.

"Yes... so wet..." she whimpers, the sound sweet, and I nearly lose control, wanting to give her the relief she needs. I slip my finger around the lace hem of her underwear.

"I am so fucking hard for you, baby; we're not even going to make it to the sofa. I am going to fuck you right here, right against this wall." My lips trail up her neck, her tits pressing against my bare flesh, and my fingers continue teasingly tracing the outside of her center.

"Yes. AJ, yes." Her legs tighten around me.

"Tell me you want it. Tell me you want me to own your pretty pussy. Beg me for it," I grit out, barely contained. I love talking dirty, and I want more than anything else for this woman, who can have anything or anyone, to beg me for what I can give her.

"Please..." she says, her hips grinding against my hand, trying to find some friction.

"Please what?" I tease, my teeth nipping the edge of her earlobe, waiting for her to say the words.

"Please, fuck me, AJ. Please own my pretty pussy."

I pull the lace to the side and sink into her so hard and so fast, her body buckles against the wall.

"Ahhhh!" she screams, grabbing on to my shoulders firmly, and I grit my teeth, feeling her warm, wet pussy wrap around me.

"That's it, fuck... that's it." My hips move rapidly, slamming her against the wall. Her body bounces with every thrust, and I pull away a little to watch her tits jiggle as her hands claw at my shoulders, trying to hang on.

"Oh my God... Oh my God," she pants over and over. This is not lovemaking. This is pure fucking, and it is the best I have ever had.

"You are such a greedy girl for my cock." I continue to thrust, bottoming out each time as her moans spur me on. I look up at her face as she looks at me. Her hands move from my shoulders, and she cups my face.

"Don't stop. Please, don't stop. Don't you dare stop," she pleads, bringing her forehead to mine, our eyes locking as I watch her mouth gape open, her eyes closing. "Don't stop... don't stop..."

"I'm not stopping, sweetheart. I need you too fucking much to stop now. I need you so much I have to fuck you hard against the wall. Need you so much I need to fuck you with your underwear still on."

"Yes... yes... yes!" Her hands grip back on to my neck for dear life.

"Fuck, sweetheart, you are going to feel me every time

you sit down tomorrow." My orgasm builds as my thrusts get harder and harder, no longer able to rein myself in.

"Every day... I want this everyday..." she moans. "Oh God, AJ... I'm coming... Don't stop..." she pleads, and I thrust into her harder, her body bouncing as my hands grip her hips tighter.

"Take it... Take all of it..." I grit out to her, and as she starts to scream my name, her pussy pulses around me and I come right along with her. Seating myself deep, I grind into her, giving her everything. She shakes around me, the two of us yelling so loud I fear someone will call 9-1-1.

I drop my head onto her shoulder, and she rests her head on the top of mine. We stand there for a moment, both breathless, the sweat building between us making our skin slippery. Then she does something unexpected. Her hands on my shoulders relax and run up and down my back, caressing my skin before her fingers start to massage my scalp.

It is tender. Relaxing. I lean against her a little more and a soft moan falls from my lips.

She chuckles. "Twenty steps to the right is the bathroom. I think we need a shower."

"Hmmmm," I growl as I lift her off the wall and walk in the direction she mentioned, my cock still buried deep, our skin still cemented, neither of us wanting to let go.

24

VALERIE

We make it to the bathroom, and he slowly lowers me to the ground near the shower. I turn on the lights, dimming them slightly, touching the wall the entire way. I don't trust my legs right now. I am still slightly out of breath, my limbs feel like Jell-O, and my muscles are shaking from the intense workout we just had. But I can barely tame my smile.

That was the best sexual experience of my entire life. Intense, hot, needy. I see him shuffle across the room to dispose of the condom, and I take a deep breath. My mind is empty. I feel free. I am shocked at what just happened. He is right with what he mentioned earlier. We couldn't make it to the sofa. He couldn't wait to have me, and that is something else I have never had before. A man who was on the edge so much that he pinned me to a wall. Sure, other men have wanted me, but usually my money, my name, not... me. Not like that.

"You alright?" he asks, and I didn't realize I was staring off into the distance. He is even bigger than I realize as I stand here in no shoes, the high heels I usually wear when I am with him offering me a few inches that are now no longer.

“Amazing. You?” I ask, grabbing some towels.

“I’ll be better when you get back over here,” he growls, and I take a few steps back toward him, placing the towels down. Leaning in, I turn on my rainwater shower, the steam misting my bathroom in an instant.

He runs his hands around my body and unclasps my bra, and I let it fall from my arms and onto the floor.

“Hmmm. Perfect,” he says, looking at me as his hands land on my waist. He pulls down my underwear, and they join my bra on the floor. I stand before him completely naked, as is he, and where I would usually turn or hide with embarrassment, I don’t move. I hold my breath and remain still as his eyes run the length of my body, and I see him start to harden again already. The appreciation in his eyes gives me the confidence I need to stand here and be admired.

His large hands circle my waist, pulling me tightly to him. Our bare bodies pushed together, he lifts me slightly, my hands holding his shoulders as my feet no longer touch the ground, and he walks us into the shower. Placing me back down slowly, he ducks his head under the spray of water, and I watch this beast of a man in my shower. His body looks like one of those carved Roman statues, all pure muscle. He glances at me watching him and raises an eyebrow.

“Here, let me,” I say, grabbing my body wash and loofah. I squeeze a little out and start to scrub his body.

"You're bruised." My brow furrows as I take in all his crevices.

"Part of the sport." His hands find my waist, holding me close.

"It doesn't look like much of a sport. I understand there is stamina, strength, discipline, and agility, but it also looks like it hurts." I see a dark-purple bruise forming on his side and wonder if he might have internal bleeding. I decide to voice my concerns. "You might have internal bleeding?" He huffs a laugh.

"I know how to take a hit. I know what my body can take," he says, his hands softly caressing my body.

"Turn," I say, and he smirks.

"You bossing me around now?" he asks, his face a little more relaxed like I am humoring him, and I almost melt into the drain. He looks so hot, I already feel butterflies below.

"You don't like people being bossy?"

"No one *ever* tells me what to do," he growls in warning, but as he does, he slowly turns, and I don't even bother to hide the grin that sweeps across my face. His back is even bigger, his shoulders high and his muscles defined. He rests his hands on the wall in front of him as the hot water runs down his back, and I move the loofah in circular motions across his skin, taking in the mass of tattoos that decorate him.

"So, were you happy with the fight, then? You won, right?" I ask, assuming he would be pleased. He turns back around and looks at me.

"I won." He nods, not elaborating.

"You're not happy, though?" I ask.

"I'm not happy a naked woman in the shower with me is asking about a fight that she shouldn't have been watching," he says, pinning me with his eyes.

"I can go anywhere I want to go," I say, full of sass.

"No, you can't. If you do that again, I will put you over my shoulder and walk you straight back out," he says, dead serious, his nostrils flaring.

"You wouldn't dare," I say to him, my eyes thinning. I like pushing him. I like standing up to him. We both know that he is going to win every time, but I can hold my own—and like to—against him.

"Just test me, sweetheart, and see what happens."

I decide to let it go. *For now.*

"You like carrying me around, don't you?" I ask teasingly as the hot water coats us both.

"I like doing a lot of things with you," he says as he steps closer. I my head a little more to look at him. My smile is sneaky.

"Yeah? What do you like to do with me?"

"I like to make you come..." Heat blooms across my body.

"Me too," I whisper, my sass now all gone, replaced with dire need.

"I like to taste your pussy." Not an air of embarrassment crosses his face. He is dead serious. "I like to watch you dance; I like the way your face lights up when you laugh with your friends..."

"Been watching me, big guy?" I tease, tilting my head.

"I also like to hear you moaning my name, wriggling on my lap... and I really like to hear you beg me for my cock," he says with finality, and I feel him harden near my stomach as I swallow, already feeling the throbbing arousal below again. He raises his hand and cups my cheek, swiping his thumb across my skin so tenderly it is surprising, before he lowers and grips on to my neck. My heart thumps in my chest as I look deep into his eyes.

"I like you doing that," I confirm, and I see his jaw clench a little as his hold on my neck tightens.

"You like my hands on your body? You like my hand around your neck?" he asks, watching for my reaction.

"Yes," I whisper like it is a dirty secret.

"You like being choked, sweetheart?" His head tilts a little as he observes my expression. I appreciate him asking me these questions.

"Only by you," I whisper, and I see him take a deep breath. I have never done anything like this. No man has ever manhandled me, picked me up, grabbed my neck. I've never had sex against a wall. But suddenly, I am feeling more in tune with my body than ever and want to do so much more with AJ than I ever thought about before.

"Turn around. Hands on the tiles." His hand drops from my neck, and I spin around and do what he says. My skin prickles in anticipation as I feel him step closer, so I know he is right behind me.

"You want me to fuck you here in the shower?" His voice is low and gravelly and right in my ear. With his chest flat against my back, he sandwiches me right between him and the tiles. My breasts push against them, my nipples pebbling from the cold.

"Yes..." I whisper, biting my lip. I feel his hand on my hip, then it coasts around to my front and dips down into my center. He's rock-hard against my butt as his other hand has a firm hold on my hip.

"I fucking love your pussy," he murmurs, his face now in my neck as his fingers skirt across my center.

"Ohh..." I start to quiver already. I am tender from earlier, but also on fire. My hips automatically move, needing more as his fingers remain on me, slowly stroking up and down.

"You want my fingers?" he asks, his tone low.

"Yes..." I pant, not afraid to tell him what I want as the hot water continues to coat both of us. I am so turned on right now, my fingers slip as I try to dig them into the tiles in front of me, but I can't get any traction. He slides a finger inside of me, and I moan, instantly wanting more.

"That's it, baby. Fuck, you are just as hungry for me as I am for you." His finger dips in and out, my hips moving with him, needing more.

"More... AJ..." I moan again, already lost in the sensation.

"My greedy girl... my good greedy girl," he rumbles as he slips a second finger inside, and I bite my bottom lip as my hips continue to grind on him. He lowers his head to my shoulder again, and he nips my skin, his teeth marking me a little before he licks and kisses the spot and runs his mouth up my neck to my ear.

"Now, promise me, sweetheart..." he starts, his fingers still moving in and out of me painfully slow. "Promise me you won't turn up to another fight." I moan as I try again to find the friction I need.

"No... I want to watch you," I murmur, my eyes closed,

enjoying his fingers, his hard body right behind me, crowding me, keeping me safe and cocooned.

"Hmmmm, wrong answer..." Removing his finger, he lazily circles my clit. My body is almost in agony as he moves so slow when my body needs hard and fast. He knows what he is doing, and it is frustrating beyond belief.

"But I..." I start to explain, but the words leave me as he sinks his fingers inside again. I see spots. It is so good, but not enough.

"No buts. I love your pussy, and I can stay here playing with it all fucking night. But if you want to come, you need to promise me," he warns, and I have no doubt that a man with his discipline could do this all night.

I bite my lower lip again, scared to open my mouth. I want to watch every fight. I want to ensure he is okay. But God, I want to come.

"Promise me, sweetheart..." he grits out, his breathing labored, and I know he is as turned on as I am. He teases with his fingers some more, pulling them out and spreading the juice slowly before repeating it over and over. It is enough to keep me on the edge, but not enough to make me come. "Promise me, and I will fuck you so hard with my cock that you forget your own name," he growls, and I cave.

"I promise... I promise... I promise... Please... Please, AJ." I barely recognize my voice as I whimper and plead with him, and within mere seconds, his hands are gone. I lose my breath as he grabs either side of my hips and thrusts inside so quickly my hands slap the tiles to hold me up.

"Oh God... Oh God..." I cry out, tears stinging my eyes as my hips move back, meeting every frantic thrust.

"Fuck, fuck, fuck... No condom," he says quickly, but the two of us are too far gone.

"I'm on the pill," I say quickly, my voice high-pitched.

"I'm clean," he grits out.

"Me too. Don't stop..."

A deep growl rumbles from his chest. One of his hands leaves my hip and runs up my front, grabbing my neck from underneath. He pulls me to him, and I arch my back, plastering my shoulders to his chest as he continues to thrust. The new position leaves me completely at his mercy. My feet dangle again, so I pull them back, wrapping them around the back of his thighs. I lean my head back a little, resting it on his shoulder as his grip remains tight and unwavering, pulling me up and down on top of him. He is a machine, and I am merely his puppet. And I love it.

"Never..." he confirms as his other hand moves forward and cups my center, his finger starting to roll quickly around my clit.

"Ohhh... Ohhhhh... *Ohhh,*" I scream, my body shaking in his arms. I have never been this out of control.

"That's it, baby. Such a good girl bouncing on my cock. Such a good dirty girl for me. Come for me. Come on my cock..." he says, breathless, as he continues to pound into me from behind, and I let go. My voice is loud as I scream in the shower, the echo amplifying it even more, my body shuddering against his. "Fuck, it feels too good, too fucking good." He growls as he jerks with his release, and I feel him inside of me, hot warmth that I have never experienced. As his grip on my neck tightens slightly, he slows, grinding into me, growling into my shoulder before slowly lowering me to the ground.

"I also love fucking you in the shower..." he says, and I laugh. Grabbing my cheek, he turns my head, pulling me close and kissing me, our lips remaining locked as the water washes us clean.

25

AJ

I moan as I start to wake. My body feels battered, my joints are sore, my muscles even worse. I dig my head further into the pillow, still half-asleep, wishing for a few more hours. But as I take a deep breath and pick up a floral scent, I'm suddenly more awake.

I rarely spend the night with a woman. We have a good time then I exit as soon as I can. I don't like chicks who are clingy, who want more. I usually wait until they fall asleep and then walk out, disappearing into the night with no desire to see them again. But I carried Valerie to her room last night after our shower, and we fell asleep in her enormous bed, until I reached for her another two times in the early morning. Now, I am rock-hard again, thinking of her amazing body. I feel warmth next to me and lift my hand to grab her, but I meet something fluffy.

"What the..." I come face-to-face with a giant rat. "Who the fuck are you?" I growl, my voice still yet to wake, and the dog looks at me before it leans forward and licks my nose.

"First and only time that is going to happen, my friend." I sit up, wiping my face. The little thing clearly snuggled into me for a bit as my other snuggle buddy has already vacated the bed. The sheets, which feel like I slept on a fucking cloud, gather at my bare waist, and I look around her bedroom in the light of a new day. This room alone is bigger than my entire apartment. Like the rest of the place, it is white, with splashes of pink, fresh flowers adorning her shelves. Her drapes are thick but open a little, and sunlight streams in from what looks to be French doors to a patio. A wide fucking patio, fifty floors up. I see an outdoor lounge and a fire pit. A fucking herb garden. Wow, how the other half live.

Then I hear some movement out in her kitchen. She must have been up a while because I smell bacon. I haven't eaten in a while, and my stomach rumbles immediately. I spot my clothes folded on an armchair in an area that can only be described as a mini living room... in her bedroom. I climb out of her soft sheets and slip on my jeans, but I don't see my t-shirt, so I stay bare on top and walk out.

I take only a few steps and see her in the kitchen. Her hair is up high on her head in a messy bun. She is stirring something in a pan, moving around the kitchen with ease, wearing nothing but my t-shirt, which fucking makes me feel something I haven't before.

"Morning..." She blushes as she looks at me.

"Morning," I say, walking toward her, wasting no time grabbing her around her waist and kissing her. I slide my hands down and palm her ass, confirming she has nothing underneath. Lifting her, I place her on the counter and stand between her legs, like I did last night.

"You okay?" I ask her, not sure why. I've never cared about any of the other women I have fucked, but this time feels a little different.

"Sore, but good," she says, her hands coasting up and down my bare torso. And I like it. "You?"

"Sore, but good." I give her a small nod. "You made breakfast for me, sweetheart?" I ask her the obvious while my heart thuds in my chest. No one has ever cooked for me before. Not like this. No one has gotten up early, made me a variety of things, taking thought and consideration into what I may or may not like. I swallow, looking at the food she has put together. As a kid, I was lucky if I found an apple to eat most days. I am surprised she doesn't have a cook or a butler, but she is fiercely independent and somewhat stubborn, so it makes sense that she wouldn't rely on others to put together a meal.

"I did. But I am a terrible cook. I knew you would be hungry, so I just... you know..." She shrugs and looks at her countertop, and I follow her gaze. There is a literal feast on offer. I spot plates of bacon, eggs, waffles, pancakes, fruit, coffee, juice. You name it, it is here. "You don't have to eat it. I mean, if it isn't any good, you don't need to pretend. I wasn't expecting you to stay, so I didn't have much to cook."

I look at her and frown.

"Not stay?" I ask her, intrigued.

"It's just that no one has ever stayed... you know..."

"No one has ever woken up next you?" I ask. I find it

very hard to believe a man hasn't completely fallen at this woman's feet already.

"I guess that they never had a good time," she says, looking a little unsure of herself. I hate that. She is literally perfection to me, and I have a really, really good time with her.

"They all sound like men who aren't worthy of you," I tell her and see her body relax.

"How can you be a complete fighting machine one moment and say sweet things like that to me the next?" She smiles.

"I'm not sweet, just being honest." I am about to say something else, when the rat barks, and I look down at it sitting at my feet. It was stealth. I had no idea it had followed me out of the bedroom. It's lucky I didn't step on it.

"You have a rat," I say to her, my eyes thinning at the ball of fluff.

"This is Bordeaux. He is my guard dog," she says, looking worried as I bend down and reach out to pat him.

"Not much of a guard dog. I didn't hear him at all." I scratch his head.

"He is small but has a big bite. Be careful," she warns as I scoop my hand around his body and tuck him under my arm. He is as big as my bicep.

"He is harmless," I murmur, my fingers scratching under the dog's chin, and it tilts its head into my hold, wanting more.

"That's weird. He barks and bites everyone who comes into this apartment."

"Maybe you just don't have the right people in your apartment," I tell her, and her eyes flick to mine.

"I think you are right about that." Arching a brow, she looks between me and her dog. "I have a lunch meeting today, but maybe we can catch up later?"

"Sweetheart, I think if you are going to cook like this and tease me by wearing my t-shirt every morning, it is going to be very hard for me to ever say no to you." I grab her neck and pull her to me. I know she likes it, so now I'll want to do it all the time. She moans in my mouth before I pull away, leaving her a little wanting. "I know you are a lawyer, but what exactly does your work entail?" I ask, and she looks at me with intrigue. "What?" I ask.

"Nothing. I just don't have many people ask what I do," she says, her smile small.

"Well, I have no fucking idea, so enlighten me." I pick her up off the counter one-handed and pop her onto her feet before leaning over and placing her guard dog on his feet too.

"I work at our family business. The last few years in the legal team. I am a lawyer, as you know." I nod and I grab a plate and start loading up on the eggs. "But I am trying to... progress things..." she says suspiciously.

"No doubt you will succeed," I tell her, not prodding, and she smiles even wider.

"You seem to have faith in me, yet have no idea exactly what I am doing." While I don't know much about being a lawyer, I can already tell she is a good one.

"Yeah, but you're sassy and have balls of steel when you walk into an all-male gym on the wrong side of town or get tickets to fight night that you have no need to be at. I have a feeling you are a woman who gets exactly what she wants."

She breathes out a sigh. "Let's hope that my plan will work, then. Coffee?" she asks as she walks along the large kitchen, and I nod as I eat. Her food is delicious, and I shovel it in, wondering why she thinks she can't cook. Working a fancy barista machine, she presses a few buttons. Then she reaches up to a cupboard to grab a cup, my t-shirt sliding up her legs, showing me the bottom of her ass cheeks, with nothing but nakedness underneath it.

I swallow my mouthful and look back over the food. She is without a doubt one of the most amazing women I have ever met. But I also can't stay long. Because I do need to go to the gym and stretch out properly and move my sore muscles. I also need to see Marcus today. Collect my money for last night. I knocked the guy out in round three just as he asked, and with the large crowd we had, I am expecting a sizable sum. So much so, I think I can announce my retirement from boxing soon.

For the first time in my life, things seem like they are truly coming together.

26

VALERIE

"I can't believe you are doing this. I am so proud of you," Chloe murmurs from beside me as we walk into my father's house together. I would much rather be with AJ. After last night, and the way he was with me this morning at breakfast, I have thought of nothing but him.

"I'm nervous. Thanks for coming with me," I say as nerves strum up my chest. I have my plans in motion, and my father is likely to start smelling a rat soon, if he hasn't already, as people in the business will talk. George and I have had conversations with other board members, all of whom are supportive of having me as the new CEO of Van Cleef Corp. Many say we need a change of leadership. Some haven't been happy with my father and his decisions in a while, and all seemed to think that I didn't want the CEO position so they have never raised it with me before. It became clear after the first few conversations that my father has been spinning his own narrative, portraying me as a young, flippant woman who just wants to shop. It was made even easier lately with the images that *Society News* have been running of me getting thrown out of a nightclub and then on the back of AJ's bike.

It doesn't take a genius to understand who is working with them. It is heartbreaking to know my own father will offer me up for gossip to get what he wants. To tarnish my name, position me as a spoiled little rich girl who still does stupid, immature things. I shouldn't be surprised, though, since he is the one trying to marry me off. I wish I had seen it all earlier. I knew he was money hungry, but I never thought it would come at the expense of me and my well-being.

I still need to get a few more board members on my side. Those I haven't spoken to yet are all good friends with my father. Men who he himself admitted to the board and who are all here at this afternoon garden party today. Plus, there is one independent. Someone who remains anonymous, who my mother put in place, who votes remotely and never shows his face. George and I have no idea who that is. We also assume my father doesn't either. This man gets the board notes, dials into board meetings remotely but never speaks, and votes like every other member. We all assume he is some retiree living in Florida or Hawaii, an old friend of perhaps my grandmother's even, but as per my mother's orders, he remains anonymous.

"So we are here to get you in front of these other board members, but what exactly is this event for?" Chloe asks as we step inside my family mansion, seeing waiters and staff running around.

"One of his afternoon garden party events. He does these a few times a year. It gives Abigail something to do, I guess," I tell her as I look around.

"There are a lot of old men..." Chloe murmurs as we step out on the back patio, and I see mostly middle-aged men milling around, talking. The kind who are overweight and balding, many with cigars.

"It's a man's world... didn't you know?" I say sarcastically. I clear my throat and roll my shoulders back. I am usually pretty confident; in law, you have to be, but my father always throws a cloak of insecurity over me and I hate it. I wore a power suit today. White, so it is feminine and in tune with the garden party theme, but it's a structured jacket and tailored trousers. I am here on business only, not here to drink and giggle with the few ladies who have perched themselves at the tables nearby.

"Miss Valerie. Champagne?" Dennis, my father's butler, asks from beside me and my smile is instant.

"Hey, Dennis. How are you?" I ask, declining the champagne as does Chloe.

"I'm well. Your father, on the other hand..." he murmurs to me under his breath.

"Anything I should know before I walk into the lion's den?" I ask. We both know what my father is like. We have always tried to warn each other over the years whenever my father is in a mood.

"Only that Mr. William Schmidt is here. Don't look now, but he is talking to your father over near the lemon tree behind your left shoulder."

I swallow and keep my face and eyes straight ahead. I should have assumed that Mr. Schmidt would be here, but these things are usually all business, and aside from me, Van Cleef Corp has no business with Mr. Schmidt. Oil is not something we have ever, or will ever, be investing in.

"Thanks, Dennis," I tell him, grateful, and he nods to Chloe and me before walking away.

"I've always liked Dennis," Chloe says, sipping some water.

"Same. Okay, let's walk in. Game faces on." I put my fake smile in place. I wish for a moment that George was here, but he, along with some of the other board members who dislike my father, never come to these things. They stick to their board requirements and never socialize with him. I am not sure why I didn't think about it before. Now I notice so many red flags with my father's leadership, it is startling.

"Hi, Valerie. How are you, dear?" An older woman approaches as I step through the crowd, and I stop and talk with her for a few moments, Chloe doing the same. Many of the ladies here are fans of Chloe's jewelry line, which is why I thought bringing her was a good idea. She is chatting with another older lady to the side, when I see my father making a beeline for me. I smile and end the conversation I am having before taking a few steps in his direction. I take a deep breath to prepare.

"What the hell are you wearing?" he whisper-yells at me, and I tense. "This is a garden party, Valerie. I thought you, of all people, would know how to dress for the occasion."

"Hi to you too, Father," I say, my voice cold. He looks

at me with narrowed eyes, sensing my change in demeanor.

“Don’t play games with me. This is your proposal and you come dressed like that?” His voice rises a little, and people nearby look at us. He notices and clears his throat, rolling his shoulders, trying to bring his anger under control. Meanwhile, I am reeling. *Proposal?*

“William Schmidt is here, and he is going to propose. An article is written for *Society News* that outlines that the two of you have been spending time together out of the public eye and how smitten you are with him. You will smile and accept his proposal with grace,” my father warns. Tears threaten to sting my eyes but in anger, not in fear. This is not what I want. This is not what I expected. But this is absolutely not happening. I look at Chloe, who is watching me with concern, then I spot Dennis over on the side, also watching me. Everyone else is laughing and chatting, oblivious to the conversation we are having. I swallow and think of AJ calling me sassy and stubborn and how he thinks I am capable of getting what I want, and I look my father dead in the eye.

“And if I don’t?” I ask him, and he looks shocked for a moment. That thought obviously never entered his mind.

“It isn’t a question, Valerie.”

“It is, actually. He will bow down to me. He will get on his knee at my feet. He will ask me a question.” I school my father sarcastically, and he doesn’t like it one bit.

“Don’t test me,” he growls, his teeth gnashing together, and I bite my tongue. Any nerves I had now all but left and only pure anger has replaced them.

“Don’t treat me like a child. I will not be accepting any

proposal. I will not be marrying Mr. Schmidt," I grit out to him, and his neck starts to go red like he is about to blow a fuse.

"It is what is expected," he grits out.

"What about what I want?" I push back.

"What you want? It appears what you want is to flaunt with losers on the other side of town. What you want, Valerie, doesn't matter. Combining family wealth is what is important. We need to compete with the Rothschilds. They need to see us as valuable, as a threat," he says. This nonsense about competing with the very men I am trying to strike a deal with is almost humorous. There is something about his words that are familiar, but I can't put my finger on it and am too angry to care.

"The Rothschilds I know very well, and they aren't like that," I tell him, trying to see if he can understand a different point of view.

"Diane was." He makes mention of their horrible mother.

"Diane is dead," I say, my voice low and threatening.

"Stop playing games." A small vein pops in his forehead, and it starts throbbing.

"I am taking my rightful place as the CEO of Van Cleef Corp." I wasn't going to show my cards this early, but he will find out in a few days anyway.

"Rubbish." He laughs like it is the most ridiculous thing he has ever heard.

"I have spoken to the board," I tell him, and he stills, looking at me with a scowl.

"You've what?" The people nearby look at us again with his increasing tone, and he plasters a small smile.

"This company was founded by my grandmother, grown by my mother, and I will be the one to take it to the next level. I appreciate you being the caretaker CEO while I was able to grow into the woman I was always meant to be. But now it is time for me to take my rightful position and for you to retire gracefully." I recite the formal words I have practiced.

"Don't be stupid. I am not retiring," he says, laughing again.

"Yes, you are." I am not playing games anymore. I loved my father once. This whole conversation breaks my heart. But he hasn't been a father for such a long time. I don't even know him anymore.

"Valerie, you won't win this game you are playing." My heart pounds harder at his threat.

"But it isn't about winning. It's about family and somewhere over the years you have lost your way. Van Cleef Corporate has firm family values, set out by my mother and her mother before her. All those decades ago, the women in my family knew the secret to success in life and in business, and it wasn't through using the money hungry tactics that you are today." I feel the strength of my mother and grandmother fill my spine, and I stand even straighter. They would be proud of me. I know it.

"Be very fucking careful, my dear daughter. Do not declare war on me." He grabs my upper arm, pulling me in to whisper. His hold is tight, and I bite my tongue so I don't show any physical pain, even though I feel like crying.

"I think I already did." I pull my arm out of his tight grasp and turn on my heel, striding away. I feel Chloe right by my side, and I hold my head high, giving Dennis a small smile on my way out. My hands shake as I reach the door, and I feel like I want to vomit.

"I'll drive. Your place?" she asks me as we get to the car.

"No. Joe's Gym. On west side." She doesn't ask questions as we make our getaway, and I look at my family home in the side mirror. Tears sting my eyes, looking at the mansion my grandmother built.

How dare he threaten me. I did declare war. Now I just need to win.

27

AJ

It's hot. The gym is crowded, and even though I am doing a light session to warm my muscles from last night, my body is coated with sweat. The air conditioner isn't working, there is no airflow, and the equipment in this place is so old I am surprised it still works. But I don't really care today, because I won the fight, I got the money, and I got the girl.

"Good fight last night, AJ," Levi comments as he sits nearby, watching me.

"How do you know?" I ask. He is underage, and I didn't see him there, but no doubt he snuck in. He always does.

"I caught it from the rafters. Security was tight on this one," he admits and I shake my head.

"You need to stop spending so much time doing things you shouldn't and more time doing things you should," I say to him, my eyes flicking back to the front window, spotting the black car parked across the street.

It's been there all day. I also noticed it yesterday, and I can't be sure, but I think it was outside my apartment when I went for a change of clothes this morning once I left Val's place.

"What's up?" Brady asks, coming to stand next to me.

"It's the car. He's been looking at it all afternoon," Levi answers for me, and I give him a scowl.

"Oh yeah? Know it?" Brady asks us both.

"No. We need to run the plates," I tell him as Cody walks up and joins the conversation.

"I can do it!" Levi says excitedly as he grabs his laptop.

"Sit down, kid," I grit out, not sure how good he is at that tech stuff, but knowing Levi, he is probably excellent at it. If he applied himself at school, this kid would go far, but he is too angry to do anything like that.

"No shit. Why?" Cody asks, ignoring Levi and now looking out the window as well.

"It's been there all day. Pretty sure it was outside my apartment this morning too."

"Marcus?" Brady asks.

"No," I say firmly. "It wouldn't be him. He paid me this morning. We are settled. We won't have trouble from him until he comes to me with another fight and I decline. He won't be happy with my retirement, but he knows it is coming, so it won't be a shock," I tell them. We have been discussing my retirement for a while. The winnings from Marcus were more than I expected.

"Anything to do with your girlfriend?" Levi asks, and the other two look at me. I don't discuss my private life with anyone. But after Valerie helped Levi out at the police station, he became eager to find out more about her. And the boys obviously know about her after spending time with her and her friends. All I want to do is be with her. After her lavish breakfast this morning, waking up in her bed with her fluff ball dog next to me, I am already itching to see her again, and it has only been a few hours.

"Don't know. Don't think so." We all look at each other, wondering what the fuck is going on. The gym door opens, and we pay little attention until Levi talks.

"Well, she is here, so why not ask her?" My head whips around, and I see her standing at the door. I watch her for a beat, looking around, her chest rising and falling quickly. Something is wrong. I don't hesitate as I strut up to her and her eyes land on me. The gym is quiet, but the fact she has been here before makes it a little less startling, and I hear a few people already back to their training.

"What are you doing here, sweetheart?" I ask her in a small growl, because I have told her she can't come to places like this.

"I need to hit something," she says in a voice that I haven't heard from her before.

"Come again?" I ask, confused. She is in high heels, a fancy white suit, and her hands are too delicate for any punching.

"I need to hit something." She grits her jaw, and I know a tense woman when I see one.

"Come on, then," I say, walking away, not waiting for her to follow, too tempted to grab her and touch her, but I don't have to look back to know that she is following me.

"Get back to work!" I bark at the gym, and all the guys get back to their training as I lead her over to a bag. She takes off her jacket and I nearly ask her to put it back on, because the singlet top she has underneath shows too much skin for other men to be looking at. But she doesn't need my jealousy right now, so I find some spare gloves and grab her hands.

"You need to hit the bag with this part of your hand; otherwise, you will hurt yourself." Not asking for information, I give her the opportunity to get out her frustrations. I don't like seeing her like this. I already want to kill someone for making my girl upset.

"Go for it," I say, standing behind the bag, holding it in place. I don't need to, as I am sure it won't even move. She throws a punch, and it lands perfectly, and my eyebrows shoot up in surprise. I wasn't expecting her strength. She hits it again, and I grab on to the bag tighter for her, watching her carefully. As I do, I notice her arm has marks on it and my blood immediately boils.

"What the fuck happened to your arm?" I seethe, now standing upright, forgetting all about the bag, needing to know what happened.

"My dad threw me a party, so my future husband could propose," she says, and possessive heat consumes my body instantly.

"What the fuck?"

"Oh, my father is a great guy, AJ. Always putting my well-being above everything else," she says sarcastically, punching the bag again. "He wants me to marry a man I don't even know!" She laughs hauntingly and hits the bag again, each punch with more strength than the last. "A man who is at least sixty years old, with three kids all older than me!" She punches the bag over and over, her arms toned, her body fit. She works out, maybe not in the boxing ring like I do, but it's clear that she exercises regularly. Something that pleases me about her, knowing that she works hard for something rather than just get a nip and tuck like many of the other rich women around this city.

"Are you fucking serious right now?" I almost roar, my anger rising more by the second, but I try to contain it.

"I wish I was joking, but my father is a piece of work. I told him today that I would not be marrying anyone of his choosing. He didn't like that." She throws another punch. Hearing her words settles me a little.

"I need to know who did that to your fucking arm, sweetheart."

"My father. The same son of a bitch who is trying to sink the company my grandmother built and who is so delusional that he is going to run my company into the ground." I try to comprehend exactly what she is saying.

"He is now on my hit list for grabbing your arm like that," I seethe. "I didn't know that fathers have the right to pick husbands for their daughters." She looks at me, her eyes flashing in anger, so I continue. "My mother is too out of her mind on drugs to bother telling me who my father is. So he sure as shit is not arranging anything for me." I take a deep breath, wondering what has gotten into me to tell her that kind of information. She nods, taking in what I admitted before sucking in a deep breath and hitting the bag again.

"I am not going to marry the man he chooses because

I know what I want. I know what I deserve. I know who I am and who I want to be," she says with so much determination, I feel pride swell at seeing her like this.

"Damn right, you are, sweetheart," I tell her as she stops punching and looks at me.

"What are you doing with your life tonight, AJ?" she asks, and my eyebrow quirks.

"I'm about to head home." My dick's already standing to attention.

"Great. I'll come."

"Come where?" I ask, imagining her coming on my cock, on my face, with my fingers. I need to move to subtly adjust myself at the thought.

"Come with you. To your place. You can cook me dinner. Pay me back for the breakfast I made for you," she says, panting slightly.

"Is that so?" I ask, not giving her an inch. I shouldn't. She will take one look at my apartment and run. She will see where and how I live and not want anything to do with me. It is the only thing that will keep us apart at this point, our economic and class differences, because I think about her constantly and have no idea how to keep my distance, especially when I really don't want to.

"Yeah, big guy, live a little," she says teasingly, walking up to me and giving me a wink. I itch to pick her up by her ass and pummel into her against the wall like we did in her penthouse.

"I'm game if you are, sweetheart." Her body now too close to mine, I have the urge to kiss her in front of all these morons.

"Let's go. I'm hungry," she whispers to me, her eyes full of desire.

"I'm fucking starving." I grab the gloves from her hands and throw them on the floor and march her out of the gym, swiping my bag on the way, leaving the boys hooting and whistling behind us.

28

VALERIE

The ride on AJ's Harley is freeing and gives me a chance to clear my mind a little. I have no idea where we are going; the streets on this side of town are not ones I have been down before. I feel at ease on the back, my arms wrapped around him, his hand permanently holding my knee. He rubs his thumb across it, his touch tender and in complete contrast to the man himself. As we pull up to a small apartment complex, I take it all in. It is dark-brown brick and on the older side. There are no garden beds or flower boxes. Graffiti is painted across a small house on the other side of the street, but otherwise it seems clean and nondescript.

"Let's go, sweetheart," AJ says gruffly, taking my hand as I step off the bike, then leading me inside. My anger and frustrations from the garden party have settled, but his shoulders seem a little higher, his jaw clenched. I look out once more to the road and see a black town car pull up slowly. It wouldn't usually be something I notice, but it looks out of place here, and I stop. AJ looks back at me and follows my gaze.

"Friends of yours?" he asks, and I get a partial view of the plate number and swallow. They are Van Cleef Security. It should make me feel better, but I have never had security before. Even when I had a stalker after college, my father still didn't offer any help by way of security, and I guess I followed his advice so I never arranged any for myself. Not even all these years later, even though my father never goes anywhere without a full security team. But there is no mistake, that car is Van Cleef Corp Security.

"No," I say, swallowing. "Not my friends." I can't count on anyone in the business like that anymore. I turn my head back to him and he looks at me, his face in a scowl, clearly unhappy before he pulls me along again. We go through the glass door and walk up cement stairs. The hallway is clutter free, painted in a shade of light blue, reminding me of an old hospital or somewhere just as clinical.

"We're here," AJ growls, and I watch him as he unlocks and opens the door to apartment 3B, seemingly tense and a bit nervous. I was so much in my own head, I hadn't given any thought to me turning up at the gym and then demanding I come back to his place. But he walks in and holds the door open, so I follow.

The first thing that hits me is that it is small. The kitchen is tiny but clean and with everything you need. There is no dining table. There's just a small sofa and a TV with a timber coffee table between the two. There is a glass sliding door that opens to a small balcony, but the view is only of the neighboring apartment block and another brown brick wall. There is really nothing here. No books, no photos, no artwork or decor. As I walk through, I take it all in.

"It isn't Harborside, I know," he says, and I spin and look at him. *Is he worried about what I think?*

"Harborside is a little overrated," I say as I watch him. He looks down at me slightly, and I take in a breath. I'm not sure where my newfound sexual confidence comes from, but I silently unbutton my blazer and slide it off my shoulder, throwing it over his sofa. It's been a tough day, and I need him.

"The view here is getting better already." His eyes burn into me as he rubs his mouth with his hand.

"What about now?" I ask, slipping my singlet top off and over my head, throwing it on his sofa as well.

"Hmmmm…" His voice rumbles deep and low, but his body remains unmoving, watching me like a hawk from afar. I don't stop as I open my tailored trousers and let them fall to the floor and I am left in my heels and a new red matching set of underwear.

"It's new. Your favorite color," I say to him from where I stand. I trail my fingers slowly across the top of my bra cup, and I see him swallow, his jaw tight as he leans against the kitchen counter a few feet away. "I got it for you." My heart races. I saw this matching set in La Perla and scoffed at myself for even thinking of owning something as sexy as this, but after spending time with AJ, I ordered it online the very next day.

He pushes off the counter and walks toward me, a deep scowl on his face. I hold my breath because he looks angry, but then he always does. Once he's standing before me, our chests almost touch, and he looks down at me, his eyes searing into mine. Then he does something startling. He falls to his knees. His hands run over my sides on the way down, pulling the soft lace from my hips, my underwear falling down my legs and I step out of them quickly.

"These are now mine," he growls, putting them in his pocket, and then his large hands smooth up the back of my legs, cupping my ass. "This pussy is also mine." His nose brushes my pelvic bone as he skirts his lips around my skin.

"I'm all yours. No one else's," I whisper, my hand coming to rest in his hair, massaging his scalp, and I see his eyes flutter closed. It feels good to say the words. It's my choice to give myself to AJ. No one has ordered it. No one has demanded it. He wants me and I want him. It is simple. Just like how life is meant to be. We haven't spoken about us, what we are doing, what we want to be. But there is no other man I want to be with right now, and clearly, he feels the same. His lips start trailing across my skin and he kisses his way down my hip. When his mouth hits my center, I gasp as he dives in with his tongue.

"Oh..." I moan, biting my bottom lip, my hand now gripping into his hair, trying not to stumble.

"I needed this... I needed you," I whine. The minute he is on me, everything else is forgotten. Whenever I am with him, all I think about is him. His large hand squeezes my butt cheek, pulling me to his face. I nearly lose my footing, until his other hand squeezes my other cheek, and I lean forward a little, both my hands now in his hair for support.

"This is... this is so good... you are sooo good at this," I moan, my hips moving a little against his face, and I tilt my head up, enjoying the moment. I have had men go down on me before. But never like this. Never at my feet. He lifts my leg slightly and throws it over his shoulder, his tongue delving in deeper, and my breath shudders as my body quivers.

"AJ... oh God... oh God... oh God..." I am not making any sense because everything in my mind flew out the minute his lips touched me. But he doesn't stop. With one hand he holds my lower back, pulling me closer; with the other, he grabs my other leg and puts it over his other shoulder. He is still on his knees, but I am piggybacking him, with my front to his face as I tremble.

His hold on me is firm, and he growls as his face remains buried, and this is yet another position I never knew existed and already want to do again and again. I remain balanced, sitting on his shoulders, but I don't know how, because my hips continue to move into his face, my breathing labored, so much so, my chest is expanding and contracting at speed. My head rolls around, pure ecstasy the only feeling I have, knowing I am safe in his arms. That he will never let me fall.

"I'm going to come... I'm going to..." I pant before my orgasm rolls through me, my body shaking as he sucks on my clit hard and flicks with his tongue. He moans, the sound vibrating on my sensitive skin, and I slump forward a little, still holding on to the back of his head so I don't collapse in a heap on the floor. I try to catch my breath as he pulls away slightly.

"Let's go," he says, full of life, his hold on my ass hard, keeping me firmly with him.

"AJ!" I squeal as he stands, keeping my legs over his shoulders, and I hang on for dear life as he walks around his sofa and into his bedroom like I weigh nothing. He throws me on the bed, my body bouncing, and I watch him rip his t-shirt off over his head and drop his shorts quicker than I can take another breath.

"Get on your hands and knees. Hang on to the headboard, sweetheart," he growls, and I immediately turn around, doing exactly what he says. I feel the bed move as he comes closer. He unclips my bra and it falls down my arms, landing at my elbows, my hands now holding the headboard tight. "This is going to be hard and fast, baby, because I can't fucking wait to be inside my beautiful wet, warm pussy." His finger circles my clit and runs up and down my center, spreading the wetness that is already building. My anticipation is so high, I can barely breathe, so I nod to him, and his hands grip on to my waist as he thrusts inside.

I cry out at the feeling of him, his size, his power, and with nothing I can do but hang on, I grip on to the headboard and let him have his way. His thrusts are strong and fast, and my breath catches in my throat, my eyes rolling back into my head. It feels so good. Having him like this makes me feel amazing, his urgency all for me.

"Fuck, this pussy is perfect. This fucking beautiful pussy of yours is squeezing my cock so hard right now..." he gasps as his thrusts becomes faster and harder.

"Yes... yes... oh... AJ..." I breathe out in reply as my body jolts on the bed, feeling my heart race and my core quiver. I love his dirty talk.

"My fucking beautiful girl, such a good girl. Look at you taking me. Fuck, I could do this all fucking day. All day, I could fuck you and still want to do it over and over again..."

I bite my lip, moaning. The bed is moving, banging against the wall. I have no idea if he has neighbors, but if so, they are not getting any rest during this late afternoon. My bra hangs loosely on my arms, hitting me in the face with each thrust, but I don't care.

"AJ... AJ..." I pant, not able to form any other words. I feel out of control, yet perfectly calm at the same time.

"That's it, sweetheart... feel me between your legs, feel me owning your pussy, your body... fucking perfect." One hand grips on to my hip tighter, the other one running around my front and grabbing my breast. "These tits, fuck, these tits are my favorite," he says, squeezing my breast and pulling at my nipple before his hand grips back on to my hip.

"AJ... I can't... AJ!" I cry, feeling my orgasm build. Sweat forms on my body, my hands white-knuckled, and I am loving every minute of it.

"That's it, baby, arch your back for me..." He groans as my body arches slightly and his hand lands in my hair. He pulls at it a little, bringing my head back to almost meet his and he slams his lips into mine, but his thrusts don't stop for even a second. I start to whimper in his mouth. "Fucking beg me, sweetheart, beg for it," he grits out against my lips, clearly almost to the edge of no return himself.

"AJ, please..." I beg, my voice high-pitched and not my own.

"Please what, baby?" He likes playing this game just as much as I do.

"Please fuck me until I come... Fuck me, AJ," I say, not making any sense, but his grip tightens even more, and his hand leaves my hair to go straight to my clit, where he pinches.

"Come for me, sweetheart, fucking come on my cock." And I do. I scream so loud, I am almost hoarse, the feeling of him grabbing my hips, thrusting into me, his hand on my clit, the sting of my hair, our skin slapping, all of it like a perfect Mozart and my body can't take it.

"AJ!!" I scream, as my body convulses, the adrenaline, the orgasm, the stress, all the buildup inside me now released. AJ growls low and deep as his thrusts speed up even move, his hands holding me tight.

"Fucking perfect... fucking mine, Val. You're fucking all mine." He grinds into me, shooting his release inside. We slow our movements, his hands continuing to squeeze, before he releases his grip and caresses my skin. His lips meet my shoulder as we both drop to the mattress, gasping. The two of us lie naked, quiet, and breathless for a beat, then he pulls me to him, sliding me across the sheets, turning me over onto my back as he leans up and hovers above me.

He looks serious, his eyes looking deep into mine as

his hand cups my jaw, keeping our eyes on each other. “You are mine now, Valerie. No other man will touch you,” he says, almost like it is a promise, before grabbing the back of my neck and smashing my lips to his. His kisses hit me so deep, I never want to come up for air.

29

AJ

I kiss her and kiss her, like I have never kissed anyone before. Because I haven't. I generally don't kiss a lot when I fuck. But kissing Valerie is now my new obsession, and I have craved it since the first time my lips touched hers and every time since. Fuck, if the boys could see me now, they would bust my balls.

She didn't balk at my apartment when we arrived. I thought for sure she would act awkward, maybe disappointed at my lack of assets, and so I felt tense bringing her here. It is nothing like her penthouse. Nothing like I am sure she has ever lived in before, and it doesn't show anything remotely like the life she is accustomed to. But this apartment is my residence and the fact that she was nonplussed about it settles me. She may be a rich billionaire with the world at her feet, but she isn't a stuck-up princess. Now as we lie here together, in my bed, which feels nothing like hers, I am surprisingly content.

I finally let her go and she sighs as I move onto my back and her body slides into my side. Her head rests on my chest as I run my hand up and down her bare back. Lying naked with a woman like this is also new. I can't even remember the last time I did it. But seeing her in the gym today, talking about arranged marriages and her being married off to some old guy she doesn't even know makes my blood boil and I cup her ass with my hand and pull her even closer, not wanting any space between us. I am many things, possessive being one of them.

"Didn't pick you for a cuddler," she comments as she herself snuggles into me deeper. Her body fits into mine just right.

"Didn't pick you for a boxing machine," I say.

"I work out. Pilates, run, and a bit of boxing with a trainer. My father doesn't like me being overweight, so it is a lifetime habit," she says, and I frown.

"You are not overweight. Your father sounds like a real dick. So he dictates everything you do, then? What you do with your body, as well as who you will marry?" I ask, trying not to sound pissed off, even though I am.

"He used to..." she says quietly. "But not anymore." Her lips meet my bare chest, and she kisses me there before laying her head down again. Warmth floods my veins.

"Why is there a car out in front of my apartment?" I ask her, knowing she knows who it is.

"It is my father's security team. He has been following me. He has photos of you and me after Chloe's showing, so he now knows where you live. I have no idea what he is doing other than trying to find something about me he can exploit," she answers honestly, and I appreciate it.

"After your fight with your father today, you came running to me?" I want to know more.

"Yes." Her voice quivers.

"Why?" I ask. I am glad she did, but I am keen to get her thoughts on what it is we are doing.

"Because you always make me feel safe," she admits, and my chest aches for her.

"Bet you that he doesn't like that you're here with me," I murmur, forcing my head back onto the pillow so I don't do something stupid like kiss the top of her head and bury my face in her soft hair. That is what a loving couple would do. That's not me. That's not us. *It could be.* The thought pops in my brain, and I shake it away quickly.

"He doesn't like anything I am doing lately. Especially the moves I am making in the business."

"Tell me about the business?"

"My grandmother started it over sixty years ago. She was a young bride. My grandfather was a factory worker and worked twelve hours a day and my grandmother, Rose, well, she wanted something to fill in the hours while he was gone. She was not content to sit around and play housewife. She was stubborn and focused," she says, and I huff a laugh.

"Sounds familiar," I say and feel her smile against my skin.

"Anyway, she was a good sewer. Made all sorts of things, and her friends and neighbors started to watch her and want tips. Soon, she was offering classes at the local community center and getting paid for it." Her body relaxes against mine, but I remain quiet, listening to the story.

"Long story short, she saved her money and started investing in businesses. First, she invested in a small butcher shop. My grandfather left factory work and managed that. Then between the revenue from the sewing classes and the butcher shop, she purchased a small haberdashery store. From there, it grew and grew. She was buying and selling businesses all over the state. Van Cleef Corp was born. We now own and invest in a wide variety of businesses, hotels, software companies, you name it."

"Sounds like she was an amazing woman," I murmur.

"My mother was an only child and stepped right into the business after getting a business degree. My grandfather died not long after, and I never met him. But between the two women, they took on more and more and grew and grew." Her fingers draw small patterns on my chest as she continues.

"And your mother now?" I ask. She talks about her father a lot but never her mother.

"My mother and grandmother passed away over ten years ago. They were flying home from a meeting in New York. The small aircraft they were on had complications. They hit the ground just outside of Quakertown."

"Jesus..." Her past is sounding just as colorful as my own, albeit still more financially secure.

"A week after their funeral, I was shipped off to boarding school, then college, and barely came home. When I did, my father was different. He met Abigail and married her within twelve months of the accident. I am an only child. For a long time, I did everything he told me to because he was all I had left. I didn't want to lose him too. So, I wore what he told me, dated who he told me, studied what he told me. If I questioned it, he would get angry, so it was easier back then to do what he asked. I wanted his approval more than anything. But now... he is money hungry and unethical and is ruining my mother's and grandmother's legacy," she says, and I run my fingers up and down her skin, feeling her shoulders tighten. She is angry, and that is good, because from what I am understanding of the situation, she is in for a hell of a fight.

"Your father sounds like a real peach," I comment sarcastically, fascinated by how the world sees her, pretty, perfect, rich, and yet her life is not that dissimilar to mine in terms of the lack of love, security, and trust that you need as a kid that was never provided. I like that I get to see this side of her. The side that no one really knows.

"I am challenging him for the CEO position of Van Cleef Corp," she says, and my eyebrows rise. *Holy fuck.*

"Good, sounds like he needs to go," I say simply, and her head leaves my chest to look up at me, wide-eyed.

"Good?" she asks, and I frown.

"You're a fucking lawyer. You're smart, you know your stuff. You got this. You will succeed, I'm sure." I believe in her. I might not know anything about her business, but I know she's capable. Her expression softens before she leans back down on me again.

"It's not about the money. I don't care about that. It is the Van Cleef legacy. The only place where I am connected to my mother and grandmother is in that business. I need to be CEO."

"It is what you were born to do," I say, getting it now. I understand the hard work and dedication she is putting in and will need to put in to win this thing. I don't even know her father, and I already hate him. Hate him for putting his hands on her and for putting anything before his daughter. I never thought I would have kids, but if I ever did, they and their mother would always come first.

"I have half the board on my side. Things are looking positive. I am also doing a deal with the Rothschilds. Something my father would despise me for, I am sure."

"Isn't he president?" I ask, assuming they are the same people, not believing that this naked woman beside me is friends with the fucking president of this country.

"Yep, nice guy too, although I mainly deal with his brothers. They are one of the wealthiest families in America," she says, like they are the guys she and her friends hang out with all the time. Fuck, maybe she does.

"I thought Van Cleef was the richest?" I ask teasingly.

"We're up there." She smiles against me, burying her face and making me chuckle.

"So what about you?" she asks me.

"What about me?" I banter back.

"You said earlier that you never met your dad?" Her head twists up, resting her chin on my chest and looking up at me. I mentally scold myself for letting that piece of information pass my lips, but in the moment, I felt compelled to open up.

"I don't really talk about it." I don't talk about my feelings. I don't like to get too deep in them. No point living in the past. If I did, I would probably fucking drown.

"I told you about my skeletons. I promise yours are

safe with me," she says, and I watch her for a beat, swallowing roughly.

"Not much to say, really. Never met my father, don't even know his name. My mom probably doesn't either." I scoff at how ridiculous it all sounds.

"And you said your mom lives out of town?" she asks tentatively, obviously remembering what I had already told her weeks ago.

"Lives in a trailer up in Wilmington now. I don't see her. She usually only calls when she needs something," I say, sounding bitter. "She is a user, has been all her life. I don't think I have ever seen her clean."

"I'm sorry about that. Seems like we both lost our parents along the way," she comments sadly.

"Seems like it." The heaviness of the conversation clouds us both.

"So Brady and Cody, have you known them long?" she asks, and the cloud lifts a little.

"Since we were kids. Their background is similar to mine. We were rough, still are. But we found our way. Now with Fortress, we are trying to get our shit together," I tell her, feeling proud at how far we have all come.

"I would say that Fortress and you guys are doing well. You were all so great at Chloe's showing. Not to mention, the numerous times you have come to my rescue..." I squeeze her ass cheek in my hand and she holds me tighter.

"Just doing my job." And I was. As I think about our situation, I find it unfathomable that the two of us even met, let alone are now sharing a bed. But I feel at ease about it. Comfortable. So I do something I have never done before. I touch my lips to the top of her head like I promised myself I wouldn't, and I bury my face in her hair, take a breath in, smelling her scent and feeling all the stress leave my body. This woman is starting to make me feel like my body is thawing out after a big freeze, and I don't know what the hell that means, but it feels good.

30

VALERIE

"I thought you were meant to cook me dinner?" I tease AJ from where I am standing in his kitchen, stirring the pot of spaghetti I found in his pantry.

"You look much better doing it than I would have," he says from where he sits on his sofa, just having gotten off the phone with Brady to check in about Club Vine security tonight. My cheeks heat as his eyes travel up and down my body. We spent all afternoon and early evening in his bed together, and now as I stand in nothing but his t-shirt, my hair pulled back and my makeup all gone, he still looks hungry for me.

I hear my phone beep with a notification. "Can you check that for me?" I ask him since I see my cell on the coffee table next to where he is. My phone has been blowing up all afternoon. I have ignored most things, so who knows what it will be this time. He hesitates, and I wait. I have nothing to hide from him, and I trust him, so I don't care if he accesses my cell.

"Notification from socials..." he murmurs.

"Oh, it's probably the girls. Or a new article in *Society News*," I say, grabbing the pasta sauce I found in the cupboard and trying to open the jar.

"What the fuck?" He stands up abruptly.

"What?" I look at him, startled, as he strides over to me.

"What the fuck is this?" he asks, thrusting my cell at me. Grabbing it, I look at the screen and see the message.

I am going to enjoy ending you, you stuck-up little bitch.

I swallow. These messages are getting worse and worse. "It's just keyboard warriors," I say to him as my fingers move across the cell quickly, and I delete and block *Valisdead123* from my social media.

"How often do you get them?" I can feel his anger rolling off him.

"Oh, you know, occasionally." I try to act like it is no big deal, but my hands shake around my phone, and I hope he can't see it.

"Look at me," he growls. I toss my cell on the kitchen counter and look up at him. His nostrils flare. "How often do you get messages like that?"

"It was just every now and again, you know, whenever there was something in the press, or maybe if I uploaded a pic to socials..." I start, swallowing over the lump in my throat. "But it has been more and more lately."

"And do they all say the same thing?" He looks at me inquisitively.

"Pretty much. All call me a whore and then tell me they want to end my life in some way, shape, or form." I watch his jaw pop.

"What does your security team say about it all?" His eyes thin.

"You don't have to worry about me, AJ. I'm perfectly fine," I tell him, hoping to see him relax.

"What. Does. Your. Security. Team. Say?" He repeats the question slowly and with purpose. He is angry. I let out a breath, knowing that I need to be completely honest with him.

"I don't have a security team," I tell him.

"Yes, you do, those guys out front," AJ says, looking confused.

"They are my father's team. I don't have a team. I don't have anyone."

"Why the fuck not? You are one of the richest women in the fucking country. Who has some sickos threatening you. You get harassed by the media and cameras every day."

"My father always told me I didn't need it. I had a stalker back—" I start to say, but he cuts me off.

"A fucking stalker? You had a stalker, and your father still didn't give you security? Un-fucking-believable." He releases a growly breath and runs his hand through his hair, shaking his head.

I turn off the stovetop so the pasta doesn't boil over while we talk about this.

"AJ, it is fine. I'm fine." Taking his hand, I bring it to my chest. "I'm safe. I'm healthy. I'm okay."

"Those messages are not fucking fine. Your father hurting you is not fucking fine. None of this is fine, Val." He is right, it's not.

"Okay. I will organize some security," I tell him, nodding to confirm it, and that seems to settle him a little.

"Good." With a nod, his shoulders deflate the slightest bit, and his hand squeezes my hip like an extra reassurance.

"In fact, I will call them right now, see if they can start this week," I suggest.

"Even better." He watches me as I grab my cell and put it to my ear, listening for it to ring.

In that moment, AJ's cell rings from where he left it on the coffee table, and he walks over to grab it. Picking it up, his head then whips in my direction.

"Security people these days... never answer their phones..." I murmur to him.

"Val," he growls in warning.

"Does Fortress want the job of looking after me or not? Because I don't trust anyone else," I say, putting my cell back on the kitchen counter and crossing my arms over my chest.

His scowl is deep, his eyes piercing mine as he walks back toward me. "Your father will not get close to you again. Your penthouse access will be managed better... You will do everything I tell you to do..." He stops right in front of me, then continues. "And I will protect you with my life," he says, softer now, and I know he means it. My heart thuds. This man is everything I ever dreamed of, and I am falling for him more and more every day.

"Looks like you got the job, then," I say, before turning back to the pasta so he doesn't see my eyes water. Because I believe in him when he says he will protect me with his life. I just hope it doesn't come to that.

31

AJ

It's been a week since Val was in my bed, and every night since, I've been in hers. The sex is fucking phenomenal and the sleepy conversations we have afterward are bonding. I now know more about her than I do almost anyone else. She has also learned more about me, and the only people who know more are Cody and Brady.

The three of us boys have discussed at length how best to organize ourselves to protect Val. I stay with her every night and have a few boys following her whenever I am not with her. The Van Cleef Security cars still follow us, though, which is something I am not happy about. But they seem harmless, so I am focusing on bigger things. Val.

I am not used to sharing my life. Not just my history and troubles but also my day-to-day hours. But everything has panned out this week. I have been to the gym to do my daily workouts. I work on Fortress with the boys, train Levi and check in on him, but my days start and end with her. It is new, and I like it.

Now as I clean up the gym from our workout today, I look at Levi who has his head straight into his laptop.

"What are you doing?" I bark, wondering what he is up to.

"Trying to hack into the pentagon," he says like the smart-ass he is.

"Stop being an idiot." I throw a boxing glove at his head.

"I am, see." Showing me his screen, I see a whole bunch of numbers and code that mean absolutely nothing to me.

"I've got no idea, but if that is what you are really doing, you better stop, because you will get put away for life." I walk across to him and slam his laptop shut. He is a smart kid, but he needs to channel it for good, not evil.

"You're no fun." He bites and puts the computer away in his bag. "How's Val?" he asks, and I look at him, raising an eyebrow.

"*Valerie* is none of your business," I tell him.

"What do you mean? She is *my* lawyer. I've never had a lawyer before, AJ. I'm feeling very loved," he jokes, placing his hand on his chest like he is in love with her himself. My heart stumbles in my chest a little at the thought of possibly loving Val.

"Stop being a smart-ass." I throw the other glove and hit him in the face, and he laughs, then his expression grows serious.

"Can I stay with you tonight?" he asks. He has stayed at my apartment a few times over the past year. But I know he sleeps on the sofas of friends a lot whenever things at home get bad.

"Where's your mom?" I ask. Zipping up my bag and standing, I wait for him to gather his so we can leave.

"She had a bad hit. She's in the hospital. Dad hasn't been home for a few days." Which means he has been on his own, probably with no food in the house, and random people knocking at his door asking for money. My shoulders tighten, the familiar feeling of anxiety and fear swirling inside of me, remembering those days when I was a kid. They were the shittiest days I ever lived.

"Why didn't you tell me? You can stay. Let me just call Val and tell her that I'll be at my own place tonight." I see a smirk on his face as we walk outside to my bike.

"Oh shit, you are sleeping fancy now, hey?" he comments, and I punch him lightly in his arm.

"Watch your..." I am about to scold him and stop short as I get to my bike. "Who the hell are you?" I ask the two men who stand near my bike in tailored suits and sunglasses, like they fell out of a *James Bond* movie.

They remain quiet and still as the back door of a black town car parked nearby opens and a man in a full, tailored, gray three-piece suit gets out. He is thin and short, angry-looking, and something about his eyes is familiar.

"AJ Steele," he says, walking up to me. I don't acknowledge him. Something about this feels off.

"John Van Cleef," he says, stepping right up to me. *Well, shit.* I straighten my spine. I want to punch him for the way he treats his daughter, but also get his approval. It's a weird feeling.

"You need to stay away from my daughter," he threatens.

"Why would that be?" I ask, my tone level, watching him and his men like a hawk. I don't trust any of them.

"Because you are no good for her," he states like I am wasting his time.

"True. But why should I? She seems to like my company."

"You're bad for her. Bad for the Van Cleef name. I know you are from a broken home; you have no money in your bank account. This bike is the only thing of value you own." Another guy walks around from the car with a baseball bat, and I grit my teeth.

"I think you need to leave," I grit out as I push Levi behind me. He takes a few steps away and lowers his bag against a tree. He rolls up his sleeves; the stupid kid thinks he is going to back me up.

"I heard that you have a record." He huffs. "Only my daughter would fall in love with a felon. She is so stupid, she probably doesn't even know." I do have a record for some minor crimes. I was in jail for less than a few weeks when I was eighteen. Not that dissimilar to Levi, although I never had a fancy lawyer to help me out back in the day. Hard times like that make a person think about their life, and that was rock bottom for me. I should be thinking he is right, that Val shouldn't want to be with a felon, but I get stuck on the words he used. *Love. Val loves me?*

"She is getting married to another man, so you need to stay away."

I almost snort. This guy is delusional if he thinks a

woman like Val could be told who she was going to marry. I know he is feeling threatened because Val is making moves to be CEO. And like a snake, he is starting to hiss.

"And if I don't?" I ask, tilting my head. He has thrown a lot of words around, but I don't yet know what he is wanting. He looks at the guy who holds the baseball bat and nods. I swallow roughly, understanding what he is about to do. The guy walks forward quickly and hits my bike.

"What the hell?" I yell as I strut toward him but am pulled back by the other two men. I struggle to get out of their grip, but with one holding me back on each arm, and Levi looking like he is going to jump in the fray, I still as they make me watch while they break my Harley, the one thing that I saved years for. The one thing that told me I could succeed in this fucked-up life.

"I know all about your little friend Marcus and your rigged boxing matches. I know all about that money you get under the table from him to fight, which no doubt has funded your silly little Fortress. I have lawyers who I pay more per hour than you will ever get, and they will ensure you are arrested and incarcerated if you even think about coming near my daughter again," he spits out, pure venom in his eyes.

I growl and start to fight again. I want him to experience pain. He watches me and sees my anger, knowing that the Harley damage hurts, but his daughter means more. His scowl morphs into a sick smile.

"I'll give her the CEO position if you leave her alone. If you try to stay with her, she gets nothing but married to a man of my choosing. Either way, you lose. You wouldn't want to stop her from her birthright, would you?"

I stop fighting, and his smile widens. He found the trigger for me and pulled it. I want Val more than anything, but I never wanted her to come down to my level. I never wanted her to suffer. Now her father will give her what she wants if I leave her alone. I don't like it, but I will do it for her.

"I know you came from nothing so have no fear of going back there. You leave and I will give her the CEO job. But be assured that if you even look at my daughter again, I will hurt her. Maybe an accident in her apartment. Lord knows that stupid dog won't be able to save her. It is entirely possible that she could burn herself cooking. She is such a terrible cook. It would be a shame to have hot oil run up her arms..." he threatens, and I want to fucking gut him. I feel sick. Losing the bike, harming Fortress, I could handle all those things. He is right. I came from nothing, but I can rebuild again. But Valerie can't be touched. She is too precious. Too precious to me. She is everything I didn't know I needed, and the last thing I want to do is leave. But she needs to be CEO and needs to be safe, and if that means I need to stay away from her to make that happen, then I will do it.

"Do we have an understanding?" He watches me closely, knowing the answer already.

"We do." I nod, my jaw tight as I grind my teeth, hating this fucker with everything I have within me.

"Good. For your trouble," he says, throwing a wad of cash at my feet. The two men holding me push me to the side as I watch them all pile back into the car and drive down the street. I look at the cash near my shoe. It is a roll of hundred-dollar bills, probably about ten thousand there, but I don't want to touch it so I kick it away from me.

"Are you alright?" Levi asks me, and I look at him. My gaze must be murderous because he takes a step back, and I pull out my cell to call Brady to bring the truck.

I'll take my bike. I'll stay away from Val. But I am not touching his fucking money.

32

VALERIE

I've been calling AJ all afternoon, but he hasn't answered. He is obviously busy. He mentioned this morning that he was training with Levi this afternoon, so maybe they went and did something together. I smile at that thought. It is so sweet that he has taken Levi under his wing. It's yet another thing that shows me exactly what kind of man AJ is.

"What's bothering you?" George asks me from across the meeting table as I place my cell down again for the hundredth time. We are at Van Cleef Corp. It is the first time I have left my apartment all week, preferring to work from home and be with AJ all night. Our nights have been a mixture of fun, deep discussion, business talk, and surprisingly tender touches. He is far from the man I first met. And I am falling for him. Hard.

"Nothing. Just trying to get a hold of AJ," I murmur as I pull together all the paperwork in front of me. We have built our reports, presentations, and are packaging everything, ready to send to each board member. I am still positive that I have six on my side, so I just need one other. Given that the other six are as dirty as my father, it is the anonymous board member my mother placed who is my only hope. At this stage, we are still in the dark to who it is.

"So this AJ. He is the one with the Harley, right? He seems to be sticking around. Usually, your friends last a few dates, and then they disappear," George asks, a small smile on his face.

"He's... different," I tell him, my smile now wide.

"What is he like?" George asks me, and I think about the question.

"He is dependable. I feel like I can tell him anything, and without saying a word, he knows it doesn't go any further than us. He gives good advice, he is empowering, and I feel safe with him," I tell George.

"Sounds like just the right someone you need in your life," George offers and I nod. The two of us understand that dependability and safety are not something I have had since my mother passed.

"But he isn't answering..." I murmur, looking at my cell again.

"Well, maybe he is busy."

"I am sure he is, but he would usually just send me a text if he missed one of my calls. It feels odd." I have absolutely nothing to base it on, but I am concerned. Something doesn't feel right. As George is about to say something, the meeting room door opens so forcefully it hits the wall, and I jump with a start as my father walks in, throwing a file on the table in front of us.

"You're done," he barks, looking at both George and me.

"What?" I ask as George and I stand up from our chairs. My heart races and George looks cross. Anxiety crawls up my throat at the way they look at each other. There is no love lost between them; they have never gotten along. I look at my father. His hair a little disheveled, his eyes fierce. The way he sounds is so abrupt and angry. He is stern, yet also smiling like he won the jackpot, and my blood goes cold.

"You're done." My father looks directly at George like he wants to slice his throat. George opens the file my father slammed onto the table, his brow crumpling as he reads the contents. I watch on silently, wishing I knew what was going on.

"You son of a bitch," George says, and I gasp, feeling dread building in my body.

"I knew she couldn't do this on her own. I should have known you were in on it," my father seethes as he points at George. George steps forward so his finger is pressing on his chest.

"You are going to ruin this company and you are going to ruin your daughter," George spits out, his face transforming with anger.

"What? What happened?" I ask, looking between both of them, panic filling my bones.

"Well, my dear daughter. George, in his position of VP, is not to be advising new leadership, especially in any takeover bids of *any* kind. It is written in his contract in black and white."

I am about to speak, but he continues.

"And your pile of shit boyfriend..." He points his finger at me, and I take a step back, my eyes widening. "I taught him a lesson this morning. That someone like him shouldn't even think about fraternizing with my daughter. Although I wouldn't put anything beyond you. You are too stupid. Of course, you can't run the company when you associate with those kinds of people. Did you know he has a record? I threw ten grand at him and he walked away. Clearly, he was only after your money." My father laughs, and I feel like I might vomit.

"What? What did you do?" I ask, the panic now clear in my voice. But my father ignores me like I am some stupid little girl who doesn't warrant further explanation.

"George, security are here to escort you out. Now that you are in breach of your contract, you are no longer employed by Van Cleef Corp. I want you to clear your desk and leave this premise immediately," my father demands. My mind is whirling, my heart thumping. I have no idea what is going on. *Did AJ leave me? Did AJ take my father's money and leave me?*

"You are a fucking lunatic!" George yells at my father before stalking past him and out the door. I sit in shock, my legs not able to hold me up any longer.

"Valerie, I have given you enough leeway. Hand your notice in to HR. You will be married to William Schmidt within the week and are not to step foot into Van Cleef Corp again," my father says, then he turns on his heel and walks out the door. As soon as he does, I stand, rushing to grab the small bin in the corner of the room, and empty the contents of my stomach. This day is proving too much.

Catching my breath, I gather my things, running out the door to my office. I grab my laptop, and instead of typing up and submitting my resignation as he demanded, I put in a formal written complaint and add it to the board papers I am collecting for each member. I then walk out of the building with George, with the promise for us to continue working together despite my father's demands. George has been in the business as long as my father has, and there is no way he is leaving it.

The car ride home is quick, but the entire way I try calling AJ to no avail. As I walk into my apartment building, my head is whirling, my heart broken. I have no idea what to do or where to go now.

"Welcome back, Miss Van Cleef. You have someone here who has been waiting for you," Victor says as I step into the foyer, catching up with his words.

"Oh, who?" I ask, looking around before my eyes land on the last person I ever expected to see, sitting back in his jeans and t-shirt on the luxurious velvet sofa in the waiting area.

"Levi?" I ask, stepping forward as concern takes over. "What are you doing here?"

"Your dad dropped this." He tosses a roll of hundred-dollar bills my way. "He threw it at AJ, actually, after he smashed his Harley to pieces. AJ didn't touch the money." I take a breath, relief filling me, but that's instantly replaced with worry and despair.

"Come up. We need to talk," I say, turning and walking to the elevator that Victor has waiting for us. I take Levi upstairs, make him a late lunch, and together we sit on the sofa as I learn all about the lengths my father will go to in order to get what he wants.

Then I formulate a plan and call in the reinforcements. I just hope it works.

33

AJ

After Brady collected me and my bike from the footpath, and I sent Levi home to stay at my apartment, I got busy with my friends and did the only thing I knew to do. Fix my bike enough so I could ride it and get the hell out of Baltimore.

If I can't be with Val, I need space. I can't be in the same city with the woman I can't have, and the chances of me going after her father given what he has done to her, to us, is very high. Luckily, the damage to my bike was purely vanity and the engine and steering were unharmed. So that same afternoon, I drove straight out of town and have been hiding here at Virginia Beach for the past few days, collecting my thoughts and trying to calm down.

Now, as I look out at the waves, I pick up my cell and roll it around in my hand. My cell phone rang almost every hour the first day, then I turned it off. She needs to have her mother's business; she needs to be CEO, and to get that, I need to be out of the picture.

I also needed time. I still have no fucking idea what to do. I have never before been so invested in a woman and it scares me. Love isn't something I ever thought I would experience. I didn't get it as a child at home, and I've never had it since. But I want Val, even though right now that seems selfish. I sigh at the conundrum. Good things never come to a man like me. I should have known that it wouldn't last.

I swallow, knowing it is time to face the music. I need to get back to Baltimore. I need to get back to Fortress, the gym, and Levi, and so I turn on my cell and wait. As expected, my voicemails are full, my text messages rolling in, and I sigh as I start looking through them all. A call comes through as I am scrolling, and Brady's name lights up the screen.

"Finally, he answers. Where the fuck are you?" Brady says, and I crack my neck.

"Sitting at Virginia Beach," I tell him honestly.

"Shit. Well, you need to come home. Right fucking now," Brady says, and I notice his voice seems a little panicked.

"What happened?" I ask, my heart starting to race.

"It's Val."

"Is she alright?" I ask, thinking about her father and the threats he made. That fucker better not have burned her, because if he has touched her, I will skin him alive.

"She is getting married. *Tomorrow*. To some Schmidt guy."

I shoot up from where I am sitting.

"What? She was going to be CEO! That was the deal. I leave her alone, she becomes CEO. Not fucking married!"

I yell as a few mothers who are nearby playing with their kids look at me with matching scowls.

"Apparently not. Old man Van Cleef fired her VP who was helping her. Told her that she will lose access to everything her mother built. She has to marry this Schmidt guy; otherwise, her father will make her pay."

My blood boils. He went back on his word to me. What a fucking scumbag. He is not even a man of his word.

"You need to come back, man. We need to do something."

"You know what he said if I do," I tell him as I pace. When Brady picked me and my bike up from the street after Val's father and I got acquainted, I told him everything. I needed to vent.

"I know, man, but as of tomorrow, we both know her life is over anyway. She has been calling for you. She wants you."

My fists clench, I am so fucking angry. John Van Cleef is a piece of work, a conniving, lying piece of shit that I now want to bury. Alive.

"Fuck!" I curse, kicking a rock, my frustration high. If I go back, that could put Val in danger, but if I don't, she will be in danger and lose everything anyway.

"Listen to me." Brady's voice is low and calm. "I've seen you with Val. I've seen the way you look at her. Hell, the way she looks at you. You two are fucking good together and had a spark from the minute you met. We don't have good in our lives, never have. But you have it now. You have met this woman who thinks the world of you. And you... I have never seen you with a woman like this before, so I know she means something to you. Man, if I had that, I would fight tooth and fucking nail to protect it. She has been blowing up our phones looking for you. She wants you. She doesn't want to be married to some old guy. She wants your fucking ugly self. So get the hell home and come get your woman."

He is right. We have never had good things. We worked hard, suffered a lot, but since meeting Val, the dark cloud that always seemed to surround me has lifted, and a little light is starting to come through. I fist my hand by my side.

"Time and place?" I grit out to him.

"George Peabody Library. Tomorrow at two o'clock. Father Van Cleef wanted it somewhere very public, wanted the world to see it. It is fucking all over the local news here."

"I'll be home tonight. We will formulate a plan. This time, I am getting the girl," I say, ending the conversation and running to my bike. I have to get back to Baltimore because Val is not marrying that prick. She is mine.

34

VALERIE

It's been a week since my world imploded. Wedding planning has been rushed. Not that I have had a say in anything. My dress is tailor made, yet still too tight. Abigail has handled everything right down to my eyeshadow color, and I don't care about any of it. I just care about AJ.

"You have balls of steel, my dear friend," Simone whispers to me. I am nervous that AJ won't show. The fact that he didn't speak to Brady until yesterday has had me on edge. But Brady has confirmed that AJ will be here, and I need to trust him. Just like I always have.

"Either that, or I am incredibly stupid," I whisper back to her, nerves coating my insides. I played the perfect daughter routine this week, all the while planning to stop the wedding somehow before it happened. I paraded myself around for days, hoping every news crew and influencer captured it for AJ to see it. Wherever he ran away to. But if he doesn't show, I have a backup plan in place. I am not marrying this man, that I know for sure.

"I admire your tenacity, your grit. Who else goes through a week like this to flush out your true love from hiding," Chelsea says in disbelief.

"What's going to happen if he doesn't show?" Chloe glances at me, worried. All the girls look beautiful in soft-pink satin dresses that fall to the floor; meanwhile, I can barely breathe in the white monstrosity that clings to my body, making me sweat.

"He will show," I say, determined. "I am his. He doesn't like to share."

The media stories have been plentiful this week and not just in *Society News*. Fake stories about how William Schmidt and I have been having a secret love affair for almost a year have been planted. Photoshopped images accompany them. Social media is having a field day, and Levi, Brady, and Cody, have all taken turns watching me whenever I have been alone. Victor has been on alert downstairs, and my friends were on constant rotation with bottles of wine and blocks of chocolate as I continually thought through my plan.

"But what if he doesn't?" Chloe pushes. I have thought about this.

"If he doesn't, then I just save myself. I say no at the altar. Publicly humiliate my father and William and cause a media shitstorm for weeks." I am ready for battle. This all ends today.

"He will banish you. He will harm you." Simone looks at me warily.

"AJ will come." I feel it in my bones. I believe AJ will

come back for me, but if he doesn't, then I know Brady and Cody will show up in a getaway car. I will run, I will hide. I can do it. My hands shake and my palms sweat. *God, I hope this works.*

"Let's hope it doesn't come to that," Chloe murmurs, as the event planner walks in.

"Oh, you look beautiful," she says, her eyes teary, and I look at her like she is insane. This is not a happy wedding day; this is my public hanging.

"She's right, you do," Chelsea says, looking at me, and I give her a small smile.

"Car is here," the event planner says, checking her cell.

"Unfortunately, it isn't the getaway car," Simone murmurs as she passes me my bouquet and the girls all grab theirs.

"Let's go." The event planner walks us to the door. I would not let anyone else up to my apartment. So instead, I have this event planner Abigail hired, who has managed most of today, her planning skills pushed to the limit.

We all fall into line. Levi is hiding in my office, and I see him peeking through the door. He looks scared, so I give him a small nod, hoping to tell him I am okay. The elevator is so quiet I can hear my heart thudding in my chest. My brow starts to sweat a little as we take it to the basement and I step out. The girls pile into one limo, and I stand still, looking at my father who waits inside the other.

This is it. This moment is going to change my life forever. I wring my hands together under the bouquet, and my stomach rolls so violently, I feel like I am going to vomit. As I step inside the car, the air thins, the reception icy, as my father doesn't even acknowledge my existence. We drive through the streets, the two of us completely silent. I have nothing to say to him. He is nothing to me and I am nothing to him. It should be sad that we are now total strangers. That there is no coming back from this, and it is. But is also a long time coming. I never really saw who he truly was before.

We pull up to the library, and my body vibrates with anxiety. Eyes wide, I look around at everyone and everything, trying to spot him, hoping he is here. I see the girls tumble out of their limo in front of us and look around just as panicky. It is bedlam. Media are everywhere; people have their cell phones out. This is chaos and carefully crafted by the very man sitting next to me.

"Chin up, dear. This is the happiest day of your life," my father says as he opens the car door and steps out. Waving to the crowd with a large smile on his face, he acts like a king to his constituents. Bile threatens to come up my throat, but I swallow and grit my teeth.

My body moves on autopilot, panicking more by the second when I still can't see AJ. I can't see Brady or Cody either, even though they promised they would be here. As I step out of the car, the cameras flash. There are paparazzi everywhere, and I pinch the skin at my elbow so hard I am surprised it isn't bleeding.

I don't even try to smile. My head continually whips around, looking at everyone, looking at the cars, the buildings. *Where is he?*

"Hey, Valerie, smile!" a pap yells out, and I scowl

toward him. I am pretending to go through with this stupid day because I was threatened, not because I want to. Regardless of the media attention and regardless of what my father says. I am not happy about this, and I am not going to fake it anymore.

I take a few steps toward the girls and suck in a deep breath.

"He isn't here," Chloe whispers as her eyes dart around and my heart rate increases.

"This way, my dear," my father grits out, grabbing my elbow hard and pulling me to the bottom of the stairs so forcefully I almost stumble. His hand digs into my skin, but I don't cry out. I don't want to give him the satisfaction, so I bite the inside of my cheek instead, already tasting the blood. My grip on my flowers is tight as I look up. This is a beautiful venue; the stone building and large steps leading up to the front door are really lovely. Just not for me. Not today.

I take one last look around as my breathing becomes more rapid. I need to decide on whether I wait a few more moments or if I bolt and run down the street now. I glance at the girls, all of them white as ghosts, and then I hear it. The roar of a motorcycle. I swiftly turn and look down the street.

"Stupid son of a bitch," my father grumbles as his grip on me tightens, and he tries to drag me up the stairs, but I remain rooted to the ground. My father laughs nervously, looking around at the crowd of people. "Valerie, start walking, or I will ensure you never walk again," he threatens in my ear, and I start to shake as he continues. "You stupid, trashy..." But he stops as I look at him, wide-eyed, and can barely breathe.

"It was you!" I say to him, disbelief and shock blanketing me.

"Get inside right fucking now," he grits out, not letting me out of his grasp.

"The message, the stalking. It was all you!" I say louder, and I hear the girls behind me gasp.

"Valerie..." His fake smile hides his bitter anger. "Get inside now," he growls; meanwhile, people are starting to notice something's happening that has nothing to do with a wedding. The cameras don't stop flashing, but the audience out here now knows something isn't right.

"How could you?" I ask on a breath, the words barely audible. I shouldn't be surprised, but I am. My father is the one who has been sending me those vile messages on social media. He has been the one who has been making me feel unsafe, damaging my self-confidence. "All for what?" Frowning, I look right at him. "After college?"

"I needed you down. I needed you frightened. I needed you to submit and do what you are told. Now get inside!" he says venomously, as most of the air leaves my lungs and my body stills in a mix of fear and anger. The roar of the bike gets louder, snapping me out of my shock, and I look around to see AJ's Harley turn the corner and ride straight up to the curb, right near my wedding car.

"Oh my God, he's here!" Chloe says, relief easing her expression.

"Run, girl!" Simone yells at me, and I do. I yank my

elbow from my father's grip, throw my flowers at his face, and pick up the bottom of my dress.

"Valerie!" my father whisper-shouts, still not wanting to cause a scene. I don't respond to him. I turn from him as quickly as I can in this stupid dress and run. I run so fast, I almost trip in my heels. AJ jumps from his bike and throws his helmet to Brady, who I only now notice has pulled up in a truck nearby, which he has left running with the door open. As I dash to AJ, he sprints to meet me, and we collide, our bodies smashing into each other, his lips on mine immediately. I hear the crowd gasp. The cameras flash incessantly. And we pull apart just as quickly, as AJ wastes no time in picking me up bridal style and running to the truck Brady exited with me in his arms.

"Runaway bride!" someone from the crowd yells, and I look over AJ's shoulder and see my girls all scattering, jumping in the other truck with Cody behind the wheel.

"Sorry I'm late, sweetheart," AJ says smoothly, throwing me in the truck. I scoot over quickly as he jumps in. Brady rides the Harley straight down the street, and we pull out and follow. People are shouting, cameras are flashing, and I turn to see my father standing there with a look of rage on his face. I stare him down and swallow roughly.

"Better late than never," I say as AJ speeds down the street so fast that I can't see the library anymore and knowing I have left my entire life as I knew it behind.

35

AJ

Cody, Brady, and I drive in convoy back to Val's apartment in a hurry. We have done defensive driving training, so we know what we are doing. I planned this for the past twenty-four hours since Brady first called me. I had to stop myself multiple times from grabbing her late last night when I got back to Baltimore, but it needed to be at the venue today. It needed to be in front of witnesses. Val is mine, and the fucking world knows it now.

I steal a look at her beside me. Dressed up in white, the gown she is wearing large, the material taking up most of the space in the truck. She looks beautiful in anything, but this is a lot.

"Don't say it. I feel ridiculous enough as it is. I can't wait to get it off," she says, pulling at the fabric, obviously aware of what I was thinking.

"Are you okay? How do you feel?" I ask her, because she seems too relaxed. Perhaps she is in shock. Brady and Cody told me she was counting on me being here. Riding in like a knight in shining fucking armor. Never in my life did I ever think that would be a phrase to describe me, yet here we are.

"Ready for the fight of my life. Seems like I also just found my stalker," she says, out of breath, and I move my eyes from the road quickly to look at her in confusion.

"Your fucking father?" I almost roar as I try to remain focused while I pull into the garage under her building. I spot some of my team positioned on either side of the roller door. They have been here since yesterday, all guarding my girl.

"He admitted it. Wanted to keep me low. Out of the company, out of the way."

"He is a fucking piece of shit," I spit out, feeling murderous.

I see the others pull up, tumbling out of the car and grabbing the elevator. "Let's get upstairs; we need to secure you inside. There is no telling what your father is going to do now," I tell her, but before I can open the door, she jumps across the seat and onto my lap in a mess of fabric and tulle and who knows what else she is wrapped in. Her lips hit mine, and it is like I can breathe again for the first time all week, and I find her waist and pull her to me. I taste her, hold her body, touching her everywhere to ensure this is real. That *she* is real. I feel her hands grab on to my shirt collar as our tongues tangle, and I lift a hand, cupping her face and diving in deeper, never wanting to stop. But I know we need to, so I pull back slightly and look right into her eyes. "I fucking missed you," I tell her quietly.

"I missed you too," she says as her forehead leans against mine.

"We've got to move."

She nods so I open the door, pulling her out and into my arms. I carry her to the elevator, not yet wanting to let her go.

I am sure we left her father in a wake of media barrage and confusion. But he made the mess, so he can clean it up. Unfortunately for us, now we have no idea of his next move, other than knowing a man like that won't stop. He will want revenge.

As soon as we are in the apartment, everyone starts talking at once and Bordeaux is barking the walls down, chasing everyone's feet. The girls crowd around Val, and questions fly.

"I can't believe that just happened," Chloe says, walking straight up to us.

"Garage is secure," Brady confirms to me.

"Got any snacks?" Levi yells, and my head whips in his direction, where I see him in Val's kitchen, currently looking in the refrigerator.

"What are you doing here?" I ask, surprised. Last I saw him, he was with me when I had the visit from Valerie's father and my bike got smashed. After that, things are a blur, and I assumed he went home.

"Looking for something to eat." He smirks back at me, and I growl. Him being here is something else I need to get to the bottom of, but Levi can wait. I look Val up and down, assessing for any damage, and my anger at this whole situation starts to unravel.

"Brady, I need you with Victor downstairs. I have a

feeling there will be a lot of people hanging around very soon." I bark orders out to the room, my eyes remaining on Valerie. It will take less than five minutes for the media to be at the front of the building, and it is going to be hectic.

"On it," he says, walking straight out the door.

"Levi!" I yell at him, and he pulls his head out of the open refrigerator as he raises his eyebrows. "Get on that computer of yours. Find out what you can about today and what is happening." I might as well put him to work. He has the skills, and we can use them.

"Pfft, easy," Levi says, shutting the refrigerator and biting into an apple and holding it with his teeth. He grabs his laptop and slouches on the sofa like he lives here. Bordeaux jumps up next to him, settling into his side like they are best friends. *How long has he been here?*

"Cody, we need more guys," I tell him, and he nods.

"On it." He pulls out his cell, taking a seat at the dining table off to the side, using it as his work desk, then he starts calling people in. We don't have many more to call, but we will get as many as we can to help us.

Brady, Cody, and I have already organized how today is going to roll and we know what we need to do. Victor downstairs is fully briefed, the security team from this apartment complex all alerted and now double in size. I have some Fortress men positioned around the apartment block, a small team working with Victor downstairs and others based in the garage. No one is coming in or out without me knowing about it. She wanted me to run her security, and that is exactly what I am going to do.

"What is going on?" Valerie asks me, her hands going

to her hips, obviously not liking being kept out of the loop.

"Ladies, thanks for watching my girl all week for me. Given the situation, you are not to go anywhere alone. Brady, Cody, or one of my guys needs to be with you all the time. Including at your jobs, if you go out..." I start to brief them, and Simone interrupts.

"We know the drill. Brady briefed us. I will be here, work, or home. That's it," Simone says, nodding.

"I've closed the shop because I knew the media would be insane," Chloe says, and I nod in agreement.

"Me too. Customers will come in for the gossip, not for beauty, so I shut my books this week," Chelsea says, and Val looks at them with concern.

"I'm sorry you had to do that," Val tells them.

"I'm not. We would do anything for you, Val," Chloe says, and the girls all hug.

"Ladies," I say, interrupting them. As sweet as this is, I need Val to myself. "I believe you have a change of clothes in the spare rooms down the hall?" I ask them, insinuating that they make themselves scarce, because the longer I see her in this goddamn wedding dress, the angrier I get. At the situation, at her father, at myself for leaving her in the first place.

"Oh, sure," Chelsea murmurs, looking at the others.

"You okay?" Chloe asks Val, not even looking at me. Val nods to her, and the girls gather the bottom of their dresses and walk down the hall in their heels, chattering the entire way.

"What's the plan?" she asks, looking up at me.

"What's the plan? The plan is that you need to get

that fucking dress off your body right now," I growl, stalking toward her. I want to burn this fucking dress and then bury the fucking ashes.

"Stop!" She holds up her hand, and I still, mere feet away from her.

"You left me," she states, pursing her pretty lips. She looks delicate now. Like the adrenaline is wearing off. Her eyes are glassy, and her bravado is thinning.

"I had to," I say, nodding, my jaw hurting from how hard I am clenching it.

"You left me?" she says again, her voice breaking, her breathing becoming more rapid. She is upset and pissed off. Good. Because so am I.

"He threatened to hurt you. He threatened your rightful position at the company your grandmother built," I grit out, trying to explain my weeklong absence, my nostrils flaring as I think about it.

"I know," she says calmly and swallows.

"You know?" I frown, trying to work out what she knows.

"Levi has been staying with me all week. He told me all about it." My head swings around, looking at him sitting on the sofa, his feet now up on her coffee table and a bowl of snacks by his side that he obviously grabbed from her kitchen without me noticing.

"What?"

"I went through with this stupid stunt today because I thought it would be the only thing to get you back," she explains, looking a little remorseful. "And Levi is currently sleeping in my spare room down the hall." I raise my eyebrows. She doesn't even know the kid, yet she opened her home to him in his time of need, when his parents are too out of it on drugs to notice he is even gone. She is kind as well as infuriatingly stupid. No man should have access to her like that. Not even fucking Levi. That will be a discussion for another time.

"I spent the last twenty-four hours planning and getting a team in place so I could come and get you," I explain. "But what if I didn't show?" I ask, wondering what she was thinking. I did wonder why she didn't run earlier, why she was going through with a wedding she didn't want.

"I trusted you to show. I knew you would come for me. You just needed a little push," she says with so much conviction, it is pulsating in my chest.

"And if I didn't?" My fists clench at my sides. I am itching to touch her.

"I would have run. Then I would have gone into hiding somewhere." She shrugs like it's no big deal, that running from your arranged marriage is just part of life. Maybe it is for her. "It was very admirable to fall on your sword for me to get the CEO position, but AJ, I don't need you to fall on any sword for me."

"I will always save you in any way I can," I tell her, ensuring she understands. My life for hers, always.

"But I don't need you to save me like that. I just need you to be by my side and cheer me on while I save myself." This woman is fucking amazing. There is no way that I will ever stand by when things get tough, but I underestimated her strength. She is strong, capable, and can do anything she puts her mind to.

"I can do that. And maybe I should have spoken to

you before I took off. But sweetheart, there is no doubt in my mind that I will always protect you. My life for yours always." It is the best she is going to get from me right now. I will always lose so she can win.

"Just promise me you won't leave like that again," she pushes. I can't win this argument because I never want to leave her side again. I take in a deep breath and step into her, our chests touching, and her head tilts up so she can look at me.

"Fine. I promise," I growl. "Now get this fucking dress off your body so I can burn the fucking thing."

"I think I'll let you do the honors," she says, grabbing my hand and leading me into her bedroom. I kick the door closed, wanting privacy, as she turns and gives me her back.

"The zipper is in the middle." She holds up her hair. I spot it, grip the material on either side, and pull, tearing the zipper from the fabric, and the dress shreds right down the middle.

"Oh my God!" she squeals, laughing, as I kick out the tulle, letting it pool at her feet.

"Step out," I demand, and she steps out of the material that gathers at her ankles. I pick it all up, like it is a large bedsheet and walk to the windows.

"What are you doing?" she asks, confusion in her eyes and a small smile on her lips.

"Getting rid of this fucking thing." I open the French doors that lead to her balcony.

"AJ?" She steps toward me in her sexy-as-sin underwear, looking like all my fantasies rolled into one.

"Gimme me a second," I tell her as I hoist the material

high and throw it over, watching it fall to the ground, settling on the street below.

"AJ!" she gasps with a surprised smile, running to where I am. We both peer over the ledge in time to see a cab run straight over the top, the dress now black, ripped some more, and floating down the street.

"Well, I guess we now know what will be on the news tomorrow..." She giggles as her eyes meet mine.

She looks tiny now without the monstrosity on her small frame, and I grab her around the waist, pulling her to me, her feet dangling as I walk us back inside.

"There, you look much better without that," I say, putting her back on her feet and closing the balcony door again. The room is quiet as I look at her. My heart races as I think about the day we have had and the fight that is coming. We stand facing each other and are quiet for a moment as the impact of the day hits us both.

"I'm scared of my father... He is... so evil," she whispers, her body starting to shiver. I rub her arms, needing to touch her and wanting to ease her at the same time.

"He won't get to you. I'll make sure of it," I tell her, knowing that he will need to get through me first.

"I just can't believe this all happened. He has completely ruined my life, and now he has me in fear for my life. Like, how could a parent do that to a child?" She looks at me for answers that I can't give.

"Well, you may share blood, but in my mind, a parent is more than blood. He has shown his true colors, none of them a quality fit for a parent," I tell her, watching her closely, concerned as I know she is about to break down.

"Thank you, AJ." Her eyes start to shimmer, tears

gathering but yet to fall. "Thank you for coming back for me." I feel her body trembling, the shock now coming to life as the adrenaline officially wears off.

"I should be the one to thank you, sweetheart." I skim my fingers down her cheek, wanting to soothe her and commit her to my memory, never wanting to forget the way she is looking at me right now. My chest feels heavy. My heart felt broken and was now patched back together, the anxiety of keeping her safe filling my bones, but I know love blooms as well and that is what scares me the most.

"I didn't do anything," she says, shaking her head, her eyes crinkling in confusion.

"I might have helped save you today, but Val, you have truly saved me. You walked into my life like a hurricane. From the moment those drinks spilled all over me, I could feel it. You have this presence that makes me feel completely at ease and riled up all at the same time. I had a deep desire to make my life better, but since you walked into it, I want nothing more than to make it my mission. Fuck, seeing you in that dress today..." I say, shaking my head, hating how close she got to being someone else's.

"AJ," she whispers, and I watch a tear fall. I run my thumb across her cheek and gather it up, wiping it from her face.

"I don't want you to be anyone else's. I want you to be mine," I tell her, barely able to breathe as I say the words.

"I want to be yours too." She nods, a sweet smile lifting her lips as her body relaxes into mine.

"Come on, sweet thing. Let me run you a bath, get you in some comfy clothes, if you even have such a thing," I tease her, and she hiccups a laugh between the tears. "Let me take care of you." More tears fall, and she nods, no longer able to talk without sobbing. I pick her up bridal style once more, happy now to know that I am the only man who gets to do so today.

36

VALERIE

Things are going from bad to worse. The only saving grace in any of this is AJ and the fact he came back for me. I broke down last night. Yesterday was too much, and even though I tried to be strong, when he looked at me as though he would crumble without me, I lost it. Having someone like AJ, big, burly, and tough, pick me up and run me a bath, sitting with me and washing my hair, soothed me like nothing else ever has. Now reality is back with a bang.

"You know, I think you have more media out in front of your apartment building than I saw at Harrison Rothschild's campaign launch," Chelsea comments, as she looks over the patio at the rows of people and cameras below.

"I gave Victor a coffee and croissant on my way up today. I felt like he needed it," Chloe says. She wears a path in my carpet where she paces. My best friend is stressing for me.

"After all this, I think I need to give him a bonus," I

mumble as I make a note in my diary to do exactly that. AJ, Brady, and Cody have been in and out all day. They are monitoring staff, hiring new guys, and Fortress has left almost all their other jobs to look after me, a fact Simone tells me Jimmy and Club Vine are supportive of so far. I have men downstairs, in the garage, near the elevator, at my door.

"You know, there is one thing that we haven't talked about in all this..." Simone says, looking at me.

"What's that?" I ask, frowning. We have been over and over everything. I am sure there is nothing I have missed.

"It is your birthday this week. I know being locked up here means no real fun, but we should have cake and a little party with the boys, maybe?" Simone says, always up for a party, and I give her a small smile.

"We have bigger things to worry about. We can celebrate next year," I tell her, and my friends all look at me with concern.

"It's your birthday this week?" Levi looks up from the sofa, where he has been perched all day, searching media articles and trying to keep us all updated on what is being said. I spent some time during the week talking to George and assembling a few team members to help in my endeavor, including a team to drip feed stories to the media. While many articles paint me in a bad light, together George and I have tackled my father head-on, his own star now falling in the eyes of the public. He is no longer considered the man of the city he once was. Without George, I have no idea what I would have done. He has supported me every step of the way, as have all my friends. I smile at Levi. He never leaves my side; he is AJ's eyes on me when he isn't here.

"Yeah, but I'm not really feeling it this year," I say with a shrug. My life is a mess. Once I get that under control again, maybe we can celebrate.

"Cool," he says simply, going back to his laptop.

"Val, check this out," Chloe says, and I step over to her and look at her cell screen. "Apparently, he flew out this morning." I look at a photo of William Schmidt walking up the stairs of a private plane.

"It says he is moving to Dubai to start a new life after being left at the altar. *Asshole.* He was always planning on moving to Dubai; he just thought he would take you with him," Simone mutters, and I sigh.

My cell rings, and everyone looks at me. This has been happening all day. Everyone is waiting for my father's call to see what the next move is. But I don't want to wait for him and then react. I need to keep momentum going on my side, maybe surprise him for once. As soon as George's name appears, I answer.

"Hey, George," I say, looking at the room of people as they all go back to whatever gossip they were reading on their own phones. I walk away for some privacy.

"Board meeting has been brought forward and is now in three days. Van Cleef Corp is in complete disarray. Your father is trying to control everything, but it appears your runaway bride act yesterday dismantled more than just his plan to marry you for foreign investment in the company. A lot of the staff have revolted. Some have left, others are demanding answers to why both you and I are no longer there," he says, and I feel sad. It is nice that people liked working with George and me so much that they are protesting, but I hate that Van Cleef Corp has come to this. I feel guilty, because if I had just done everything my father wanted, then everyone would be happy. But I roll my shoulders back and fill my lungs with confidence, because there is always a better way, and my father was continually too lazy and too money hungry to consider other options.

"Have the board packs gone out?" I ask him. We had all our board papers collated and packed, ready for each board member, and this week while I was playing the good daughter and having bridal dress fittings, George was working from home, sending out the board papers, along with calling stakeholders and supporters. My father might not like him, but George is well respected in the business community and has a lot of connections.

"Everything has been delivered and signed as received. No doubt your father also got his own pack and has now seen the strategies you are proposing. I dare say the collaboration with the Rothschilds will anger him like fingers down a chalkboard," he says, and I scowl.

"He probably didn't even look at it. I am sure he flipped through it and then threw it in the garbage." I take a breath and think about the situation.

"You need to lay low for a few more days. The board is instructed to vote on three matters. One, keep leadership as is with no changes. In the current climate, that would be stupid," George explains.

"I agree." I nod even though he can't see me.

"Two, they vote to replace your father with you. We have a strong business case for this, but again, given the current situation, they may also see this as a risk," he adds, and I hold my breath.

"What's the third option?" I ask, already knowing it, but asking just the same.

"Three. They replace your father with new leadership. Someone entirely separate from the family and the company history."

"Are you sure they can do that? My family built this company; surely, they can't just take it?" I ask, feeling frustrated.

"Well, the business rules state that they can't unless they see complete reputational damage occur. At the moment, Van Cleef Corp is all over the media."

"Yes, because my father tried to marry me off to a man for business interests," I say, rubbing my eyes.

"Just stay safe and in contact with me until the board meeting."

"That's easy. AJ has me in complete lockdown," I tell him. I can't walk outside or go to the Van Corp Offices to speak to staff, and I can't put my case forward to the media. I know this complete lockdown is necessary because my father is a real threat, but it doesn't mean I like it.

"I must say, seeing you run to that man and him throwing you in that truck is a video on *Society News* that I have watched on repeat," George admits. "I'll be there later tomorrow. I look forward to meeting him. In the meantime, I can start pulling together some things for AJ and your security team," George says, and I smile.

"Thank you. I think you will like him. I think the two of you will get along well."

"Any man who can protect you, Valerie, is already a firm friend of mine." My heart warms. I now understand why my mother loved George so much. As I hang up, I think of her. Of what she ever saw in my father, of what she would think about this entire situation and what he is doing.

Then I think of AJ, and I know regardless of if I become CEO or not, I have already won. Because he came back. He came back for me.

37

AJ

"I still can't believe this is her place," Brady says, whistling low in appreciation, looking over Valerie's penthouse apartment before he sits on the sofa next to Levi. He slumps in exhaustion. It's day two of lockdown and we just got back here after walking the perimeter, ensuring everything is tight as dusk approaches.

The media are still camped outside, which itself provides protection because no one is coming in the front entrance for fear of being photographed. So far, we have updated all the locks and installed extras, and we have coded new passcodes into the entry of the complex and common areas. We've conducted daily security briefings with Victor and the security team from the complex down in the foyer and now have full access to their own security systems and processes. Considering this is our first full-time personal security gig, the boys and I have it under control, and I am not cutting any corners.

"Stop being a dick," I tell him, as Cody sits at the

kitchen counter, tapping on his laptop. Valerie is in her home office on a call, as her phone hasn't stopped all day. I don't know how she does it. Her world is imploding, yet she is calling staff from Van Cleef Corp to ensure they are all okay, speaking to business associates, trying to get in touch with board members. It is full on.

"So I have secured an overnight team. I have our top ten guys. One will always be downstairs, and I have another two always at the Van Cleef Corp office. Incognito, of course, and then we will work in rotating shifts with Valerie from there," Cody says, having put the people together.

Her doorbell rings, and I strut to the wall and pick up the phone.

"Victor?" I ask. We have gone through this with him all day, practicing exactly the key words he needs to say so he remains inconspicuous to anyone else. We need Val secure and protected, and that includes anyone who has access to this building.

"AJ. George is here. Miss Van Cleef's associate," he says. I run my hand over my face, because there is still so much I need to know about her contacts. I look at the time, noting it is almost six, not late, not early.

"Send him up," I say, putting the phone down and going to the front door to wait.

"What about comms?" I ask Cody. All three of us went through training years ago to become the security team we wanted to be. In addition to working in the field either at shopping malls or recently Club Vine, and the physical training we do, over the years we have completed everything from defensive driving training, first aid and medical, to various gun licenses, and terrorist training. This kind of job, protecting Val, is the kind of job we always wanted to do. The shopping malls and nightclubs were merely for revenue until we could find out how to get into the fold of personal and business security. Seems like Val has fast-tracked that for us.

"Got the team cells so far, and still working on other comms," Cody says, and I nod. There is a knock at the door, and I look through the peephole and see an older man with a briefcase.

"AJ, I presume," he says, looking at me with a raised brow as I open the door.

"George?" I ask, and he nods. I put my hand forward for him to shake, which he does. If Val trusts him, then so will I. I step back to let him in.

"Right, boys, what do you need?" he asks as he walks to the kitchen, places his briefcase on the counter, and sits on a stool near Cody.

"What are you offering?" Brady asks, standing from the sofa and walking over to him, watching him closely.

"Well, I have arranged cars, a few Escalades. One is downstairs already and the others are on their way; they should be here tomorrow. The glass is bulletproof, and each car has a tracker. I have wired a few hundred thousand to your account to help pay for any incidentals, and I have secured a three-bedroom apartment one floor down here in this building so you are always close to Valerie. You can use it as an office, for meetings, and can take breaks, or have privacy as you need throughout the day. It also has direct access to this floor with a private staircase in case you need to get here quickly."

"Um, thanks?" Cody says awkwardly as we all look at George in surprise.

"Security of one of the wealthiest women in the country doesn't come cheap, and Valerie has made it clear that you are the team she wants. She has put me in charge of helping her manage her business affairs, and her safety and security is paramount, especially now," George says, and I sigh. The help is great, the money even better. I feel odd taking it from Val, but it is for our services, and we can't protect her if we don't have what we need. And we need to pay staff, as we are down to our last few dollars already.

"I appreciate your foresight," I tell him.

"I have also had an offer from the Rothschilds," he says, looking at me, and I frown in confusion.

"What's that for?" I ask.

"They have a great security team, one of the best. Harrison is currently president, as you know. They have been through this kind of thing before. I am not sure if you are aware, but their mother often ruffled their feathers, not unlike Valerie's father is currently doing. Seems the boys and Valerie have a fair bit in common. They offered to send a few of their security guys over to help out, talk through strategies and the like."

My eyes widen. *The first family offered us security team members?*

"Sounds like something we would be interested in," I say diplomatically.

"Shit, yeah, that would be great," Brady says like a teenager, and I shoot him a look. He sees my reaction and clears his throat. "I mean, that is very nice of them," he mumbles, and I shake my head at the guy who wanted Fortress to secure jobs in the top end of town, because he needs a fucking etiquette lesson.

"Oh! Hey, George," Val says as she walks out from her office, and my eyes rest on the woman that I can't believe is mine. She is wearing jeans and a white shirt, and her hair is up and she has glasses on that make her look like a naughty librarian. My hunger for her is instant. The past few days we have made up for my absence, but with the current issues and the continuous people in this apartment, we have barely been alone. Not as much as I would like to be.

"Hi, Valerie. I am just sorting out the security financials and getting the boys what they need," George tells her, and she smiles.

"Thanks, George. I have no idea what I would do without you." I watch their interaction as she gives him a hug. They are close, almost looking like what a father and daughter should be like.

She pulls back from him and instantly comes to me where I am on the arm of the sofa, sitting on my lap and falling back to rest on my chest. My arms curl around her waist, pulling her to me, keeping her secure.

"Boys, let me take you downstairs to your new apartment. I have the kitchen already stocked with food, and you can set all this up down there and we can leave these two to it for the night," George says, and I smile. He might be pushing seventy, but he knows what needs to be done, and I nod at him in appreciation.

"Can I take Bordeaux?" Levi asks from where he is still sitting on the sofa. He has barely moved for days, his head stuck in the computer, the dog near his side. I never thought the name of a wine region in France would fall from Levi's lips.

"Sure. Keep him close to you, though. He doesn't like strangers," Val tells him, and I watch Levi pick him up, hug him to his chest, and follow the three others out the door.

"Ahhh, do you hear that?" Val asks, looking at me with a small smile.

"No, what?" I'm on alert in an instant.

"Silence..." she whispers and takes in a deep breath, relaxing into my arms.

"You've been working hard," I tell her, looking at her, worried. She is holding up pretty well, considering her life is exploding.

"So have you," she says, her hand coming up to cup my face.

"You don't need to worry about me, sweetheart." I kiss the side of her head where it rests on my shoulder, knowing she has so many other things to be concerned about right now.

"Maybe not, but I like to worry about you. I like to think about you. I like to talk to you. Have you here with me." I swallow harshly at her words.

"I like being with you too. I can't stop touching you, ensuring this is real. That I have met someone like you." My heart thuds. I have never been this open and honest with anyone before. I have never met anyone who gets me the way Val does.

As I kiss her neck, breathing in her scent, my arms

wrap around her tighter. I could eat, I need a shower, I need sleep, but I need her more.

"Let's go to bed," she says quietly, and I lean down to kiss her as I stand. Her arms wrap around my neck, and I pull her ass up so her legs circle my waist. It feels good to have the penthouse to ourselves. It feels good to have her safe in my arms. I walk with her slowly, our lips on each other, the two of us taking our time, not our usual rushed selves.

"AJ..." She pulls back a little, her eyes finding mine.

"Yeah, sweetheart?" I ask as I close the bedroom door and walk us to her bed.

"Make love to me?" she asks as I lay her down. No one has ever said that to me before. Val and I have slept together plenty. Our sex life is mind-blowing and one of the reasons I fell for her so damn hard and fast.

I look at her and swallow roughly as my hands move to her front and lift her top from her body. I don't know what to say, so I decide to show her my response with action.

"Come here, sweetheart," I tell her softly, wrapping my hand around the back of her head and kissing her again. Tonight, I will take my time. Tonight, I will make love to my girl.

38

VALERIE

AJ kisses me so softly, so sweetly, I nearly lose my mind. How a big man like this can give me the most tender of touches that make me melt. With his body over mine, his hand on the back of my neck, his lips work me over like only he can.

Our bodies move together almost as one as he kisses down my jaw to my neck, his fingers slowly opening the button and zipper of my jeans before I shimmy out of them.

"Who knew you had such a soft touch, big guy?" I tease him with a smile. I like this side of him. I like that I am the only one who gets it. The only one who gets to see him like this. To the outside world, he is hardened. A brute.

"You're worth taking my time with." His words coast across my neck as he peppers kisses against my skin. I run my hands down his back, grabbing the bottom of his shirt and pulling it up. With my top and jeans already on the floor, he is too covered.

"One day, I want to hear all about these tattoos," I whisper, my lips now brushing his bare chest, kissing each illustration that adorns his skin. They are large, a mix of words, drawings, shapes. Separately, they stand on their own, but together, they are magnificent.

"Right now, I just want to hear you moaning my name, sweetheart," he growls as his hand delves into my underwear and his finger circles my clit.

I bite my bottom lip as my body arches at his touch. "AJ... that feels so good," I moan, my eyes closed, my head pushing back into the pillow as my body vibrates for more. Every touch from him makes my senses come alive.

"I fucking love it when you arch your back for me," he says, then his lips travel down my chest to my bra. This time, his other hand is there, pulling the cup of my bra down and his mouth encloses around my nipple. My skin feels like it is on fire with need. My body aching, my mind only on him, this moment, us together.

"AJ..." I moan. He feels like he is everywhere, and his slow, seductive touch is making me quiver.

"I'm trying to take my time... but you moaning my name like that is making it hard to keep in control."

I smooth my hands up his back, feeling his muscles, his torso hard, strong, and safe, before I delve my fingers into his scalp, pulling at his hair. He growls his appreciation as I massage his head. I may be stressed, but he is as well, the two of us in new territory and both in fear for our lives. His hands move to my waist, and he slowly pulls off my underwear, his mouth following and kissing down my body.

"Mmmmm..." I bite my bottom lip as his hands move

straight back up my legs and he buries his mouth in my center.

"Fuck me, this is too fucking good..." he grumbles against my skin, and I smile as my hips start moving against his face, his tongue exploring, still taking his time. His hands graze up my sides to unclip my bra as mine remain buried in his hair. I pull the straps from my arms, flinging the lacy number across the room.

"Come here," I whisper to him, the room now dark as night has fallen, the streetlights outside giving us a small glow through the window. He kisses his way up my body and my hands land on his jeans. I feel him hot and hard as he takes my lips with his for another soul-burning kiss. Pushing his jeans off his body, I take his underwear at the same time, and he kicks them off his legs.

"Spread those beautiful legs, sweetheart. Let me in..."

I do what he says and move my legs and he positions himself between them. I look at him hovering above me, this man. I would have never in a million years thought that the two of us would be remotely compatible, but he feels like my second half, my soul mate, the one I have been waiting for.

"AJ..." I whimper as he starts to push inside. Our foreheads meet, our eyes focused on each other, his swirling with so much desire, need, and complete devotion. He grits his teeth as he pushes inside, and I lose my breath as he bottoms out.

"You feel good, baby," he says, kissing me again, and I loop my arms around his neck as our movements become synchronized. We are not frantic, we are not rushed, our bodies move together like they know exactly what to do. Our lips taste each other, his hips push into me, brushing my clit with each thrust, my body becoming hot.

"AJ... this is amazing. You are amazing," I pant. The sweat builds between us, even though we are going slower than ever before. It is a new type of arousal. My eyes water at his tender touch. It's like nothing I have ever experienced and nothing like I thought this man was capable of. My breathing starts to shudder, my body moving a little quicker. I feel out of control as I feel the high approaching.

Our foreheads remain connected as his eyes bore into mine, my mouth open, our breaths mixing, and I hear him breathing harder as well.

"Come for me, sweetheart. Let me feel you let go." Sweeping his tongue across my lips, he cups my breast, pulling my nipple, and thrusts into me more powerfully. My body feels overwhelmed in a good way, as one hand hits the bed at the side and I grip on to the sheets, my fingers white-knuckled. My other hand grabs his shoulder, my fingernails digging into his muscles. He hisses slightly as he leans down and bites my lip, and I let go. I gasp before my entire body begins to shudder, the sensual feeling overwhelming as my legs shake around his.

"AJ... Oh... AJ!" I cry out, and he swallows my moans. A deep growl leaves him and rumbles against my lips as he thrusts hard once more and then comes. His arms hold my body tight as he pulses into me, his chest rumbling, our bodies laced with a light sweat, and we pant together as we come down from our high. We stay like that, kissing for a moment, before AJ falls onto the mattress next to me and pulls me into him. We remain silent, the two of us taking in what just happened, and I realize in that moment I am utterly and totally in love with him.

39

AJ

I wake up feeling like I have slept for a year. The bed is comfortable, the early morning light still a soft glow, and the feeling of small kisses against my skin makes me smile and my dick hard.

"What are you up to, sweetheart?" I grumble, my morning voice sounding rougher than I expected.

"Kissing all your artwork," she says, her naked body draped on top of mine. She doesn't stop as her lips touch almost every inch of my chest. I huff a laugh and open my eyes. Her messy bed hair and pink cheeks make me feel things I never have previously. Before Val, it would be a rare occurrence if I woke up in the morning with a woman beside me. Even when it did happen, it was usually because I was too exhausted or too drunk to leave during the night. But I have been in her bed and woken up with her numerous times now, and it is my favorite way to start my day.

"Come here," I say gruffly as my hands find her waist. My dick is ramrod straight this morning and the only thing on my mind to fix the situation is her. Last night, I tried to be soft. Sensual. I had no fucking idea what I was doing or if I was doing it right, but I did what felt right to me and I made love to her. I've never done anything like that before, and it connected us more. I felt it right in my core, and I want to do it again. It was a test for me. To see if I could resist her just enough to go slow and steady. It was hard. My feelings for Val are intense and the need to have her hard and fast is what I crave.

"AJ!" she squeals as I lift her up, her light body easy to maneuver. She knows what I want, her legs falling to either side of me immediately as she straddles my waist.

"That's better," I praise, as my large hands run up and down her soft bare thighs. This is the best sight I have ever seen. Her curves, her tits, her hair hanging down around her shoulders, and the big smile on her face that I know is there for me.

"You're throbbing..." she murmurs, her hand coming to my cock that is standing to attention right in front of where she sits on me.

"What are you going to do about it?" I teasingly ask her as she gives me a few small pumps in her hand. When my hips jolt a bit, her body jiggles, her tits wobbling.

"This..." She lifts a little, and with me still in her hand, she positions me at her entrance and then slowly sinks down on top.

"That's it, sweetheart. Look at how good you take me," I grit out, watching my dick slide into her.

"Ohhh, that feels so good," she moans a little as she lifts up and down on top of me, and I am mesmerized, her naked body all open right in front of me to take in, to look at, to watch. I run my hands up her thighs, skimming up her waist, and then I cup her tits, molding them in my hands as her movements speed up.

"That's it, baby. Ride me. Fucking ride my cock."

She moans my name how I like it, her hands cupping around mine on her breasts as her hips move faster.

"Fuck, you're beautiful, such a good fucking beautiful girl with my cock buried inside of you..." I grip on to her waist and pull her on and off me, my need for her now urgent.

"Oh God..." She starts to whimper, her body now at my mercy as I thrust up into her. Her hands grab on to my forearms as our pace increases.

"I want to bury myself so deep," I growl, needing this, needing her.

"AJ... AJ... AJ!" she screams as her body convulses, and her mouth drops open. She looks so good, bouncing on top of me, bare, no inhibitions. Her face looks almost pained in ecstasy and her hands grip on to me hard as I don't relent. I thrust up into her harder, my core muscles working overtime, needing to feel her come for me.

"You look so fucking beautiful when you come," I grit out before I shoot my release. "Fuck..." I groan, my orgasm strong. Her hands rest on my chest as we both pant before she flops down on me exhausted.

"That's the cardio workout you need to do every morning," I tease as I kiss her head, her hair spread across my chest, and she chuckles. I caress up and down her bare back, tracing her sides, feeling her curves.

"Speaking of starting the morning..." she murmurs

"We should get up before everyone comes in today." I don't want to move. I want to lie here with her naked body on top of mine, and I want to do that all over again. But my boys will be up soon. They will barge in here to get me for our daily walk around the building and check-in with Victor.

"Let's hit the shower," I say, sitting up and lifting her off my chest, positioning her in my arms so I can carry her to the shower.

"You don't have to carry me everywhere," she says as she snuggles into my chest, and I walk into the bathroom and turn on the shower.

"But I like it," I tell her honestly. I feel like if she is in my arms, then this is all real. Not some dream or my imagination. She is safe and I feel safe with her. Like, if we are together, then nothing else matters. As long as we have each other, then everything else will be alright.

"I can tell." She smiles as I place her on her feet under the spray, and I watch her as she soaks her body. "So I wanted to talk to you about something..."

"About?" I ask, ducking my head under the stream of water, wishing it would wash all the bad shit in my life away.

"I want to go into the Van Cleef Corp offices today."

I pull out of the water and look at her like she is crazy.

"No," I say sternly. She is not leaving this apartment. It is what her father is waiting for. He hasn't made a move yet because he can't. But I know he is waiting for her to leave. I am sure he has plans to take her, kidnap her, mistreat her. That is not going to happen.

"But I need to go in, see the staff. Tell them I am fine

and things will be okay," she says, and I shake my head.

"It isn't safe." There is no way in hell she is leaving this apartment.

"But I need to show the board that I am strong and capable under pressure. That I won't just hide when things get tough. They need to see what kind of leader I can be." She's not letting it go and my shoulders feel tight.

"We don't know what your father is thinking, we don't know what he has up his sleeve. Here, you are safe," I grit out to her, trying to make her understand.

"But I need to be seen in public. I need to make a statement," she pushes back on me, looking frustrated that I am not condoning it. "I can't keep hiding."

"Val, I said no."

"AJ, I need to get out." She demands as my nostrils flare.

"No," I say sharply, because if I say anything else, I will yell.

"AJ, it has to happen sometime. I need to force his hand." I know what she means. Nothing will happen while she is here, and I know we need to make a move, but I don't want to.

"I can't protect you as well outside of these four walls," I grit out.

"You don't need to worry. I'll take a team. You don't need to protect me. I will be fine."

"You are not leaving this penthouse!" My voice rises, the shower not drowning out our heated discussion.

"Why not?" Her sassy confidence is in full effect.

"Because he will find you, because he will take you from me, and he can't do that, because I fucking love you!" I yell, and we both still. The running water is the only sound as we both stand together in shock.

"What?" she whispers, her eyes wide.

"I fucking love you, alright," I snap as I step out of the shower and grab a towel, my heart thumping, my head a mess.

"Wait..." She scrambles to turn off the water and follow me. I take a deep breath. I feel like I am going to have a fucking panic attack. *I love her. I fucking love her.* What if she doesn't love me? What the fucking hell have I done. I lean on the sink and hang my head as I try to get myself under control.

"AJ," Val says softly, her hands running up my arm. "Look at me." I squeeze my eyes shut for a moment before opening them again and taking a deep breath. I stand up and turn. I need to take it like a man.

"I love you too. I think I did from the moment you picked me up and threw me out of Club Vine," she says, a small smile coming to her face. I sigh in relief and my shoulders lower as I swallow hard. For years, I felt unloved. If your own parents can't love and care for you, what hope is there to ever find true love? I never thought it was for me. But I found it. And she is standing right in front of me. A small smile threatens my lips. *She fucking loves me too.*

"Don't be scared. This is a good thing." Her smile widens, and I can't help but smile back at her. I reach out and cup my hand around her waist and pull her tight, looking at her now beaming. Kissing her gently, I feel her melt into my arms. I pull back slightly and look at her before our conversation re-emerges in my brain.

"The answer is still no," I tell her sternly, and she pouts. She is about to come back at me when my cell rings. I am immediately on guard with how early it is.

"Get it," she says, stepping back, worry on her face.

I swiftly walk back to the bedroom and grab my phone from the nightstand. *My mom?*

"Hey, Mom," I answer as I sit on the bed and look at Val, who leans against the doorframe, watching me with concern.

"AJ. I'm in a bit of trouble," she starts cautiously. It has been months since I last spoke to her. Being in a bit of trouble means she has a dealer to pay and no money to pay him.

"How much?" I ask, lowering my eyes, feeling like shit that Val sees this side of me.

"Just a thousand."

"A thousand? Jesus, Mom, what the hell?" Anger takes over.

"Don't shout at me, boy! I've seen the newspapers. I see you are shacked up with that rich woman. A thousand dollars is mere change to you now," she spits out, the bitter tone that I am so used to hearing from her making an appearance. I don't like her referencing Val or her money.

"Don't you even say her name." I love my mom. In my own fucked-up way. But I love Val more, and nothing and no one will come before that. Not even the woman who gave birth to me.

"Just come down here and give me some cash. I need it before five," she demands and I wonder for a beat what would happen if I said no. Closing my eyes, I sigh in defeat. I know exactly what will happen and I can't let it. Death or severe assault. I have barely a grand in my personal bank account, so I will take it all and give it to her and then figure out the rest after.

"Alright, Mom, I will come today. See you soon," I say, hanging up and feeling like shit.

"Is she alright?" Val asks, coming to sit next to me on the bed.

"She just needs some cash. I need to go see her today," I tell her, still not looking at her, embarrassed and ashamed that at thirty-three, I am giving my mom money that she can spend on drugs because her habit is one that she can't break. It is barely seven a.m. and already this morning is too emotional.

"Okay, well, you go. Do what you need to do. I'll stay here today. I won't go anywhere until you are back with me." I look up at her, and she nods, confirming her words. A feeling of warmth spreads across my chest at her giving up her need to go out today and waiting for me. I don't want to choose saving my mom or saving Val. I would make a choice if I had to, but I don't want to have to do that, and the fact Val understands makes me love her even more.

"I promise not to be gone too long. Just the day. Brady and Cody will be here to watch things," I tell her, hating to leave her.

"Go get ready, I'll make you breakfast." Leaning in to kiss me, she ties her robe and walks out to the kitchen. I watch her walk away and already can't wait to be back. To be back home with her.

40

VALERIE

AJ left over an hour ago, and I sit at the dining table, holding my cup of coffee and looking at the morning sun through the window.

The apartment is quiet. I don't even have Bordeaux here to keep me company as he is now best friends with Levi and downstairs with him. My mind wanders to work. To the board. And the anonymous board member. I try to think about who it could be. Is it a man or a woman? A friend of my mother's, someone I know, or perhaps someone I don't? I know I still have the support of the six board members, so my life now rests in the hands of this anonymous person. I run my finger around the rim of my coffee cup and silently hope and put good vibes out to the universe that this person will make the right decision.

There is one more day until the board meeting. It's not lost on me that it falls on my birthday. It is either going to be the best present or the worst, depending on how they vote. The doorbell startles my thoughts.

I walk over to the door and peek, seeing George standing on the other side.

"Hi, George," I say, opening the door. He looks pale, his brow furrowed, and my stomach feels heavy when I spot him. But he isn't alone. Dennis, my old family butler, stands next to him, holding a box in his arms.

"Dennis? Nice to see you, but what's going on?" I ask, opening the door wider, knowing something isn't right.

"Hi, Valerie. I have some things that you need to know," Dennis says as he and George step inside. Closing the door, my heart rate increases.

"You need to take a seat," George says, and I really start panicking.

"Okaaaayy," I say, apprehensive as I take a seat, and now I really wish Bordeaux was here sitting on my lap.

"Valerie. As you know, your mother hired me many years ago, before she even met your father," Dennis starts, and I nod. Dennis has been with my family for a long time.

"I know."

"Well, back then, things were a little different. Your mother and your grandmother, they were fearless, and they really changed the way of doing business. Van Cleef Corporation was innovative, and I believe that is what made it really special." Dennis continues, and my eyes flick between him and George.

"I know. That's what I want. I want to take us back in that direction. Not the chasing money and losing friends like the business my father has established," I say, wondering what my parents' butler is about to tell me.

"When your father started showing an interest in your mother, it was quick. I believe the term people use now is 'love bomb.' I believe he love bombed her and she fell pregnant with you. They had a shotgun wedding and, well, the rest is history," Dennis says, looking melancholy.

"Thank you for telling me this, but I am confused as to what it has to do with me now?"

"Your mother always thought of the future, and over the years, she started to become more aware of the type of man your father was. So she made some business changes..." he says, his voice trailing off.

"What changes?" I ask, my stomach in knots.

"She made me the anonymous board member of Van Cleef Corporation." Thank God I am sitting down because I would have fallen over.

"Really?" I breathe out, in shock, but also happiness.

"Yes. As a butler, I hear many things in that household and come across various paperwork and materials. Over the years, I have gotten a good handle on exactly what your father is planning and the reasons behind it. Your mother saw an opportunity to ensure he is kept honest by implementing me as the anonymous board member, to be in place until you took over as CEO." A small smile comes to Dennis' face.

"She was so smart..." I murmur, thinking about my mother.

"She was. She had great foresight. Excellent ability to strategize and see the bigger picture," George says.

"So, what does all this mean? Do I have your vote?" I

ask, my stomach now lurching into my chest. Dennis looks down at the box at his feet, and my heart stutters. *Is he not going to vote for me?*

"There has been some... progress on that matter..." George says cryptically.

"What is it? What's happened?" I sit on the edge of my sofa.

"I remembered last night about some files," Dennis says, and my brow furrows.

"Files? What files?" I ask, a bit confused.

"Your mother's files." He paces my living room. "I remembered she had a box of files stored away. She told me to access them in case of an emergency. I think at the time she meant if your father died, not that he was threatening you," Dennis says.

"What? Where are they?" I ask, keen to see them. Keen to have any contact with my mother.

"They were in a safety storage facility on the west side," he says. "Your mother thought they would be safer in an area of the city that none of her contacts would think to visit." He shakes his head, half smiling at the memory of her.

"So we go get them," I say, standing, ready for action.

"I went last night. I have been up all night looking through them." He swallows roughly.

"And?" I ask, my hand immediately coming to my elbow to pinch the skin. A nervous tick I am now aware I have, thanks to AJ pointing it out.

"You have a trust fund," he says, and I still.

"A what?" I ask. "Wouldn't that be something that was in her will? She already left me some money. That is how

I bought this penthouse." But he already knows all this; George and Dennis were both with me, even way back then.

"I know. But this is something additional. Your mother was a very smart woman." I take a breath, willing tears not to come as I think about her. George looks a little teary too, thinking of his own memories with her.

"So what does the trust fund say?" I ask.

"It comes into effect on your twenty-sixth birthday." He looks at me closely.

"My twenty-sixth birthday..." I say, a new nervousness, mixed with fear coating my insides. *That is tomorrow.*

"That is how old your mother was when she had you," George confirms, and my eyes widen.

"So what is it?" I ask, looking at them both, knowing whatever it is, it is big.

"The trust fund states that on the day of your twenty-sixth birthday, you will become majority shareholder of Van Cleef Corp. It means the board needs to consult with you before making any formal decisions and you will have the final say. It means Van Cleef Corp will be yours."

I stumble and fall back onto the sofa.

"What?" I ask, barely able to breathe. "My mother left me the company?"

"Even back then, she knew you were the rightful heir." George nods as he sits in the armchair next to me.

"I don't understand. How come I didn't know this? My father surely would have known of my mother's wishes?" I ask George.

"In the paperwork, it clearly states that if you are not

interested in the company, have a different career, provide no value, are married with children and prefer not to be involved in Van Cleef Corp, then the trust fund becomes null and void," Dennis says, and I let the words sink in.

"My father hid it," I say, not believing any of this is happening. I wish AJ was here. I feel like I need his steady hold and his thoughts on this.

"Dennis and I have talked about this all morning. We thought that your father wanted to marry you off to get oil money and international expansion opportunities, and maybe that was true, but I suspect that your father really wanted to get you married so that you don't get the trust fund. If you married William Schmidt and moved to Dubai, then the trust fund would have become void and your father would get full ownership, and Van Cleef Corp would've become all his," George says.

"I can't believe it. My twenty-sixth birthday is tomorrow," I say, shocked. I feel a little dizzy and I am glad I am sitting back down. "I think I am going to throw up." I clutch my stomach. This is too much. *A trust fund? My birthday.*

"My father obviously knows my birthday is tomorrow..." I say quietly, looking at George.

"That is why he was trying to get you out of the company, trying to get you married. Once he knew you wanted to be more involved, he tried to steer you away from the business, but when you became adamant you wanted more involvement, he was desperate." I jump up and start to pace.

"So who else knows about this?" I ask George, and he shakes his head.

"No one. Just the three of us."

"So my father knows he has one more day to get the company?" I ask him, and George nods.

"He is desperate. He will do anything, and today is the last day he has to make a move. After today, the only way he will get the business is if you die, but we can mitigate that threat by adjusting your will," George says, and a chill runs through me. I don't believe my father would kill me, but I also didn't think my father was capable of hurting me like he has.

"So what do we do?" I ask, looking between Dennis and George, because I have no idea of the next steps.

"I will call your lawyer, get a meeting today, and finish updating your will," George says, and I nod, almost on autopilot, still in shock. "Where's AJ? We need to plan. We need to pull the board together immediately, and everyone close to you needs to be locked down for their own safety. If your father is as desperate as I think he is, and he can't get to you, then he will go after someone close to you. Anything to cause you pain and try to get you to come to him," George says.

"AJ's gone," I say quickly, my panic starting to rise. "He went to see his mother today. She needed some help." George looks at me in horror.

"By himself?" George asks.

"I'll try to call him." I feel dread in the pit of my stomach.

"I'll get the boys up from downstairs. I will also call in the police chief," George says, already pulling out his cell and dialing numbers.

"I'll call the board," Dennis says, and I stare at him for

a beat because I know today is the day my life will change. He gives me a small, comforting smile and a nod. "You've got this."

I just need AJ here with me. I need him home and safe.

41

AJ

Being on my bike, riding down the highway, has always been one of my loves. There is something about the freedom I feel, the wind on my face, the graceful way the bike curves around corners, the sun on my skin. But today, I would rather be anywhere else. I took my time riding here, stopping along the way numerous times because I am procrastinating. I don't want to see her. I don't want to be anywhere near the trailer park I grew up in. The memories from my childhood still haunt me, and I prefer to push it all to the back of my mind and focus on the present. On Val.

As I slowly pull into the familiar front gates of my childhood home, I look around at the space. It looks like it has gone downhill since I was last here. The grass is long and in need of cutting. A few trailers look like they came off second best in wild weather, and there at the end of the long road, I see my mother's trailer. Old, but sturdy. A bit like her.

I ride up to the trailer and park the bike, kicking

down the stand and turning off the engine, and I am met with eerie silence. Stepping away from the Harley, I put my helmet on the seat and look around. When I pull out my cell, I don't have service. Another reason this place is so crappy. Some people would find this relaxing, being out here surrounded by forests. But I know the dangers that lurk. I spot the place where Brady's trailer used to be, long gone now, just a dead patch of grass left behind.

"Mom?" I call out, preferring not to go inside her home. I can't remember the last time I set foot in there. While I come here to check on her and drop off cash a few times a year, I never go inside. I can't. I don't even want to be outside it, but I can't leave her when she needs me. So here I am. I hear the TV blaring. It's not unusual, but every time I visit, she is straight out the door, shouting at me about needing money already. Patience is not a trait she holds well.

"Mom!" I bark out, hoping she hears me. Although if she didn't hear the rumble of my bike, then she is unlikely to hear my voice. I see no people, no cars, no other noise. Something feels off, but I can't put my finger on it.

"Mom!" I bang on her trailer door. As I wait for her response, I look around some more. Her neighbors are farther away, the plots next to her now empty. There are no kids playing, which is a good thing, as they should all be at school, but I grew up here, and Brady, Cody, and I always hung out here, so it is weird to see it so deserted.

Anxiety crawls up my spine as frustration nips at my shoulders. I don't want to waste time. I need to be back in

Baltimore. I need to be with Val. The last place I need to be is here, paying off my mother's drug debts.

"Mom!" I yell again and open the door. I am immediately hit with heat and a musty smell. Looking around, I can see the kitchen from where I stand, and it looks like a dumping ground of rubbish. There's barely an empty space on the counter.

"Mom?" The place looks like shit and smells like shit. But this is what happens when someone is a user. This is what I grew up in. Takeaway wrappers are on the floor, empty bottles of alcohol nearby. I breathe through my mouth so I don't smell the neglect of my childhood. I pay her account here at the trailer park every month so she always has a roof, but other than that, I have nothing else I can give her. Until she calls me needing money to pay her drug debt in order to not be physically assaulted. Then I always come.

I spot her sitting in the armchair in the living space, one of the game shows she likes watching on the TV. As I step toward her, she doesn't even look up.

"Mom?" I say quieter, wondering what the hell is going on.

"I knew my boy would come," she says, her voice low.

"That you did." A man's voice sounds from down the hall, and I jump back in surprise.

John Van Cleef. He looks a little different from when I last saw him. He is still in a suit, but he needs a shave, and by the looks of the dark circles under his eyes, I would guess he hasn't been sleeping much either.

"What the hell are you doing here?" I ask, livid, looking between him and my mother. She finally looks up at me. Her eyes are a little glassy, red, and her pupils are pinpoints, heroin clearly in her system.

"Your mother has been very accommodating. Pity you didn't take after her," he says, walking toward her slowly.

"You need to keep away from her," I warn, not liking him anywhere near me or my mother.

"AJ. That is not how you treat visitors," my mother scolds me, but her words are slurred. I have no idea how much she has had, but she isn't in her right mind.

"Yes, AJ. That is not how you treat visitors," he repeats sarcastically, and I grit my teeth. I want to end him. I step forward to do just that, then he lifts his hand and I still. He holds up a syringe.

"Your mom has got all she needs now," he says with a sick smirk on his face, handing it to my mother.

"Stop, Mom!" I shout as she takes it from him. "Don't!"

"But I need it, baby. You know Mommy needs her medicine," she tells me like she did when I was fucking five years old.

"Stop, Mom!" I stride toward her but stop short as I hear the click of a gun. My eyes dart to Valerie's father holding a handgun, aimed right at my head. I look back down to my mother who is five paces from me, and before I can move again, I see her push the needle into her arm, the sharp edge piercing her skin.

"Mom... please..." I choke out, knowing that whatever is in that needle is not something she will recover from. My heart tears in my chest, anger vibrating through my body, but I can't move. The gun is aimed firmly, and she won't stop. No matter what I do, what I say. My mom has been an addict her entire life. She can't live without it.

"Ahhhh, that's better." She sighs, and I watch her take a big breath in, then slump back farther in her armchair. My eyes are glued to her as she looks up at me, and she smiles before they roll to the back of her head.

"What the fuck did you give her?" I spit out as I reach for my cell to call 9-1-1.

"Put your fucking phone down," he growls.

"She OD'd. She can't take the pure stuff. She is too used to dirty drugs, dirty lifestyle," I bite out, knowing he doesn't give a shit, but my mom has nothing to do with his fucking money grab.

"You have ruined my fucking life!" he shouts. "Let's face it, you were never cut out to be a billionaire, and I am never going to let you be with my daughter. She should be married by now. She should be enjoying her honeymoon. She should be halfway around the world in Dubai, making babies, away from *my company*!"

"But instead, she is screaming my name every night and taking over her rightful position at the company by day," I grit out. We both know I am not good enough for Val. But I love her, and she loves me.

"You have no father. No mother," he says, looking down at my mother's slumped figure in the armchair. "And you sure as hell are not having Valerie."

I try to think about this situation clearly. My mother's chest stopped rising and falling minutes ago. By the time 9-1-1 gets here, it will be too late. Whatever was in the syringe was too much, too strong. I swallow harshly, pushing the emotion down. I have a gun raised at my head, so I know that I will be lucky to get out of here alive, and I sure as fuck don't want to die here, in this trailer, next to this woman. I struggled my entire life to make something of myself, to get out from this trailer and away from her drug-affected lifestyle. I worked too hard to get away, just to die right back here where I grew up. I need to get outside to have at least a small chance of survival.

"If you are going to shoot me, then let's go outside where you can shoot me like a man," I seethe, not showing fear. I want to wrap my hands around his throat and take away his last breath. I want to grab that gun and shoot him right between the eyes. But I can't do any of that in this cramped trailer. If I can get outside, I have more room to move, more places to run, more opportunity to overpower him. I suspect he likes a challenge, just like his daughter, and I am right, when I see his nostrils flare.

"Get the fuck down those stairs." He waves the gun, and I wonder for a brief moment if he is actually on some type of drug as well because he is fucking crazy. I step backward slowly, not giving him my back, and I walk out of the trailer.

"Go slowly... no sudden moves or else I will shoot you where you stand," he threatens as my feet touch the gravel outside, and I take a few large steps backward, trying to get as far away from him as possible. I don't stop stepping as he walks out, and I am already farther away from him than I was inside. But his hand is still raised, the gun still pointed at my head.

"You have nothing left to live for. I spoke to your landlord, and you've lost your apartment. Your Harley is being repo'd in about an hour..., but don't worry, I will ensure it goes to scrap metal. And that little hobby you had called Fortress. I had a friend of mine from the tax office hide some incriminating evidence in your financials that the IRS are going to be very fucking interested in. You and your little friends will be bankrupt before the end of the week."

I grit my teeth.

If what he says is true, it is checkmate. At this rate, I will be surprised if I don't go to prison. If this is what is coming for me, I can't help Valerie, just like I couldn't ever help my mom. I am not the man either of the women in my life needed.

"Wow, that is so nice of you, Mr. Wilson..." Valerie's voice comes from the side, and I spin around to see her, along with Brady and Cody, plus another few guys I don't know stepping toward us. *Mr. Wilson?*

"What the hell did you call me?" her father yells at her. *What the hell is she doing here?* The group of them look like they just arrived and were hiding among the spare trailers.

"Your name. *Mr. Wilson.* That is your name. Van Cleef was my mother's maiden name, my grandmother's name, the name you took when *you married* into this family. The name that you have now tarnished," she says, and although I can hear the tremor in her voice, she looks pissed. But she needs to get out of here, it isn't safe. *What the hell was she thinking coming here?*

"I haven't fucking tarnished anything. You and your fucking felon here have ruined *everything*!" he yells, spit flying from his mouth as I move a little to the side, putting my body in front of Val's. Her father waves the gun around in his hand. He is desperate, and desperate men do stupid things. *My life for hers, always.*

"It doesn't really matter. I already got AJ a new bike. He is moving in with me, so he no longer needs that apartment—you have saved us the hassle with that. Not to mention that the IRS is currently being sent this live recording, as is *Society News*, and oh, that's right, where are my manners, this is Detective Skimmer from the FBI. He works in the white-collar crime division. Unfortunately, for you, he only started this past month, so he isn't on your payroll yet," Valerie says, and I swallow. I left her for half a day, and she organized all this? I watch her with admiration. Coming to my defense like no one has ever before. Then I hear sirens in the distance.

"You fucking bitch," her father seethes, and while he is looking at her, I take another small step back. He is now like a wild dog being backed into a corner. I spot both Cody and Brady taking a stance and ensuring Val is somewhat behind them too. I spot both George and Levi with some other guy I don't know over near the car, Levi with a camera held high, obviously filming. I also see my Fortress team members strategically positioned all around the trailer. The whole fucking team is here.

"Now, now, is that any way to speak to your daughter? The rightful heir of Van Cleef Corp, and as of tomorrow, the new CEO." She is in boss mode, but we all still need to be careful.

"No one will believe it. This recording is doctored,"

her father says, waving the gun around again as he starts to look panicked.

"Oh, but according to the trust fund that my mother left, Van Cleef Corp is mine on my twenty-sixth birthday, and believe me, the first duty of business will be your immediate removal from the company."

"You fucking bitch, just like your mother. I only married her for the money, and now you have ruined that."

I take another step back, watching him closely. Val needs to be removed now. He is right on the edge. I look at Brady, and as he meets my eyes, we share a nod in agreement.

"Thank you, I take that as a compliment," she says. You'd never know how nervous she is. She's running off anger alone.

"Fuck you!" he yells, and I jump as he fires the gun. I hear Val scream, and out of the corner of my eye, I see Cody grab her and pull her down to the side, covering her body and running her back to the car, where George and Levi are scrambling to get inside. I feel a sharp burn in my chest as her father shoots another round, and I fall to the ground as more shots go off around me, and then it is quiet.

"Subject down. I repeat, the subject is down," I hear before I see men everywhere, jumping out from behind the trailers, running out from behind trees. These aren't my men. I think they are local police, maybe even the FBI. Some run in my direction and past me to where Val's father is. I lie still on my back, trying to breathe, but it hurts like a motherfucker, and then my vision starts to go.

"AJ! AJ!" I hear Val's screams, and I turn my head and see her running toward me. She falls to her knees and cups my head in her hands.

"My life for yours, Val. Always," I whisper, then the lights go out, and all I see is black.

42

AJ

My body feels heavy, and I groan as I move my head to the side.

"Don't move too much," I hear Val say softly from next to me. Her voice is like an angel, and my body, although sore, immediately relaxes having her with me.

"I feel like I have been hit by a truck," I murmur, trying to get a gauge on what's wrong with me.

"Not a truck, but you did just get out of surgery," she says, and I open my eyes. I squint, looking at her perched on a chair that she has pulled right up to the bed. Her hands hold one of mine. The room is white, stark. The bed linen is scratchy. I am in the hospital, that much is clear.

"No wonder I can't move my arm," I say, looking across to my other arm that is wrapped from shoulder to wrist and in a sling across my body. I wiggle my toes and move my legs. They feel heavy, but otherwise, they move okay.

"No other injuries."

I turn my head back and look at her. I let my eyes wander from her head, down her body, and back again. She looks tired, like she has been crying, but she is still beautiful to me.

"You alright?" I ask, praying she didn't take a hit.

"I'm fine. My bodyguard jumped right in front of the gun and took two bullets for me." Lowering her eyes, she takes a big, shaky breath in. I squeeze her hands, and her eyes shoot back to mine.

"Just doing my job." Watching her, she huffs out a laugh as a tear runs down her cheek.

"Don't cry, sweetheart. We are okay," I tell her, trying to comfort her, the stress of the entire situation now overflowing.

"I just saw you lying there, blood coming from your chest. I was so scared," she whispers as another tear falls. I reach up with my good hand and cup her face, wiping the tears away with my thumb. "I just didn't know what else to do. We got the police involved; we took helicopters to Wilmington…"

"Come here," I tell her as I move to the side a little.

"AJ. Stop, you shouldn't move." Standing up, she looks worried.

"Come here, Val. Lie with me."

"Lie with you?" she asks, taking in my injury as she bites her lip.

"Come here," I growl, and she finally lets go of a breath and climbs onto the bed. It isn't big enough for us both, but I pull her in tight, our bodies sandwiched against each other, and I feel her body relax into mine.

"Just don't ever jump in front of a gun for me again, okay?" she says, trying to pull herself together.

"That's a promise I am not making to you, sweetheart," I tell her honestly. "What happened to my mom?" I ask her, even though I already know the answer. Val's head buries into my chest, and my lips immediately find the top of her head. Her rose scent wraps up my nose, and I take a deep breath, her hair tickling my chin. I feel my throat getting a little tight, my heart thudding hard. I close my eyes, still picturing her sitting in the armchair, and I swallow roughly, trying to push the sadness down. I wait for the words from Val, needing the confirmation.

"She passed away. I'm so sorry, AJ. She had an overdose." I feel her tears seep through my shirt, so I pull her tighter. "Brady and I organized a funeral home to look after things, and they are waiting for you to make some decisions."

I don't have words. I feel heartbroken since it was my mom. But I also feel relieved. She is finally at peace and no longer chased by her demons. I kiss Val's head again, feeling grateful to have her by my side, knowing that as sad and low as we feel now, we still have each other.

"Brady, Cody, and I have been talking with the police. They want to interview you."

I don't know how long I have been here, but I'd assume they would want to speak to me at some point.

"And your father?" I ask, my nostrils flaring, thinking about that man and all that he has taken from me and tried to take from his daughter. My shoulders stiffen, but I slowly relax again as I feel Val's fingers run up my bare chest. I trail my hand up and down her arm, and I can see her hand shake a little.

"He, ahh..." She pauses as she weeps. Again, I pull her even tighter, wishing I could take away all her pain. She clears her throat and continues. "He died at the scene. Police shot him twice in the chest after he shot two bullets into you. There will be a private burial later this week. George is helping me manage it."

I don't know George well, but I am extremely grateful for him and everything he has done for Val.

"It will be okay, sweetheart. I got you," I tell her, needing her to know that I will always be by her side and there for her whenever she needs me. Losing a parent is hard. Couple that with the past few months that Val has experienced, and it is a wonder she is still standing.

"And Van Cleef Corp?" I ask, the words she was saying at the trailer park now coming back to me. "You got a trust fund?"

She slowly explains everything that she and George found out and talks to me about Dennis.

"The board has agreed to meet in sixty days to talk over the change of leadership. They will take care of the business for me now as I get my life together. I am confident by then things will be a little more sorted." There is obviously a lot we need to do between now and then, but I like her optimism.

"So you want me to move in, then?" I smile against her.

"I never want you to leave me again." My reaction is instant as I pull her even closer to my side. My shoulder aches, the throbbing increasing, but I don't care. All I care about is this woman. Everything else is a distant second.

"I can promise you something else, Val," I tell her, and she takes a breath.

"What's that?" she asks in anticipation.

"Whether in your penthouse or a shitty apartment on the other side of town, I promise that wherever you are is where I will be," I say firmly, leaving no room for questions.

"I love you, AJ." She looks up at me, and I see all that love shining in her eyes.

"I love you, sweetheart," I tell her, then I take her lips with mine.

AJ - SIX MONTHS LATER

"Here, I got you a coffee," Brady says, pushing a takeaway coffee cup in my direction as he walks into the meeting room at Van Cleef Corp.

"Took your time," Cody says, looking up from his laptop and leaning back, clearly waiting for the caffeine hit.

I roll my head to relieve some tension and look at my two friends. "Okay, so how are we positioned with the new guys?" I ask, getting down to business. It has been over six months since the incident and life has been crazy. It took months with police statements, physical therapy, and getting up to speed on our new working arrangements, but the three of us sit here as partners in Fortress, the new security firm responsible for not just Val, but for the entire Van Cleef Corp. But I never leave Val's side. Where she goes, I go. That will never change.

"We have twenty new guys who have passed their physical and background checks. We have them scheduled for some training with us next week. Assuming they pass all the training, they should be ready to be deployed in the business within the month," Cody says, and I nod. As Val arranged, the board looked after the company for exactly sixty days, and then she stepped into her new CEO position. She worked hard those first few months to clear her name, increasing staff morale and pushing new deals. Her work ethic is unsurpassed and one of the many things I admire about her.

It's not only work that has been busy for Val. She is still trying to finalize her father's estate. Her stepmother, Abigail, has become a recluse. Val purchased an apartment for her in Florida, where she now lives. The family mansion where Val grew up sits vacant now, with Val hiring builders for an entire redevelopment. The plans are being drawn up, and I am not sure if living in such luxury is going to work for me. I still find her penthouse amazing.

"Just in time for Tennessee," Brady adds. With the next hotel that Van Cleef Corp is opening in Tennessee, new security guards will be needed, for both opening week and ongoing. Val kept her word, and she is collaborating with the Rothschilds and also Whiteman's Whiskey. Neither deal went sour due to her father, which I know she was extremely grateful for. The project came together ahead of schedule and below budget. Val's will to succeed and prove everyone wrong has fueled her. The board members are happy, George is her deputy, and the two of them are unstoppable as they currently look at where to expand next.

"Speaking of which, is that President Rothschild?"

Cody asks, looking wide-eyed at the glass wall of the room that shows us the reception area. I look out and see a tall man in a full suit, his smile wide, standing at reception, with about six people swarming around him and another five security people behind him. George and Dennis, Val's new chief advisor, shake hands with him, and then I spot Val. I knew she had an important meeting today, and now I know who that was with. She smiles at him, and he leans down and kisses my girl on the cheek.

My eyes thin, and a small growl rumbles from my chest as I watch him and his team get into the elevator and leave.

"Easy, tiger, they have been friends for years, remember," Brady says, as Cody chuckles, and I throw my pen in their direction. I keep my eyes on Val, and she spots me, her smile widening as she walks across to our meeting room.

"Hey," she says, strutting in with Bordeaux at her feet and closing the door behind her. After a few months in the top job, Val implemented some new rules at the company. One of which was work-life balance, where people can work from home when and if they need to. Another one was to bring your pet to work day once a week. Bordeaux loves it. As he walks in beside her, he immediately runs around the room, smelling everyone's shoes until he comes to me and jumps up on my shins.

"Hey, boss," Brady says to Val cheekily as I scoop up my little pal and put him in my lap, where he lies down and makes himself comfortable. George brings in his cat, that is the most antisocial animal I have ever met. Some guy in finance brought in a fish tank, keeping his tropical guppy in his office. It is certainly a talking point that has brought a lot of laughter to the office at a time when everyone needed it. Including Val.

"Hoping I could talk to you for a minute?" she asks, and the boys take the cue.

"Be back later. We'll go to the kitchen and see if Sheryll in accounts has brought in any more of those chocolate chip cookies," Cody says, and he and Brady leave the room, closing the door behind them.

"What is it, sweetheart?" I ask her, frowning, wondering what is going on that she can't talk about in front of the boys.

"I have a new project I need you on," she says, coming to stand by my side.

"Sure, what's happening?" I ask. She is being a little coy, and my heart beats a little faster. I lift my hand and run it up her leg, resting it on her hip.

"Hawaii."

"What is it? New hotel? New business venture?" My head immediately goes to how many new guys I now need to hire and if I have the time to train them before they need to be deployed.

"No. A vacation. Me and you. Two weeks of uninterrupted beachside relaxation. After we have the Tennessee opening, I am leaving George to run things for a few weeks so the two of us can relax."

I smile immediately, my hand squeezing her waist. I have never been to Hawaii. I only recently flew to Tennessee when Val had to head there to check out the construction. Other than that, I haven't traveled much.

"I think Brady and Cody can manage things for me," I

murmur, already liking this idea. Just the two of us. Her naked, in bed, screaming my name, on repeat. I really like the sound of this. My dream of having her all to myself and lying in bed with her all day long is now going to become a reality.

"Levi can look after Bordeaux and the apartment." I know she has already planned it out. No doubt the hotel is booked, things in motion.

"You won't get him out of his," I remark, because Levi has taken over the three-bedroom apartment downstairs from us. Fortress still uses it as our base when we need to, but now that Val isn't confined to the penthouse, the apartment downstairs is more of a meeting point the boys use. With Levi having ongoing issues with his family, having him closer to us, eating well, working out, and helping Fortress on the side, he actually attends school and is passing all his subjects, which is something that both Val and I are very happy about.

"So how about it? Are you ready for some relaxation time? Fun in the sun?" she asks me with a bright smile.

"Wherever you are is where I'll be." I remind her of my promise.

"Good. You will love my new red bikini," she teases as she wiggles her eyebrows at me and leans down, giving me her lips.

"It's going to look much better on the floor at your feet," I murmur on her lips and relish her laughter, grateful that I have finally found my happiness.

. . .

To grab a bonus scene to see where Val and AJ are now download it HERE or scan the QR Code below

ALSO BY SAMANTHA SKYE

TANNER

My new neighbor happens to be the **grumpiest billionaire** in Whispers, but his gravelly voice and golden brown eyes make this city girl weak at the knees.

When my life imploded and I lost my job and my fiancé in a matter of weeks, I didn't know what my next step should be. Then I received an inheritance that would change my life forever.

Moving to a **small town** and renovating the old farm house was a step in the right direction. But bickering with my startling good looking, yet much older neighbor was not part of my plan.

Tanner Whiteman owns the largest whiskey distillery in all of the country, and now he wants my land. It's the only thing that I have to my name and there is no way I am letting him take it.

It is clear I am not cut out for country life and Tanner has no trouble pointing that out. Although as his eyes linger a little longer and his words take new meaning, even the **massive age gap** is not enough to stop us.

But something does. Something Vicious. Something unexpected. And not even the local **billionaire** knows what is coming.

www.books2read.com/tanner1

ALSO BY SAMANTHA SKYE

The Billionaires of Whispers

Tanner

Hudson - Coming 2024

Connor - Coming 2025

Sawyer - Coming 2025

Sutton - Coming 2025

Griffin - Coming 2025

The Baltimore Boys

The Charming Billionaire

The Arrogant Billionaire

The Damaged Billionaire

The Secret Billionaire

The Bossy Billionaire

The Billionaire Babe

Men Of New York

My Legacy

My Destiny

My Fight

My Chance

Boston Billionaires

Coming Home

Finding Home

Leaving Home

Building Home

ABOUT THE AUTHOR

Samantha Skye is an international bestselling author. A country kid turned city slicker, she writes spicy and suspenseful contemporary romance novels that leave you hot under the collar and on the edge of your seat.

Samantha lives in Melbourne, Australia and when she's not plotting her next novel, she can be found travelling and chasing the sun.

To join in the conversation join Skye's The Limit Facebook group here;

https://www.facebook.com/groups/skyesthelimitbooks